WILLIAM AND MURRON RODE ALONG THE RIDGE TO A GROVE, FROM WHICH THEY COULD SEE A BREATHTAKING LOCH. THERE HE TURNED TO HER IN THE MOONLIGHT ...

'I have fought. And I have hated. I know it is in me to hate and to kill. But I've learned something else away from my home. And that is that we must always have a home, somewhere inside us ... When I lost my father and brother ... I thought I might die of grief alone! I wanted to bring that grief to the people who had brought it to me ...

'But later I came to realize something. My father and his father had not fought and died so I could become filled with hate. They fought for me to be free to love ... I had to stop hating and start loving.'

He squeezed her hands. He reached with trembling fingers and combed her windblown hair away from her face, so he could see it fully.

'But that was easy. I thought of you ...'

ABOUT THE AUTHOR

Randall Wallace was born in Tennessee. He is the author of four previous novels, including *The Russian Rose* and *So Late into the Night*. The *Washington Post* wrote of him, 'The reader is held. Wallace knows how to shift scenes, how to build plot and subplot and tie them together, how to create suspense with teasing foreshadowings of hidden pasts and untold histories.'

Randall Wallace now lives in Southern California.

RANDALL WALLACE

BRAVEHEART

A SIGNET BOOK

SIGNET

Published by the Penguin Group
Penguin Books Ltd, 27 Wrights Lane, London W8 5TZ, England
Penguin Books USA Inc., 375 Hudson Street, New York, New York 10014, USA
Penguin Books Australia Ltd, Ringwood, Victoria, Australia
Penguin Books Canada Ltd, 10 Alcorn Avenue, Toronto, Ontario, Canada M4V 3B2
Penguin Books (NZ) Ltd, 182–190 Wairau Road, Auckland 10, New Zealand

Penguin Books Ltd, Registered Offices: Harmondsworth, Middlesex, England

First published in the USA by Pocket Books, a division of Simon & Schuster, Inc. 1995
Published in Signet 1995
10

Printed in England by Clays Ltd, St Ives plc

Acknowledgments

The journey of *Braveheart* has taught me about clanship, that bond of loyalty and shared devotion that unites across time and miles. I have seen in new ways how those who have loved me, taught me, stood by me, helped me, forgiven me and prayed for me have become a part of all I do.

Such a bond goes beyond thanks; but there are some who, because of the miles they walked on the path that led to this book, must not go unmentioned here. They are:

Evelyn and Thurman Wallace, my mother and father, for the legacy of their example that all freedom begins with freedom of the spirit, and that it has a price, paid in the currency of love. And my sister, Jane Wallace Sublett, who, by loving me so consistently through victory or defeat, has helped me accept both, and fear neither.

James W. Connor, who, even before I did, believed I would write novels someday.

Dr. Thomas Langford of Duke University, who taught me that deeds were the finest sermons, and who opened my life to the possibility that every prayer was a story, and every story a prayer.

Judy Thomas, who helped me believe that all writing should sing the silent music of the soul.

James J. Cullen, whose screenplay about heroism and honor was the first—and still is one of the finest—I ever read, and whose poetic glories inspired me to attempt such a work of my own.

Rebecca Pollack Parker, who, when the inspiration for *Braveheart* was but a spark, embraced it in the lantern of her spirit, and nurtured it to flame.

Lisa Drew, editor of this book, whose relentless faith in my novels has brought me back to writing them.

And let me not forget Blind Harry, roving minstrel of Scotland, who kept alive the tales of William Wallace.

And always and forever, my wife, Christine, and our sons, Andrew and Cullen. Among all the other gratitudes for my family, there is this: to write truly of love and women of strength, one must know them—and I know Christine. And the spirits of our sons are a constant revelation of God's sweetest strategy: He gives us a gift so great that we would give our lives in return.

This book is for you all.

To Scottish friends I lift a glass
To you, who've kept alive
The memory of heroes past
Across dark moors of time

To you who know this simple truth
And show it near and far
It is the tales we tell ourselves
That make us who we are

So let us drink to Scotland fair
Its sorrow and its solace
And lift our glasses in the air
To you and William Wallace

And to the Clan that bears his name
My sisters and my brothers
I'd rather be a man in your eyes
Than a king in any others.

Randall Wallace

Prologue

I will tell you of William Wallace.

I first encountered his story when my wife and I came upon the statue of him that, along with one of King Robert the Bruce, guards the entrance to Edinburgh Castle in Scotland. I am an American; I had grown up in the American South within a family I knew to be Scotch-Irish, and although I had always been interested in history, I never thought much about our roots extending beyond America. We were dirt farmers from Tennessee. What I am trying to say is that I never thought of our having famous relatives.

Songs of William Wallace have been sung for hundreds of years, and not just by Scotland's poets alone—even Winston Churchill wrote, with keen admiration, about Wallace's courage and spirit. But to me, an American, his story seemed lost, a great treasure of the past, utterly precious for our time, lying neglected and forgotten. His story began to speak to me, to haunt me; it entered my life as divine gifts do, quietly, overwhelmingly, irreversibly.

Historians agree on only a few facts about Wallace's life, and yet they cannot dispute that his life was epic. There were times when I tried myself to be a fair historian, but life is not all about balance, it's about passion, and this story raised my passions. I had to see through the eyes of a poet.

No one knows what William Wallace whispered into the ear of the woman he loved most. No one else heard the words he spoke to God when he prayed. And the words he shouted to his army, when the men who fought behind him were desperately outnumbered, were recorded only in their hearts and can be read there.

In my heart, this is exactly how it happened . . .

THE
BOY

1

THE SCOTTISH HIGHLANDS ARE A LAND OF EPIC BEAUTY: cobalt mountains beneath a glowering purple sky fringed with pink, as if the clouds are a lid too small for the earth; a cascading landscape of boulders shrouded in deep green grass; and the blue lochs, reflecting the sky. In summer, the sun lingers for hours in its rising and setting; in winter, day is a brief union of dawn and twilight. In all seasons the night is a serenade of stars, singing white in the silence of an endless black sky.

Elderslie lies between Glasgow and Edinburgh, at the gateway into the Highlands. It was in the shire of Elderslie, in or about the year 1276, that a contingent of mounted Scottish noblemen converged on a farm nestled in an isolated Scottish valley. The noblemen wore sparkling chestplates and woolens colored with the richest dyes of the day; even their horses were draped in luxurious cloth. But they had left their armed escorts far behind, for this was a meeting of truce, and the terms were that each nobleman could be accompanied by a single page boy. The nobles had agreed, for each knew that their country needed peace, and to have peace, Scotland's crown must have a head to wear it, and they had to have a meeting to establish just whose head that should be.

3

Their old king had died without an heir. The rightful succession belonged to an infant girl, called the Maid of Norway, and the nobles of Scotland sent for their new queen. The Vikings, cousins to the Scots, agreed to bring her down on one of their ships.

On the English throne in London sat King Edward I, known as Edward the Longshanks because of his lengthy legs. He disputed the ascension of the baby to the throne and claimed the right to chose Scotland's new monarch lay with him and him alone. Longshanks was a Plantagenet, a line of rulers renowned for their ruthlessness and accused by their enemies of worshiping pagan deities that delighted in cruelty. And so when the baby died on her journey south, there were those who said she had been smothered and Longshanks was to blame.

It may have been a lie or a half-truth with some other man behind the murder. There was plenty of ruthlessness to go around; Scotland's nobles fought with Longshanks and with each other for the throne. Alliances were made and broken; nobles grew richer each time they switched sides, oblivious to the suffering of the commoners whose lands and lives they controlled and whose welfare they neglected.

As the hostilities wore on, even the nobility began to suffer. Trade suffered; crops failed because the farmers who tended the fields were forced away from them so often to fight for the nobleman who owned them. So Longshanks invited them to talks of truce. He chose the most warlike of the nobles, the ones most insistent that their country remain independent. Although they were the most stubborn, they were the ones bravest enough to answer the call to come unarmed, with one page boy only, to discuss peace.

And so it was that the nobles appeared on the misty, muddy roads that converged on the prosperous farm of a man called MacAndrews, who had been willing to offer up his spacious barn as a private place to discuss such a noble thing as peace. The nobles, riding in from opposite directions or coming in on the same road at

4

cautious intervals, eyed each other suspiciously, but the truce held. One by one, they tied their horses outside MacAndrews's farmhouse and entered the quiet barn, with their pages.

Among the other farmers of that shire was a man named Malcolm Wallace. He owned his own lands, where he had built a stone house as a gift to his wife, though she had died in childbirth the year it was completed. Like his friend MacAndrews, Malcolm Wallace was a patriot; he wanted Scotland ruled by Scots. This was a dangerous opinion, and those who held it kept it secret; it was the measure of MacAndrews's trust for Malcolm Wallace that he was the only neighbor to whom he whispered about the great occurrence that had been set for his barn that morning, and Malcolm had promised to drop by when the meeting was over.

So midafternoon of that same day, Malcolm Wallace stopped his work and saddled a horse. John, his eighteen-year-old son, did the same and together they mounted up for the ride over the ridge and into the next valley. Watching them from the loft of the barn, where he had been gathering eggs, was seven-year-old William.

William had his father's blue eyes. He had sometimes stared into the still water of a loch and stared at himself, trying to make his features grow into an exact replica of the face of his father, who he was sure was the finest man ever born. William idolized the strength of his father's silence, the power in his hands, his arms, his shoulders. But most of all he admired the strength of his father's heart. He had heard other men bluster and boast. But his father never made loud predictions. He simply did what he was going to do, and let that say it. Once William had been on the road to the village with his father when they met a neighbor returning from the marketplace with a fine new horse. Malcolm had stopped the man and in a quiet voice asked for the money the man owed him. The man

5

claimed to be freshly out of money and pointed to the horse as evidence. It also seemed to William that the man had looked at his father with a squint of defiance, but William was never sure because the look, whatever it was, vanished when Malcolm hit him with a single blow to the middle of the chest. The man crumpled and lay like a log in the road. Malcolm took the horse and thanked the man, who never moved as they rode off.

It was that same horse that William looked at now.

His father and brother were halfway up the rise when they heard hoofbeats behind them and turned to see William riding bareback, talking to the horse through his knees, a natural rider. He stopped the horse beside his father and looked steadily at him from beneath the blond thatch of his hair.

"Told ya ta stay," his father said.

"I finished my chores. Where we goin'?" William said.

"MacAndrews's. He wanted us to visit when the truce was over." Malcolm spurred his horse, and William fell in line behind his father and brother.

They rode on, over the hills of emerald grass dotted here and there with the purple flowers of wild thistle.

They stopped high above the next valley and looked down at the MacAndrews farm. The ground in front of the house was pitted from the hooves of many horses, but they were nowhere to be seen now. The house was silent; the whole place looked deserted.

Up on the hill, Malcolm Wallace felt both sons glance at him. They didn't like it either. "Stay here," he said. He meant William.

The boy watched as his father and brother spurred their horses and rode down the hill. They pulled up at the barn and looked around. "MacAndrews! . . . MacAndrews!?" Malcolm yelled.

They dismounted. Malcolm found a pitchfork. John lifted the woodpile ax. They moved to the door of the barn and pushed it open. They waited for a moment on either side of the door; in a country where stealing livestock was an art form, it paid to be careful. But no sound came from within the barn.

Makeshift weapons held high, they darted inside.

John staggered. Malcolm, whose heart had borne many deaths, felt that heart skip in his chest.

Hanging from the rafters of the barn were thirty Scottish noblemen and thirty pages, their faces purple and contorted by the strangulation hanging, their tongues protruding as if they were tasting the dusty light.

Malcolm stabbed the pitchfork into the ground in useless anger; John gripped the ax as he followed his father through the hung bodies of the noblemen to the back row and saw the one man in commoner's dress, like theirs. "MacAndrews," Malcolm said quietly, then he and John spun around at the sound of the shuffle behind them.

William stood there near the front door, gazing up at the hanging bodies.

"William! Get out of here!" John barked.

William frowned in bewilderment. "Why would MacAndrews make so many scarecrows?" he asked.

Before his father and brother could think of anything to say, William, with a boy's curiosity, touched the spurred foot of one of the hanged noblemen. It was too solid; realization flooded over him. "R—real!!! . . . Ahhhhhgggg!" he yelled. He turned and ran but knocked back into the feet of the hung man behind him. In blind panic he darted in another direction and ran into another corpse and another; the hung men began to swing, which made it harder for William's father and older brother to fight their way to him.

"William! *William!*" Malcolm called after him.

Then, worst of all, William saw the pages, boys like himself, hung in a row behind their masters.

Finally his father and brother reached William and hugged him tight. There in the barn, among the swinging bodies of the hung nobles, Malcolm Wallace threw his arms around both his sons. They gripped him back. William was shaking, but within the circle of his father's powerful arms he felt the pounding of his heart subside and could hear sounds again instead of its throbbing inside his body.

"Murderin' English bastards," his father said.

2

OUTSIDE THE WALLACE FARMHOUSE THAT NIGHT, THE COTtage looked peaceful, the windows glowed yellow into the night. Inside, John rose and closed the shutters of the kitchen, where men were gathered.

In his bedroom, young William lay tossing in nightmarish sleep. He mumbled in smothered terror; he twitched.

In the blue grays of his dream, William stood at the door of the barn and gazed at the hanged knights. Their faces were garish, horrible. Then one of the heads moved and its eyes opened! William wanted to run, but he couldn't get his body to respond, and the hung nobleman's bloated tongue burst through his lips, and the ghoul moaned, "Will—iam!"

William tore himself from sleep; he looked around and swallowed back his tears and panic.

Then he heard voices coming up from the kitchen. Many voices, low and angry. He climbed quietly down from the upper corner space where he slept beneath the roof thatch that kept out the rain and cold, and tiptoed down to the doorway of the kitchen. He stopped in the shadows at the dark rim of the candlelight.

A dozen tough farmers were huddled around the kitchen table. William's brother John was among them, and William recognized the others. Some lived close by, a few lived several valleys over, but they were all men his father trusted; at one time or another he had seen his father walking and talking quietly with each of them. But he had never seen a meeting like this before.

Redheaded Campbell, scarred and missing fingers, was stirred up. "Wallace is right!" he barked to his friends. "We fight 'em!"

But MacClannough, a slender man with fine features, was counseling caution and countered, "Every nobleman who had any will to fight was at that meeting."

"So it's up to us! We show them we won't lie down and be their slaves!" Malcolm Wallace said in a voice so hard and low that William felt chilled.

"We can't beat an army with just the fifty farmers we can raise!" MacClannough said.

"We don't have to beat 'em, just fight 'em," Malcolm said. "To show 'em we're not dogs, but men."

Young William watched from the darkness as his father dipped his finger into a jug of whiskey and used the wet finger to draw on the tabletop. "They have a camp here," Malcolm said, looking from face to face. "We attack them at sunset tomorrow. Give us all night to run home."

The next day Malcolm and John saddled horses and led them from their barn; they were checking the short swords they had tucked into grain sacks behind their saddles when William came out of the barn with his own horse.

"William, you're staying here," his father said.

"I can fight," William said.

These words from his youngest son made Malcolm pause and kneel to look into William's eyes.

"Aye. But it's our wits that make us men. I love ya, boy. You stay."

Malcolm and John mounted their horses and rode away and left William watching them go. At the edge of their oat field they turned in their saddles and waved to him.

William waved back and watched them until they disappeared on the curving trail up the valley.

3

THE PEACE OF THE SUMMER TWILIGHT HAD BEGUN TO SET-tle over the Wallace farm. The wind whispered across the straw thatch of the rooftops, and the chickens scratched lazily around the barn. All was strangely quiet.

Then William and his friend Hamish Campbell, redheaded like his father, ran from the rear of the house and ducked in beside the barn, breathless, gasping. The two boys pressed their backs against the wall. William peered around a corner, then shrunk back and whispered, "They're coming!"

"How many?" Hamish shot back.

"Three, maybe more!"

"Armed?"

"They're English soldiers, ain't they?" William demanded.

"With your father and brother gone, they'll kill us and burn the farm!"

"It's up to us, Hamish!"

Hamish leaned forward for a look, but William pulled him back and breathed hot words into his friend's ear: "Not yet! Here he comes; be ready!"

They waited and heard heavy footsteps. Then from around the corner three enormous, ugly hogs appeared. The boys hurled rotten eggs. The eggs slapped the snouts of the pigs, who scattered as the boys charged, howling.

The sun went down on their play. The boys walked

toward the house, beneath a lavender sky. The house looked so much darker and emptier now. "Wanna stay with me tonight?" Hamish asked.

"I wanna have supper waitin'," William said.

"We'll get those English pigs tomorrow," Hamish said.

"Aye, we'll get 'em," William grinned.

The sky had gone fully black and the stars were hard and bright above the house when William's face appeared at the window and he looked toward the distant hills, where he saw trees and heather, but no sign of life. He turned back to the cook fire he had built in the grate and stirred at the stew he had made. He spooned up two steaming bowls full and set them out on the table.

But he was only hoping. He looked out the window again; he was still all alone. So he left a candle burning on the table beside the stew and moved up the stairs.

Night thawed into a foggy dawn, and William rose from his bed, where he had huddled, afraid to sleep, through a night that seemed to have no end. But now, with gray showing through the cracks of his board windows, he rose, dressed, and moved down the hall. He stopped at the door of his father's bedroom and saw the undisturbed bed. He moved on and passed the door of his brother's room, also unrumpled.

In the kitchen he found the two cold bowls of stew beside the exhausted candle. He spooned up his own cold porridge and ate alone.

After his breakfast, William was in the barn loft, shoveling corn down to feed the hogs, when he glimpsed something coming. He saw an ox cart rumbling down the curving lane. Its driver was Campbell, with MacClannough walking behind it. The farmers glanced up at William, their faces grim.

From his perch in the loft, William saw what the neighbors had brought: the bodies of his father and brother. The cart stopped; Campbell, with a bandage

11

around his left hand where more of his fingers were now missing, studied the back of the ox as if it could tell him how to break such news. The butt of the ox seemed to tell him to be matter-of-fact.

"William . . . Come down here, lad," Campbell said.

William looked away, he took quick breaths, he looked back, but the bodies were still there.

4

THE OUTSIDE OF THE HOUSE WAS NOW SURROUNDED BY horses, wagons, and neighbors. The undertaker arrived in his hearse, preloaded with coffins.

William sat at the kitchen table, weeping, holding the bowls of stew, hugging them as if they were his family. A neighbor woman moved up beside him. "Poor dear. That's cold," she said. "Let me get you something hot."

She reached for the bowls, but he held tightly to them.

"There now, darlin' . . ."

"Get away from me!" William said.

"Now, now." Suddenly he was fighting her for the bowls; the stew spilled over her skirt, and the crockery bowls shattered. William burst from the room and rushed out into the yard, where all the neighbors had gathered. His wild grief disrupted the solemnity; they gawked at him. He looked everywhere, instinctively trying to find his father and brother. He spotted the ox cart, empty now, standing beside the shed, and ran toward its open door. Campbell saw him going and yelled, "William!" but it was too late; the boy disappeared inside the shed.

There on a makeshift table lay the bodies of Malcolm and John Wallace. As William watched, the undertaker wrapped a cloth strip around his brother's lower jaw and tied the ends of the strip into a knot at the top of his head. William's father had already been bound for death this way.

Old Campbell, the big grizzled redhead, stepped into the door, following William—but what could he say now? The undertaker went on with his work. William approached the table; the bodies didn't look real to him, certainly not like his father and brother. He saw the wounds. The dried blood. The undertaker poured water from a bowl and scrubbed off the blood. But the wounds remained.

Campbell, MacClannough, and several others who had been gathered around the kitchen table in the Wallace house only two nights before now carried the bodies of William's father and brother to the two new graves, dug into the rocky soil beside the grave of Mary Wallace, its cairn weathered and overgrown with moss. The mourners were gathered in a circle around the three graves as the parish priest droned in Latin, and they tried to hold onto expressions of stoic grief, but the sight of the boy, standing alone in front of the graves of his dead mother as the bodies of his father and brother were lowered with ropes into the ground beside her, had all of the neighbors shaken. He stood alone, and they seemed afraid even to look at him.

At the foot of the graves, and just outside the circle of mourners, three of the farmers were whispering. "We gotta do somethin' with the boy," MacClannough said.

"He's got an uncle in Dunipace," Campbell told him.

"Malcolm had a brother?" MacClannough asked.

"A cleric. Don't think they got along. I sent a lad to fetch him."

"What if the uncle don't come?" Stewart asked.

They all thought about that question for a moment.

"You don't have a son, MacClannough, how about you?" Campbell asked.

But no one was anxious to adopt a grieving, rebellious boy. MacClannough looked at his wife and two daughters. His youngest daughter was five; she was a beautiful girl with long auburn hair, and she clung to her own mother's hand as if the open graves were the mouths of death and might suck her parents in, too.

Then the girl did what no one else there had thought to do; she moved to the softly weeping William and held out to him the thistle flower that she had carried to the graveside.

William looked up at her, and their young eyes met—children encountering grief for the first time. Everybody at the funeral had seen the gesture; it even stopped the local priest in the middle of his droning. As the girl moved back to her mother's side, the priest had lost his place in the liturgy of death and could only mutter, "Amen. Rest in peace."

As the gravediggers shoveled dirt over the coffins, Campbell and his son Hamish moved to William and took his shoulders.

"Come on, lad. Come on . . . ," Campbell said.

They all filtered back toward the house. Outside the house, Campbell slipped the undertaker some coins as final payment. The undertaker climbed up into the wagon box and lifted the reins; but before he could snap them a figure appeared riding toward them. A lone, stiff figure that made everyone pause.

The figure drew closer. It was Argyle Wallace in black clerical priestly garb. He looked like a human buzzard; his face was craggy, permanently furious.

"You must be the relative of the deceased," the priest said.

Argyle only glowered at the man, who retreated. Argyle dismounted and glared at William.

"Uncle Argyle?" William said.

"We'll sleep here tonight. You'll come home with me. We'll let the house and the lands, too—plenty of willing neighbors."

"I don't want to leave," William said.

"Didn't want your father to die either, did ya? But it happened."

The people wanted to stay and eat the food they had brought, but a contingent of English soldiers rode up, a dozen mounted men carrying lances. The leader of the soldiers looked down at the funeral bunting.

"Someone dead from this household?" the leader asked.

"We just had a funeral, isn't that what it means in England as well?" Argyle said.

"What it means in England—and in Scotland, too—is that rebels have forfeited their lands," the leader answered. The mounted soldiers behind him shifted their pikes and eyed the unarmed farmers.

"My brother and nephew died two days ago when their hay cart turned over," Argyle said. "Their graves have been consecrated, and any man who disturbs them now incurs eternal damnation." Argyle's eyes burned like the hell fires he spoke of. "So please. Dig them up."

Outmaneuvered, the leader reined his horse away. Several of the farmers spat on the ground. Argyle glared at them.

"Funeral's over. Go home," Argyle said.

That night inside the kitchen, William and Argyle sat together at the table. Argyle had laid out a proper meal with exact place settings.

"Not that spoon, that one's for soup," Argyle told the boy. "Dip away from you. And don't slurp." They ate in silence for a few minutes. Then Uncle Argyle asked, "Did the priest say anything about the Resurrection? Or was it all about Judgment?"

"It was in Latin, sir."

"Non loquis Latinum? You don't speak Latin? We shall have to fix that, won't we? Did he give the poetic benediction? The Lord bless thee and keep thee? *Patris benefactum et* . . . It was Malcolm's favorite."

Argyle knew nothing about tucking a boy in bed;

15

that was clear in William's bedroom that night when he stood awkwardly idle as William scrubbed his face at the washstand and crawled into bed. His bushy eyebrows and narrow lips moved toward each other as if to join in a kiss somewhere at the tip of his hawkish nose, and his eyes blinked so rapidly that he gave the appearance of a bird who has just been rapped in the face and now has no idea what to do next, which in fact was very much Uncle Argyle's situation at the moment. All day long he had known exactly what to say and do, but now he was baffled. "Had enough to eat?" he demanded of William, and the boy nodded. "You've washed your face? Yes, of course, you just did that." His eyes narrowed as if at last he'd caught the boy trying to get away with something.

"I always say them as I'm falling asleep, so my dreams will be open to God all night long," the boy said.

"Who told you that?"

"My father."

There was a long pause. William wondered if he had done something wrong. "Good night, Uncle," William said.

Argyle grunted and started out. Then he stopped, turned back, and leaned down over William, and with great tenderness the grizzled old uncle kissed his nephew on his hair.

Alone in the kitchen, Argyle sat down by the hearth and stared at the embers. He had ridden all day, ever since he'd gotten the news of the death of his brother and his nephew John. All day his mind had buzzed with the practical issues: how he must save his brother's land from confiscation, see to their proper burial, and see to the raising of this son Malcolm had left behind. He had accomplished it all; Argyle Wallace was a man who accomplished everything he set out to do or died trying. The boy would come home with him, that was settled. Argyle had never had a boy around, or even a wife for that matter, but Argyle was

16

an ecclesiastic, and the teacher in him liked the challenge of this wild colt of a nephew.

Malcolm was dead. That was that. When things couldn't be changed, they had to be faced, dealt with. Argyle had done that. But now he sat by the fire and he wanted no sleep, and all he could think about was the time many years ago when he and Malcolm were boys and had just gone to their bed in the loft of their father's house. Argyle had insisted that his brother pray properly on his knees by the bedside, as Argyle always did. And Argyle remembered how, so many years ago, Malcolm had told him that he had decided to pray from within the bed, so he would fall asleep with his dreams open to God.

Malcolm's huge broadsword now lay beside the hearth, next to Argyle's hand. Argyle lifted it and turned the tip to the floor, so that the handle stood before his eyes like the cross.

He began the benediction: "The Lord bless thee and keep thee . . ." Then tears of grief spilled down the old man's cheeks, and he wept beside the fire.

5

DURING HIS SLEEP THAT NIGHT, WILLIAM HAD MORE nightmares. Once again the boy stood in the doorway of the barn and looked at the garish, hung faces in his nightmare. Then a mangled hand came from behind him and grasped his shoulder; William gasped, but the hand held him gently. He turned and saw his father and his brother! They were wounded, bloody, but they smiled at him; they were alive! William wept with joy and reached to hug them, but his father stretched forth a forbidding hand. William kept reaching out helplessly. His father and brother moved past him to the hanged knights. Two empty nooses were there. Before the boy's weeping eyes they put their heads into the nooses and hoisted themselves up. William's grief exploded; his tears erupted and he awakened in his bedroom with tears flooding down his face.

A dream! Still upset, still grieving, he got up and went looking for his uncle.

William moved down to the room where his uncle would be sleeping. He opened the door. The bed had not been slept in. He moved downstairs to the kitchen, but his uncle was not there either. For a moment William thought that his uncle might have abandoned him. Then the boy heard a strange, haunting sound—distant, carried by the wind. He moved to the window and saw only moonlight. He opened the window and heard it more clearly: bagpipes.

William lit a candle and threw open the door. Wind rushed in and blew out his candle. But he heard the pipes, louder in the wind.

William was barefoot and cold, covered only by his nightshirt, but he stepped outside. The sound of the pipes was growing louder. He moved through the moonlight, drawn toward—the graveyard! He stopped as he realized this, then forced himself on.

He moved to the top of the hill where his ancestors were buried and discovered a haunting scene: two dozen men, the farmer/warriors of his neighborhood, were gathered in kilts—and, among them, a core of bagpipers. The pipes wailed an ancient Scottish dirge, a tune of grief and redemption, a melody that, with some modification, has come down to the modern time as "Amazing Grace."

Then William saw his uncle standing at the fringes of the torchlight. Uncle Argyle must have heard them and walked out, too. But what was he doing holding the massive broadsword?

William moved up beside his uncle. Argyle glanced down but said nothing.

"What are they doing?" William whispered.

"Saying good-bye in their own way—playing outlawed tunes with outlawed pipes." They watched as the farmers stood encircling the graves, the music flowing through their veins. Some prayed; some wept; some, their lips moving without their hands making the sign of the cross, seemed to mutter private vows. Argyle whispered, half to William and half to himself, "Your daddy and I, we saw our own father buried like this, dead from fighting the English."

William took the sword from his uncle and tried to lift it. Slowly, Argyle took the sword back.

"First learn to use this," Argyle said. He tapped William on the forehead with the tip of his finger. "Then I will teach you to use this."

With an expert's easy fluidity, he lifted the huge sword. It glistened in the torchlight. The music played; the notes mingled with the smoke of the torches, hung in the air, swirled in the Scottish breeze, and rose toward the stars.

The next morning, William and his uncle rode off in a farm wagon. William held his possessions in a small bundle in his lap. The wagon rattled, lightly loaded with a few of his father's clothes, the wooden chest that held the dress William's mother had worn when she and his father had married, and, wrapped in a length of woolen cloth woven in the pattern distinctive to Wallaces was the broadsword his father had carried into his last battle and his friends had brought back with his body.

William glanced at his uncle as if afraid of his disapproval if he should look back. They reached the top of the hill on the road that led out of the valley where the Wallace farm lay. The horse blew with relief as the road leveled out, and the wagon rolled easier as it stretched ahead.

And there William did glance back just once to see the deserted farmhouse.

THE
REBEL

6

YEARS LATER, AN ENGLISH SAILING VESSEL RODE AT ANCHOR at the Pas de Calais. The entire southwest of France was under the control of Edward the Longshanks, the English king, yet still this vessel was surrounded by a contingent of soldiers, half of them attired in the silks and plumes of an honor guard and the other half in the practical battle gear of fighting soldiers. The former unit had arrayed themselves upon the main deck, whereas the rougher fellows stood in guard positions upon the docks. Out on the water, halfway between the shore and the horizon, rode three warships, swiftest in the English fleet, on watch for the pirates who plied the channel or the Spanish or anyone foolish enough to accost this convoy on this day.

A lookout on the topmast of the flagship was watching the shore, not the sea, and when he sang out, "There! Coming!" the sailors poured up from belowdecks and the parade soldiers lined the rails.

Six French knights, armored as light cavalry, galloped up the road, and then a carriage, flying from its corners the fleur-de-lis, gold on a French blue background, sped into view. Its quartet of jet black horses was lathered and sweating; its wheels drummed sudden thunder on the rough planks of the dock. Six more horsemen rode behind.

The procession lurched to a halt beside the ship, and the captain stepped quickly across the flat timbers bridging to the dock, and there he swept the hat from his head and bowed low. Footmen sprang from their perches at the rear of the carriage; one opened the carriage door and the other placed a golden step below it. From the carriage emerged the brother of the king of France, himself a prince. He was thirty-eight years old, fair-haired and handsome; he wore the finest clothes that anyone on the ship had ever seen.

But he was not the one they had sailed across the channel to meet. Stepping from the carriage into the sunlight was Isabella, his niece, daughter of the king of France, bride-to-be of Edward, son of Longshanks, king of England.

The captain had seen the sun, after a storm-tossed night at sea, rise above the alabaster cliffs of Dover. He had seen the Milky Way on a night so dark and calm that the stars reflected on the black surface of the water and the ship seemed suspended in the heavens. But as he lifted his eyes for his first look at the future queen, the breath left his body, and he knew he would never see anything nearly as beautiful as this blue-eyed woman who kissed her royal father upon his cheek and floated across the bridging timbers into the ship as the sun played upon her yellow hair.

Her name was Isabella Maria Josephina Christiana Marguerita Rochamboulet—well, she had more given names than she had years—And those were just the Christian names. Her family names and titles, in a world where inheritance of crowns depended upon connections of blood and marriage, were a litany as long as the Latin Mass. She had been educated in languages, for which she had great talent, and music, in which she had little, but had received no instruction at all in the art of politics, and it would be years before anyone realized that her gifts in that arena were greatest of all. But she was a woman, and a beautiful one. Yet she could have been utterly unremarkable and still have found herself on this ship, bound for the same destination, because of all those names and titles.

Longshanks had chosen her to be his daughter-in-law because her connection to the throne of France reassured the French nobles of their prospects in the kingdom he sought to create through the union of the two realms. And the king of France had allowed her to accept the proposal because he too wished to see France and England under one crowned head, though with Longshanks already old and his son reputed to be weak, the French king had a different expectation from Longshanks about whose head would wear the crown.

As Isabella stood at the rail and watched the sails fill with breeze, she was aware that nothing she had ever accomplished or said or thought or felt had ever had any result whatsoever. She was a princess already; she was going to be a greater princess still. People would bow and curtsey and would obey her every whim, agree with her every opinion. But she was on her way to marry a man she had never met in a country to which she had never wished to go. No one had ever asked for her consent in the arrangement. She had no power at all. Isabella would only have one man, and he was already chosen. She was a virgin—a royal physician had certified that—and once she married she was forbidden to have any relationships beyond those with her husband. To violate this law was treason.

Beside her stood Nicolette, her friend, her confidant, her lady-in-waiting. Nicolette had dark hair, beautiful dark eyes. Isabella had sometimes wished to have hair and eyes like Nicolette's. Just to be different. But what would it matter?

It was a clear day. The sun was bright. Isabella looked toward the horizon and her new home. They said you could see England from far off on a clear day. She looked toward her new home and gripped the ropes to the sails as the ship rolled through the waves.

Nicolette looked at her lady's face and saw that it looked sad. Nicolette was not surprised. She had seen that face laugh many times, but not since they told her of the engagement. Still she would make the best of it, Nicolette knew that. Isabella seemed frail with that narrow waist and those eyes like a painted doll. But when you looked into those eyes, you knew—you always knew—that she would do what must be done.

7

"HOW DO YOU LIKE IT SO FAR?" NICOLETTE ASKED AS THEIR carriage rolled across the cobblestones of London. They had just entered the city after two full days' journey from the coast. They had seen much of England and only ten minutes of its capital city, but still Isabella knew her friend was referring to London; she was used to Nicolette's sense of humor.

Isabella smiled. "It's a dream."

"It is a nightmare."

"It isn't Paris, that's what you're saying."

"It stinks."

"Paris stinks. We're just used to the way it smells."

"Paris smells like rotting flowers. London smells like rotting fish. If you prefer fish to flowers, then that is up to you."

Isabella laughed. Even in this bone-jarring carriage, with the rain falling and the French guards riding before and after the carriage weighted down by the mud, Nicolette brought warmth and laughter. "London is gray and dirty," Isabella said, "but the people are hardy. Did you see that man back there at the bridge? He was waiting in the rain, had been for hours, I would guess, but he kept the bridge clear of traffic for us to pass. We didn't have to stop and wait;

26

he was already keeping it clear because he knew sooner or later we would be along. The people are efficient."

"Maybe they are stupid. Why else would a man sit out in the cold instead of waiting in a tavern by the fire and coming out only when there is a carriage there to make his job necessary?

"I don't think they are stupid," Isabella said. "I think they are afraid."

8

HER WEDDING DAY.

Isabella woke in a fur-covered bed with four posts carved into angels. They all turned inward as if to watch over her. The canopy that stretched above their halos was woven with patterns of golden thread that caught the light of the fireplace, a cozy blaze maintained all night long by a silent-footed ancient attendant. But neither the wooden angels or the soft bed or the warm fire had made her sleep deeply; several times throughout the night she had opened her eyes to see the flickering gold reflections above her. Now as the princess looked up she saw the gold washed out by the gray of a London morning seeping in at the edges of the window curtains, and she squeezed her eyes shut again and said to herself, "My wedding day."

Many times, as a girl growing up on a castle estate in the country outside Paris, she had imagined this day; she and Nicolette many times had described to each other what colors they would wear, the cut of their dresses, the flowers they would wear in adornment. About the age of fourteen they had begun to include their dreams of a bridegroom in their discussions. He would be handsome, tall, strong. Of course, they were children then, with immature ideas. Isabella was seventeen now, and her thinking was far more mature.

Now she understood that she was a princess, soon to be a queen. She knew her duties: fidelity, respect, maintaining an appearance that would support her husband's pride, and the obligation—greatest of all—to provide him with a male heir. These were utterly natural; she had no doubts she would be a perfect wife.

But she had other expectations, and they caused her some uncertainty. She hoped her new husband would want to share his thoughts, his feelings, his dreams with her. She knew this was a radical hope, but she saw it as her only chance for happiness. Isabella had always known herself to be headstrong. She had ideas; she liked to express them. She had been warned about this many times by the older ladies of the court who had undertaken her instruction in the responsibilities of royalty. They would practice flattery with her: how to widen her eyes in admiration when a man expressed an idea, how to be breathless with his brilliance. She remembered how Madame Bouchard, sent to her from the king of France, had tried to instruct her.

"Now, my darling, suppose I am your royal husband and I come to you and say, 'I am so proud of my new flagship! It is the largest and finest in the world!' What do you say?"

"I ask him who built it."

Madame Bouchard blinked for a moment, sucked her lips between her teeth, and said, "That could work, that might be a good opening. And how would you continue the conversation?"

"I would ask who his sailing master would be and if the master and the builder knew each other."

Madame Bouchard frowned. "No, you see, my darling, the point is not to make your husband talk or to cause him to answer questions unless they are to lead up to the main embrace of this verbal dance, which is to tell your husband that he has accomplished something wonderful. Something spectacular. Something that a lesser man would never have conceived, much less attempted."

"To polish his pride," Isabella said, nodding thoughtfully.

"Yes!"

"To nurture confident feelings about himself."

"Exactly!" Madame Bouchard said, new hope in her voice.

"Then I would also be sure to ask him if the sailing master and the builder not only knew each other, but had spent time together sailing vessels of the builder's making."

"No, no, no, child, why would a queen possibly wish to engage the king in a conversation about details in which even a man could not find the slightest interest?"

Now it was Isabella's turn to look baffled. "Because you said it was about his pride. About his confidence."

"And so it is! But—"

"So what if he brought this ship out before his people, even before another king, and his great ship should sink?"

"That could never happen! What are you—"

"Oh, but it did happen! I heard my father and his friends discussing it, though it was some years ago. The king of some seafaring nation wanted a grand warship to display his power by sailing up and down the coast of his country. He had a favorite builder and ordered the largest vessel the builder had ever made. He had a favorite captain and he put him in command. They launched the ship, it looked glorious, and the king ordered many of his subjects out to the shore to watch the great ship as it passed."

"My darling, I don't see how any of this could be of interest to your future husband unless you wish to put him to sleep."

But Isabella could not be reined in once she had the

bit in her teeth. "Since the builder had been ordered to make the ship as grand as possible, he had added extensive carvings above the waterline; he had given it a wide flat bottom to make it ride high in calm seas. He had given it tall masts. But the sailing master was unfamiliar with such a design. He packed on sails to make the ship look more impressive. And there, just off the coast, on a fine sunny day, in front of several thousands of the king's subjects, the ship hit a light cross wind, flipped over, and sank without a trace."

Madame Bouchard sat motionless, like one of the mummified saints at the cathedral. Isabella was afraid her teacher still didn't understand the point she was trying to make.

"His pride, you see? Wouldn't it be better to ask him those questions that guaranteed he would not make such a mistake?"

Madame Bouchard was blinking, coming back to life.

"Of course, it would never be necessary for me to tell my husband such things after he had had a ship built."

"Precisely," Madame Bouchard said.

"I would have informed him of the importance of good planning when he first mentioned the idea of building a ship, and then he could be very proud of himself."

Madame Bouchard was speechless again.

"And confident," Isabella added, hoping to please her.

But Madame Bouchard, quivering from the tip of her nose like Isabella's uncle Pierre, who died of palsy, stood without another word and left the room.

Lying in her bed now, on her wedding day, Isabella wondered what had ever happened to Madame Bouchard. She hoped her old teacher was still alive. She hadn't looked healthy at all that last time they saw each other.

What if her betrothed, Prince Edward, son of Longshanks—what a peculiar name; did his subjects dare use it openly?—was a sullen man, suspicious, always watching others for the thoughts they kept hidden, as he hid his own? She had observed many of that kind of man in the courts of France, and surely there were many like that here. It would not surprise her, but she would be disappointed. She had met the prince but once, and that at a distance, nodding to him from opposite sides of a U-shaped table at a dinner given in her honor to welcome her. The prince and his friends had sat on one side and the princess, with her attendants from France and the new ones now provided her from the English court, had sat on the other. The center table was empty; Longshanks was in Wales, someone had said, advising his military advisors.

The prince was a slender young man with fine features. She had not spoken to him except to curtsey and say, "The pleasure is all mine, m'lord," after he had said he welcomed her with great pleasure before sitting down to start the meal. But she had watched from the corner of her eye while exchanging whispers with Nicolette. She had noticed young Edward had a quick smile, though he kept watching his friends as he smiled as if he needed their approval. A strange habit in a prince.

Isabella of France lay there in her English bed and thought on all these things without opening her eyes.

Nicolette, moving soundlessly by her bed on her way to tend the fire, thought, *What a strange girl this princess is, frowning in her sleep on her wedding day.*

She sponged her body in warm water scented with the petals of roses brought live all the way from Italy. She put on new undergarments, and a whole flock of attendants, chattering with excitement, dressed her for the wedding. Yards and yards of fabric, light as air, bleached white, wrapped around her shoulders and flowed to the floor; a royal blue bodice hugged her waist; tiny gold chains adorned her shoulders and a necklace of diamonds embraced her throat. Two more

31

attendants brushed her hair, plaited and coiled it, then placed the veil, falling like a cloud from her head to her waist. Nicolette oversaw it all, inspecting each button, each chain, each buckle; snapping instructions; making adjustments; and always beaming.

The attendants kept flapping; it seemed the more beautiful she became, the faster they worked, until finally Nicolette clapped her hands together loudly and said, "It is done!" They all stopped and looked at the glory they had created, a princess they would all be proud to serve.

Isabella turned to the polished silver mirror and studied herself. She barely recognized the reflection. It was rare for royalty to show gratitude—servants were expected to do no less than their best, and appreciation was thought to ruin them—but Isabella turned to the women who had dressed her and said, "Thank you. I . . . thank you."

It seemed to embarrass them. Nicolette stepped forward and commanded, "Tell them we are ready."

The attendants snatched up all their spare cloth, their shears, needles and pins, and hurried out; but as the last one was leaving Isabella said, "Wait. Tell them I need a few more minutes. Just a few. Alone with Nicolette."

The last attendant curtsied and was gone.

"Last-minute nerves?" Nicolette asked.

"No, I . . ."

"Well, what is it?"

"I need . . . to speak with you."

"Of course. What about?"

"I . . . we must talk."

"You just said that! Please, Isabella! Would you stop this fidgeting? Don't you understand we have the whole country waiting? What could you possibly need to talk about now, enough to keep the king, the prince, the elite of the entire kingdom standing around scratching their noses?!"

"Sex."

At that moment another attendant knocked on the

outer door and called, "M'lady, please! We are all ready!"

"Tell them to wait!" Nicolette shouted, then snatched the door open and barked even louder. "We are *not* ready!" She slammed the door and spun around to face Isabella. Nicolette's features were frozen for some moments in a blank stare as she tried to consider what to do next while concealing her concern. It only made her appear to Isabella to look panicked.

But then Nicolette shrugged and moved to Isabella, taking both her hands in her own. "Now," she began with the patient tone of a grandparent speaking to a confused child, "haven't we talked about such things many times before?"

"Yes, we have, of course we have. But you were always telling me how it came about. How you met, the first glance and then the second one, the one with real meaning, the brushing past each other, the sudden kiss in a dark corner of the palace corridor, the rendezvous—"

"Yes! Yes! Exactly! Exactly!" Nicolette's head kept nodding and nodding.

"But you've never told me about the actual thing. The actual thing itself."

"The thing. The thing. The actual thing itself," Nicolette repeated, and then, when there was another knock at the door, she bawled at the top of her lungs, *"We are not ready!"*

Nicolette began to pace. "The thing. Yes, of course. The actual thing itself . . . Weren't you listening when I told you all my stories?"

"I *was* Nicolette, I *was* listening! But I need to know exactly what to do!" Isabella felt her own rising panic and was angry at herself for it. It was not like her to lose her head this way; whatever was the matter? She liked to be in control; and with her intellect coupled with her position of privilege, she always had felt in control of every situation. But now she was about to step into a secret, intimate place, about which she

33

knew absolutely nothing. And no one would tell her, not even Nicolette! Suddenly Isabella began to suspect that her friend may have lied when she was describing her many romantic liaisons.

But Nicolette had not lied. She was an experienced lady of the court of France, even if she was still only nineteen. And while Isabella, reared in the expectation that she would someday wear a crown, had been wrapped in the regal requirements of chastity, the customs of Nicolette's life had been just the opposite. It would be many years before she delighted some nobleman or even a royal cousin by consenting to become his wife; until that time—and, the truth be told, even after that time—she would enliven the world of court romance like a willing participant at a royal ball, doing one of those dances in which everyone is always switching partners.

"Isabella!" Nicolette said in a demanding tone that only she could take with her friend, and only now. "You mean you know nothing? Absolutely nothing?"

"I tell you I can't think of anything to do! With you, with everything you've ever described, there is some kind of—of—of courtship! Some kind of gradual . . . But I haven't even spoken to the prince, not really!"

"Madame Bouchard! She's the one who should've told you!"

"She isn't here!"

"All right, all right, listen to me, this is what you do! Tonight, when you are in the bedroom waiting . . ."

"Yes?"

But suddenly Nicolette didn't know what to advise either. "Yes, let me think, let me think. Well, you don't really have to do anything. Exactly! That's it! He will come in and *he* will know just what to do!"

"What if he doesn't?" The two young women stood blinking at each other. "I mean, I don't know anything about such things, but did he appear to you to be someone who knew a great deal himself?"

Another knock at the door, and a voice from outside pleading, "Please, ladies! Please!"

"All right," Nicolette said decisively. "You will lie down upon the bed, you will close your eyes, and you will say as softly as you can, *'I am ready.'* Do that, and everything will be . . . acceptable."

" *'I am ready?'* " Isabella repeated.

" *'I am ready.'* "

Arm in arm, the princess and her lady-in-waiting moved to the door. Nicolette opened the latch and pushed the door open, revealing dozens of relieved attendants dressed for the wedding and perspiring in their scarlet smocks trimmed in white ermine. "I am ready," the princess declared, and with a slight glance at Nicolette and a faint smile upon her lips, the future queen of England walked slowly into the corridor to join the great procession that would take her into Westminster Abbey.

9

THE WEDDING WAS A BLUR FOR HER. IT WAS NOT THAT SHE missed all the details; quite the contrary, she felt and saw so many things that she could scarcely take them all in. Her attendants looked so beautiful, with flowers in their hair, sewn into garlands draped around their shoulders, strewn in petals at their feet; the flames of a thousand candles danced in ranks in the abbey to the tunes of harps and lutes; and the faces of the dignitaries crowded into the pews, all of them watching her.

But there was one face that would wipe all of this from her memory: Edward I of England, Longshanks himself. She saw the king for the first time in her life as she reached the altar of the abbey; she was just about to kneel to receive the initial blessing when she became aware of his presence. It was strange, this presence of the king; she had been with kings before and knew the strange sense that came into one's stomach when a king was about. All attention was directed to him, and yet everyone pretended to be looking away. She sensed that same breathlessness as she came to the end of her walk down the abbey's central aisle and looked in the direction that everyone else was pointedly not looking. There she saw Longshanks.

He was tall, as tall as they had said. But nothing she had heard, in France and later in the court in London, had prepared her for what she was seeing now, for he was handsome. There was no doubt about that. It was in his carriage more than his features; he stood like a statue, like a living statue, with the posture of a man who has never questioned his own judgment, has never had to. He was dressed in the grandest clothes of the kingdom; he wore his crown lightly as if he had been born with it on, and in effect he had. The face itself—well, some people had told her it was cruel. Certainly the nose was too long, the chin too sharp for his face to look kind. But his long dark hair was luxurious, the skin smooth, the—

The eyes! He turned them to her just then, and it was then that she understood what everyone had meant. There was no feeling in them, none at all. They were dead eyes, like one of those Greek statues in which the shape of the irises had been carved but the pupils had not. When he looked at her, it was clear to Isabella that he felt nothing. The young beautiful princess was used to being appraised, considered for her beauty, her value to the realm. Or if not appraised, then admired. But this man showed nothing, and Isabella was sure beyond doubt that he felt nothing. She had heard a story about him, how his wife had died while visiting him during a campaign against the Celts in Wales. Longshanks, so the story went, had been shattered by grief; he ordered her body carried back to London on the shoulders of his proudest soldiers. Wherever they stopped to rest and set the litter bearing her body down upon the earth, his builders were ordered to erect a cross. In the Norman French of Longshanks's court, these were called *chère reine* crosses, for "precious queen." English commoners, in that peculiar mongrel tongue they called the English language, corrupted the term into charing cross. It was the decree of a grieving man, a romantic, a man with a heart. The story had put Isabella off guard. This man who looked at her now, with those dead eyes, had no heart and no soul.

She went through the rest of the ceremony, repeating her vows wherever it was expected of her. Prince Edward became her husband in the same mechanical way. They did not kiss; they were not expected to. Later, Isabella would not remember the ceremony at all.

But she would never forget her first look at those eyes.

That night the attendants prepared a special wedding chamber for them in the new royal apartments she and Edward were to inhabit together. A table was placed before the bedroom fireplace and a special dinner laid out upon it, with lamb, fowl, fish, fresh fruits, vegetables, pastries—every rich food the kingdom could provide. And wine, too, and more flowers, all arrayed for them in the bedroom. A small army of servants must have worked on it, and yet they had all disappeared now, like magic fairies. Only Nicolette remained, and only for a moment. She gripped Isabella's hands in her own, stared as if she had just spoken—though she had uttered not a word since their time together before the ceremony—and nodded, not once but many times. Then Nicolette too left her.

Isabella thought the prince would arrive at any moment. She sat down beside the fire to wait, for ever since she had seen her father-in-law, she had felt cold. But her new husband did not arrive. The ice in the wooden bucket around the wine melted, and an attendant tiptoed in to replace the water with more gray chunks from the palace ice house. Kitchen servants tiptoed in to take the food away and warm it again, but still Edward did not come.

Isabella fell asleep in the chair.

Later—she did not know how much later—she awoke to the sound of male laughter and the rattle of the latch at the door. Someone was fumbling at it as if it were locked, but of course it was not. Edward staggered in. He was drunk. He was accompanied by another young man, the same one who had been with him at the first royal dinner she had attended.

They stopped laughing when they saw her; then Peter, her husband's friend, burst into laughter again.

Isabella smiled, trying to understand the joke. But now her husband seemed to see no joke; he was looking at her. He then turned to Peter and stared blankly at him.

"I shall wait outside," Peter said and laughed again. He left them, closing the door loudly.

Edward stared at her.

She stared at him. She rose from her chair.

He did not move.

She moved to him. He said nothing. There was sweat on his brow; his breath stank. He smelled as if he had vomited recently.

She knelt before him and kissed his hand, then rose. He did not move.

She walked to the bed, still fully dressed, and lay upon the fur. "I am ready," she said.

She heard the door close and Peter laugh. Her husband had gone, and she was all alone.

Her wedding night.

10

THE NEXT MORNING, ISABELLA BREAKFASTED NOT IN THE royal apartments, but in the dining room of the guest quarters where she had previously stayed. When Nicolette found her, she was already half through with her meal. "There you are!" her friend sang brightly. "And up so . . . early." Nicolette's tone changed the instant she saw Isabella's face. She sat down immediately and leaned close, her eyes asking the question.

Isabella spoke softly, barely above a whisper. "I was ready. I suppose he was not."

Nicolette's tongue tried to wet her lips, suddenly dry. She seemed to want to say something but was saved from the effort by the arrival of a trim young man dressed in the bright livery Prince Edward had designated for all his personal servants. He handed Isabella a folded, sealed message on a small silver tray and said, "From your husband."

As soon as Isabella lifted the note, the messenger bowed sharply and took his leave. With a glance at Nicolette, the princess broke the seal, unfolded the single paper, and read the words scrawled there. "'The king directs me to attend a meeting this morning at the first chime. I am otherwise engaged, also at his direction. You will attend in my place and report to me afterward in the royal apartments.' It is signed 'Edward.'"

Just then the first chime of morning rang. Nicolette looked across at her friend. "You are late," she said.

Longshanks stood at a map nearly as tall as he was and stabbed with his narrow finger at the land north of England, marked as endless hill country dotted

39

with fortresses and shaded in other areas so impassable the mapmakers had left them bare. "Scotland! *Scot—land!*" he barked at his advisors. They sat at a grand table in clothes that made their shoulders look wider, their chests thicker. Some even wore polished armor to conferences like this one in order to enhance their status as military men. But none of that made them less afraid of Longshanks.

"The French will grovel to anyone with strength!" he said in a voice deep and powerful and relentless as the sea. "But how will they credit our strength when we cannot rule the whole of our own island?!" Longshanks shouted.

He punched the map again, then saw the princess enter silently and move to the window along the far wall.

"Where is my son?" Longshanks asked.

She stopped suddenly, realizing the question was meant for her. "Your pardon, m'lord, he asked me to come in his stead," the princess said.

Longshanks's eyes expanded in fury; it was frightening to see. "I send for him—and the little coward sends you?!"

"Shall I leave, m'lord?"

"If he wants his queen to rule, then you stay and learn how! I will deal with him."

He spun back toward his generals. Ignored, the princess settled silently onto the cushions of the window seat.

"Nobles are the key to the Scottish door. Grant their nobles land here in England. Give our own nobles estates in the north. Make them too greedy to oppose us," he said.

One old advisor spoke up hesitantly, "Sire, our nobles will be reluctant to relocate. New lands mean new taxes, and they are taxed already for our war in France."

Longshanks glared at him but took the point. The wheels spun in his brain. His dark eyes fell on the princess. He stared, his eyes cold and blank. She felt chilled, and yet it was as if he was not looking at her at all, but at some lifeless echo that inspired a dusty memory. What could he be thinking of?

He turned back toward his advisors and revealed his inspiration. "Then let our nobles be real lords in Scotland. Grant them *prima noctes,* 'first night.' When any common girl inhabiting their lands is married, our lords shall have sexual rights to her on the night of her wedding. That should fetch just the kind of lords we want to Scotland."

Princess Isabella, tucked against the far window, upon a goose down sitting cushion by the damask curtains, felt a draft must have blown in, so cold did her back become. Vivid emotions flooded through her in a confusing swirl. Young women . . . on their wedding nights . . . She had just experienced the emotions and uncertainties of her own wedding night, and she felt for any girl in the same situation. Isabella was young, perhaps naive, but she sensed that princesses and pauper girls must all be alike in their hearts. This was against all she had been taught, but her experience, her recent experience, told her it must be true! If anything, she, in the last days, had come to envy common girls who, she fancied, were free to marry for love. But now, here loomed the enforcement of an old tradition whose only purpose, as far as she could see, was to destroy love and families. If the true purpose of marriage, as the Church taught, was procreation, then the right of a lord to copulate with a common girl in his dominion on the first night of her marriage would mean that her husband could never know if his firstborn child was of his seed or the nobleman's. What a savage, perverse law!

And on top of that, why had the king been looking at her when he thought of it?

Then Isabella's heart went cold. Longshanks was looking at her again. He was smiling lewdly at her. She lowered her eyes, stood, and left the room.

11

THE PRINCE AND HIS MUSCULAR YOUNG FRIEND PETER
were stripped to the waist and fencing in the royal
apartments. They paid no attention to the knock or to
the princess as she entered. She watched them—they
were dancing more than fencing. Edward lost his
sword; it clattered to the polished floor. He looked up
at his wife as if angry at her for having seen his
clumsiness.

"What is it?!" Edward snapped. He had a bark like
his father, as if imitating Longshank's face and tone.
But the son's sound seemed to say, How long must I
suffer? whereas the message in the king's tone seemed
to be, How long before I make you suffer?

"You directed me to report to you when the king's
conference was ended," the princess said.

"So I did! And what was so important about it?"

"Scotland. He intends—"

But Edward and his friend were fencing again, the
clanging of their blunted swords so loud that she
couldn't hear herself.

She tried again. "He intends to grant—"

But Edward lost his weapon once more, and now he
whirled on her. "Shut up, would you! How can I
concentrate?!"

"His majesty was quite keen that you should understand—"

"All so very boring! He wants me to learn to fight
too, so *let me do it!"*

For an instant, anger flared into her eyes. She
glanced at Edward and at the young man with him
just before she turned to walk out. But Edward had
noticed her glance.

42

"Stop there," he demanded.

She stopped but did not turn around.

"Do you disapprove of Peter?" Edward asked.

He lifted his hand and drew his friend Peter to his side. Still the princess did not turn around.

"No, m'lord," she quietly said.

"Turn around. I said, *turn around!*"

She braced herself and turned. But she could not brace herself enough for what she saw: Edward nuzzled Peter, the prince's bare chest to his muscular friend's bare back, both men glistening with sweat and sexual excitement.

The princess's eyes quivered, but she did not look away.

"Now, my flower, do you understand?" Edward asked.

"Yes. I had thought that . . . I was loathsome to you. Perhaps I am. If I may be excused, m'lord."

"You may," he said.

She started to leave as quietly as she came, but her husband yelled after her, "Don't worry, m'lady, it is my royal responsibility to breed. And I assure you, when the time comes, I shall . . . manage."

She closed the door softly on her husband and his lover.

12

FAR NORTH OF LONDON, UP WHERE THE FIRTH OF FORTH and the river Clyde cut the great British island nearly in half, seven horsemen galloped along a wet road, the hooves of their horses slapping sharply, smacking mud high onto the horses' flanks and across the legs of the riders. They rode with military precision as a bodyguard; in the center of their formation was a young man, barely in his twenties. His hair was dark brown, his moustache and chin whiskers smartly groomed in the fashion of Norman nobility. His shoulders were broad, his chest thick from hard practice with the heavy broadsword he wore at his waist. The tunic over his chain mail displayed a scarlet cross, and one of the riders beside him carried a banner that snapped in the wind, flashing the same noble colors.

They wound into Edinburgh, Scotland's royal seat, city of its last king. The road grew more crowded, but the peasants and free merchants scrambled aside to let the riders pass. At the steep hill up to the castle their horses labored, but the young man spurred his horse into the lead and through the gates without pause. A clatter of hooves upon the cobblestones, a snapping of the guards' pikes in salute, and Robert, 17th earl of Bruce, had arrived.

Gathered around a massive table in the central room of the castle were two dozen noblemen, supporters of the Bruce's claim to the vacant Scottish throne. As young Robert strode in, still spattered with the mud of his ride, the others stood and bowed their heads in respect. Robert waved his solemn acknowledgment and took his seat at the center of the table; the others settled in respectfully. Young Robert glanced to his friend Mornay, another young noble similarly attired in fighting armor, and gave him another nod in personal greeting, as he did to Craig, a balding, gray-haired nobleman.

Old Craig was not only leader of the council, he had long been a friend and ally of the Bruce's father. He spoke up immediately. "Young Robert, we are honored! And your father is well?"

"He strained his leg so that it pains him to ride, but he sends his compliments." Robert glanced around the table to include all of them, for noble pride was never to be slighted. Then Robert, as was his habit, plunged right into business. "He hears Longshanks has granted *prima noctes.*"

44

"Clearly meant to draw more of his supporters here," Craig said.

Mornay, lean, dark, and fit, though not so handsome as young Bruce, had been impatiently awaiting his friend's arrival and now gave vent to the sentiments that had been pushing to get out. "The Balliols have endorsed the right, licked Longshanks's boots so he will support their claim to the throne!"

The comment set off a storm of hatred, like the first flash of lightning brings the rain. The competition for the crown of Scotland had only grown uglier in the years since the death of Alexander, Scotland's last king, and the untimely death of his infant successor. Alliances had been made and broken; meetings made to discuss alliances had broken into brawls, cousin had killed cousin, brother had murdered brother. Two families—Balliol and Bruce—had emerged as the leading contenders. Most of the noblemen, and the commoners, too, seemed to favor the Bruces; they were more instinctively warlike, they exhibited a decisive ruthlessness, and the Highland clans had always respected action more than words. There was never any doubt that the Bruces acted for their own self-interest; many times they had earned English favor—and the corresponding rewards of huge tracts of land along the border areas—by suppressing renegade uprisings among the Lowland clans. But the clans, autonomous tribes under chieftains who held the power of life and death over their members, lived by fighting with and stealing from each other, especially from the Lowlanders, so they were unoffended by the Bruce family's persecution of their neighbors to the south. Alliances with the English king were another matter, yet they saw that for every treaty made there was a treaty broken. To them it seemed that the Bruces clasped one hand with the English only to draw them close enough to punch them with the other.

Several times the Bruces had been captured and imprisoned by the English. They had always been released when it seemed to Longhanks that the headaches he suffered over the rising power of the Bruces had been less painful than the torments of unchecked marauders along the northern borders of his kingdom.

The Balliols had been troublesome, too, but although they were as pugnacious as the Bruces, they seemed to have a preference for diplomacy. Longshanks had seen this and had endorsed John Balliol as heir to the Scottish throne. The support of Longshanks—his threats to opponents, his bribes to supporters—swung a majority of the noble families of Scotland into the Balliol camp, and a consensus of nobles had declared John Balliol king. No sooner had this happened than Longshanks insisted the new king come to England and pay him homage, thus declaring himself a servant of the English crown. Balliol had resisted, for to do so would have shown him to be no king at all. Longshanks responded by laying siege to Balliol's castle and taking him prisoner. From prison Balliol had given in and announced his homage; Longshanks accepted the subservience and kept Balliol locked up anyway.

So now all of Scotland was even further divided. Some Scottish free men said their king was in prison; others felt the man in jail was no king at all, and they looked for another. The Scots continued to fight among themselves. Longshanks was happy, because they were no longer fighting him.

Hatred and anger ran strong in the deep veins of the Scottish spirit, and those emotions were vividly expressed around that great table in Edinburgh Castle as young Robert Bruce met with his supporters. Bruce let them give tongue to their passions; it was useful to allow them to let some of the heat out, so they could be led.

But finally Mornay brought their choices into focus. "If we fight now," he said, "we will have the commoners' support."

Robert now said what he had prepared to say even before he set out for the meeting. "My father believes it is too soon to step out alone. He says we must lull

Longshanks into confidence by neither supporting his decree nor opposing it." Young Bruce glanced at Mornay, who saw in the look that he too would rather fight than talk, rather act than wait. But Bruce's father had long been known for the shrewdness of his instincts, and no man there would dispute the elder Bruce's council.

"A wise plan," Craig announced, ending the meeting.

The allied nobles filed out, making friendly conversation about the bounty of the harvests from their lands, expansions of their castles, improvements of their horses' breeds. Young Bruce went with them, promising each that he would carry their fondest greetings to his father.

Then just before he mounted his horse for the ride home, Robert found a moment with Mornay. Mornay's brown eyes sparkled, deep and intense; his grip on Bruce's hand was strong, purposeful. It reminded Bruce once again that his friend was ambitious—and growing impatient. Mornay leaned close to him and whispered, "This diplomacy is a game for old men."

Robert grinned as if Mornay had just joked with him; he did not want these men to see them whispering, for private exchanges tended to make the hands of some men—and especially of these men—seek the handles of their swords. He climbed into his saddle and waited as Mornay, with as fine a contingent of mounted men as any in Scotland, leaped onto his own horse. They rode side by side to the gates of the city, and then, as their paths home parted, Bruce said to Mornay, "Don't worry. The time for you and me is coming."

13

BARELY A DAY'S JOURNEY FROM EDINBURGH, BUT IN A different world from the royal city with its fine residences overlooked by the noble fortress, lay Lanark, a village of mud streets and stone houses, with thatched roofs and the persistent aroma of peatmoss fires. Lanark was a market for farmers, a gathering place for fairs and festivals. Such a festival, this one of planting, was then taking place in the open grassy area at the edge of town. Flutes chortled like birds, notes sparkling in the air; girls wove garlands among the locks of their hair and bounced and spun to the music; children chased each other; old men laughed. Farmers carted in fresh bread and wheels of cheese; villagers brought out casks of beer or strings of smoked fish.

All of this happened before the guarded gaze of English soldiers. Some were battle-scarred veterans with missing eyes and ears, others were pimply boys away from home for the first time. They had been told from birth that the Scots were little more than animals; they knew that even the Romans, conquering Britain a thousand years earlier, had decided these wild people who went into battle with their bodies painted blue and had been known to strip naked in battle and build defensive walls with their dead, were better left alone. This was a country that could not be subdued; English kings may not have known it, but their occupying troops knew it only too well. They moved about only in groups, rested only with sentries posted, and learned never to turn their backs on anyone. Although Longshanks had decreed that no Scottish civilians could own weapons, even the women carried blades tucked among their clothes. The garrison at Lanark was headquartered in a stronghold near the village center. They were commanded by a man named Hesselrig, who held the official title of sheriff of Lanarkshire.

Hesselrig's men had standing orders to subdue any disturbance and direct orders not to disturb the festival as long as it was peaceful. Hesselrig himself approved of the celebration. If the countryfolk were enjoying themselves, it implied they were coming to accept English rule. So it was that his soldiers watched the village streets and the roads to the festival, giving all who approached it a careful appraisal.

And so it was that they took special notice of the young man who came riding in from the hills beyond the village. His eyes were that green that only Scots and Irish seem to possess, his hair light brown when he passed the shadows beneath trees and showing blond when in a shaft of sunlight. He sat his horse as if born there, his back straight, his hands relaxed on the reins. He had a look of lean, rippled power. He looked dangerous.

He was in his midtwenties. Many men had fathered entire families by then and already looked old. He had a sheen of health like a man who had eaten selectively and avoided too much drink—rare for a man who appeared capable of taking what he wanted. And, as the apparent owner of a horse—and a fine one, too, with long legs and a deeply muscled chest, clearly capable of speed—he could have been a knight. Knights of the Middle Ages lived on the mercenary cusp between the peasantry and the nobility. Owners of a horse, weapons, and possibly a small stronghold, they were upwardly mobile in a society that knew death well and valued the ability to cause it. This young man wore the smock of a farmer, but his hands, noticed by the first sentry he rode by, bore old nicks and sundry scars about the knuckles, such as one might see on a fighting man.

The soldiers all noticed him and nudged each other as he passed. He carried a dead wild goose hanging

49

across his saddle; he stopped his horse at the edge of the clearing and surveyed the scene of the festival. Farmers were roasting a pig; women were comparing handiwork; young men were tossing a caber—an unbranched tree trunk roughly half the size of a modern telephone pole—in the traditional Highland games. And these people too were noticing the new arrival, especially the farm women with daughters of marriageable age.

Also watching were the fathers, husbands, and suitors of the local women. At the edge of the clearing was Campbell, his red hair and beard now streaked heavily with gray, and with him his old rebel friend, MacClannough. They watched as the young man dismounted and tied his horse to a willow. And in the way he moved, the way he carried himself, they saw the reflection of the friend they had loved and buried many years before.

"MacClannough . . . ," old Campbell whispered.

"I see him," MacClannough said.

"Could that be . . . William Wallace?"

They watched as one of the English soldiers, backed by three others, moved up and shoved the young Scot from behind, determined to provoke him there and then if he had come to make trouble. The young man lurched forward for two quick steps and recovered his balance easily, then turned calmly as if he had expected the provocation. "Hey, boy! You hunt this bird?" the soldier demanded.

The green eyes fixed themselves on the soldier.

"It's against the law for Scots to own bows. You shot this bird?" the soldier continued. His comrades, enjoying their role as intimidators, surrounded the horse, pulled the goose from the saddle, and began prodding the bird's feathers for evidence.

"I hit it in the head. With a rock," answered William Wallace—for William Wallace it was.

The soldiers didn't believe a goose as plump as this one could be brought down with anything less than a fine bow. But they couldn't find any puncture wound on the bird. William reached his hand out for the return of the goose. The soldiers dropped it onto the ground. Slowly, William picked it up and headed into the clearing.

The farmers watched him coming and mumbled among themselves.

"He wrote to Dougal, saying he would be taking over the farm again," Campbell said.

"He *wrote* Dougal? How did Dougal read it?" MacClannough asked.

"Had the priest read the letter, didn't he?" Campbell said.

Also among those who noticed William's arrival—but pretended not to—was Murron MacClannough, grown now into a stunning young woman. Her long auburn hair reminded people of those years long ago; she wore it the same way, straight and full down her back. Her dress was plain, like the grass that surrounded a wildflower. She was the most beautiful girl in the village, maybe in all of Scotland, and the soldiers who hassled William noticed her, too.

William reached the food table; farm women were preparing the feast. He tossed his goose onto the table as his contribution; the women smiled and began plucking right away. One of them spoke up quickly, taking her chance before the others could. "Young William Wallace, back home! How good to see you here! Have you met my daughter?"

The daughter mentioned was missing teeth. William nodded to her.

His smile was gentle, but had it outshone the sun it would not have been as bright as her hopes, and she lowered her head in disappointment. But then she raised her face in surprise as William took her hand and gave her a respectful bow.

He moved away from the table, passing through the crowd like a stranger. Then he glanced toward the knot of girls. He saw Murron. She saw him, then

51

looked away. Did they remember each other? He moved toward her; she was shy, her eyes downcast, but then she raised them and looked at him.

They moved closer and closer together. Just as they were about to reach each other, a huge round stone thumped to the earth at William's feet.

He looked up and saw one of Murron's suitors—the broad, muscled young man who had just tossed the stone in William's way.

Suddenly every young man, every old man, every young woman and her mother, every child in the whole village, seemed to be watching to see how William would handle the challenge.

He first tried to move around the bigger man, but the broad young farmer cut him off. Then William seemed to think he recognized the big redhead.

"Hamish?" William asked.

And it was his old best friend, Hamish Campbell, but Hamish wouldn't admit it or be put off from the challenge. He pointed to the huge stone. "Test of manhood," Hamish declared in a voice grown deep and full and threatening.

"You win," William said.

"Call it a test of soldiery, then. The English won't let us train with weapons, so we train with stones."

"The test of a soldier is not in his arm. It's here," William said and tapped his finger to his temple.

Hamish stretched out his hand as if to show William something in his palm. "No. It's here," Hamish said and with a sudden movement he slammed his fist into William's jaw, which dropped him to the wet ground.

A few men moved to interfere, but Campbell, MacClannough, and the other farmers who were the true leaders here stopped their neighbors from interfering. Hamish stood over William and waited for him to get up.

William blew out a long breath and cleared his head. "A contest, then," he said. He stood. With a deep grunt he hoisted the huge stone, eighteen inches in diameter. Straining with the effort, he lugged the stone to the line the burly young men had scratched in the rocky field. Beyond the line were the muddy dents from previous tosses. William took a run and heaved the stone.

It arced heavily through the air and landed with a muffled thud, making a new dent well beyond the other marks in the field.

People were impressed, everyone but Hamish, who was pursing his lips in contempt at the toss. William glanced at him and seemed almost to apologize for the length of the toss, saying, "I still say this is no test. A catapult can throw a stone farther than a man can."

"That depends on the man," Hamish said sharply. He walked out, lifted the stone, and lugged it back to the line. He retreated a few more steps, took a short run, and heaved with a great groan.

The stone flew and passed William's mark by a couple of feet. People laughed and whistled. William nodded, impressed.

"Can you do it when it matters? As it matters in battle? Could you crush a man with that throw?" William wondered out loud.

"I could crush you like a roach."

William walked to the dent made by Hamish's throw.

"Then do it. Come, do it."

Hamish scowled at William, at everybody watching. William didn't move. The green eyes seem to laugh at him. Hamish lifted the stone and carried it back to the line. He glared at William. William stood calmly.

Hamish backed up for his run and looked once more at William. William yawned.

"You'll move," Hamish said.

"I will not."

Hamish backed up a few more feet for a longer run.

"That's not fair!" Stewart, another of the farmers, called out from among the knot of men around old Campbell, Hamish's father.

53

"He's tired; he should get a longer run!" old Campbell argued.

William seemed completely unafraid. He leaned down, picked up a small smooth stone, and tossed it up in the air casually, like a boy lost in daydreams on a midsummer's day.

Stung by this show of calm, Hamish took a furious run and heaved. The stone flew through the air, missed William's head by inches, and buried itself halfway into the earth behind him.

William never flinched. The people cheered.

"Brave show!" old Campbell called out.

Hamish was miffed; it was as if William had won. But what had he done except stand there? "I threw longer than last time!" Hamish shouted and glared first at William, then at his father and the other elders.

"An ox is strong but not clever," his father boomed back.

"An ox is stupid enough to just stand in one place!" Hamish countered. Everyone considered this, while Hamish seemed both surprised and particularly proud of his reply.

"That's not the point," William said. He turned, walked double the distance Hamish threw, turned again, and hurled the rock he held! It whistled through the air, hit Hamish in the forehead, and dropped him like a shot. *"That* is," William said.

Everybody cheered and laughed. They surrounded William. "A fine display, young Wallace!" Campbell shouted.

William took a tankard of ale from a farmer, walked over, and tossed the cold liquid into Hamish's face. He awoke and, his eyes uncrossing, saw William's hand outstretched to him. Hamish accepted it, and William groaned, pulling his huge friend to his feet.

"Good to see you again," William said.

"I should'a remembered the eggs," Hamish said.

They grinned and embraced. Music played and the dancing began again. For several minutes William accepted the greetings of his father's old friends, nodding to each. Then, when he had paid respects to all, he began to move across the clearing to the knot of young ladies.

Again he drew nearer and nearer to Murron—then passed her and moved to the girl with the missing teeth.

"Would you honor me with a dance?" William asked.

The girl was thrilled. The young handsome man danced with the girl with the missing teeth.

"You've taken over your father's farm?" the girl asked as they went spinning along in the dance called strip-the-widow.

William nodded.

"They say he died long ago. Fighting the English," the girl said.

"He died in an accident with my brother. Their cart turned over," William said.

The music ended, and William gave the girl a gracious bow of thanks. She glowed. As he escorted the girl back to her beaming mother, it started to rain. Everyone gathered up the food and scrambled for shelter.

Everyone but William. He stood out alone in the rain and watched it fall.

14

THAT NIGHT, WILLIAM WALLACE STOOD IN THE DOOR OF the farmhouse where he had slept as a boy, where he had kept his last vigil waiting for his father and brother, the place he had left long years ago with his uncle Argyle. In the time since then the place had been used by a succession of tenant farmers, and several of the more prosperous of the local farmers had wished to buy it. Uncle Argyle had refused the first two offers without telling William, but the most recent one, coming two years ago, caused the old man to sit William down, tell him about the previous bids for the house and lands, and let him choose for himself what to do with his inheritance. William had refused the offer, sending word that he planned to work the land himself. His return seeming imminent, all the tenants had vacated. The house had been empty since that time; William's return was delayed for reasons that the select group of local farmers who received communications from Uncle Argyle (through the village priest) never heard explained and found mysterious.

Now one wall, needing daubing, admitted the wind. The table where William had once laid out the dinner of stew that his father and brother would never eat was still there; constructed by his father, it had survived the years of use, and the scars upon its surface made it look sturdier than ever, but it was the only furnishing that seemed usable. The straw sleeping mats were filthy; William had already carried them outside and replaced them with clean straw from the barn. The bedsteads had long ago been removed; he didn't know who had them, but he was sure that Uncle Argyle or old Campbell had seen to it that someone worthy had them. Other than the one wall, the house seemed in good enough repair. Ah, well, the roof leaked, a trickle of cold water had begun to fall on William's neck. The roof needed thatch, that was to be expected.

None of that was important. He could take care of all that. But now something else occupied his thoughts—or rather drew all his thoughts away, so he couldn't think at all.

He stood at the open door of the farmhouse and gazed out at the rain.

Hard against a steep hillside, beside a meadow ringed with trees, stood the MacClannough house, a thatched cottage with wood plank windows closed against the storm. The aromatic smoke from a cozy fire in its hearth curled up out of its chimney and mingled with the rain. Inside the house, the old man was in his chair, the wife was sewing, their daughter Murron was embroidering something, and there was a knock at the door.

"Who can that be in this rain?" Mrs. Mac-Clannough wondered.

Her husband stood and opened the door to—a horse! The animal stood just outside his doorway as if the beast wished to come in! Then the farmer recovered from his surprise and saw that the horse had a rider: none other than William Wallace.

Both man and horse were drenched with rain; huge steady drops exploded over them. Young Wallace smiled as if he had just come calling on a bright, warm Sunday and said, "Good evening, sir. May I speak with your daughter?"

Mrs. MacClannough stood bug-eyed at her husband's shoulder, and then Murron appeared behind her stunned parents.

Wallace persisted. "Murron, would you like to go for a ride on this fine evening?"

"The boy's . . . the boy's insane!" Murron's mother sputtered.

"It's good Scottish weather, madam. The rain is fallin' straight down," William said and grinned again, but he was losing hope.

Farmer MacClannough was still stunned, but his wife's words were all the quicker. "She absolutely may not, she'll—*Murron!*"

Murron had grabbed a cloak off the back of the door; she ran out and hopped up behind William, and they galloped away. Her parents stood in the doorway and looked at each other.

In a long, wordless, exhilarating gallop, William and Murron raced along the heather, up hills, and through streams swollen with the rain. Then the rain stopped; the moon came out behind broken clouds, and a billion stars, washed clean by the storm, shone in the black depth of heaven. William pulled the sodden reins, drawing the horse to a halt, and they sat there together on the warm horse's back, the mare breathing and blowing yet seeming to feel the sudden beauty of the night, and Murron still pressed against William's back. They just sat there together, the two of them, neither saying anything, neither feeling the need to.

Then, at last, William spoke without turning to face her.

"Thank you for accepting," he said.

"Thank you for inviting," she said.

"I'll invite you again. But your father thinks I'm crazy."

"You are," she said. "And when you invite again, I'll come again!"

He lingered; he seemed to want to say something more, or perhaps it was just that he didn't want the night to end. Finally he nudged the horse with his heels, and the mare made her way back down into the valley.

They reached the door of her house. William hopped off the horse and reached up to help her down.

The moment she touched the ground, they looked into each other's eyes . . .

But the cottage door was snatched open so quickly that there was no time for a kiss. "Murron, come in!" Mrs. MacClannough snapped.

William walked Murron closer to the door. They turned and looked at each other again. She waited for him to kiss her.

"Murron, *come in!*" Mrs. MacClannough said even louder.

Still Murron hesitated, and when even then he did not kiss her, she knew he was not going to. She lowered her eyes and started into the cabin, but then William grabbed her hand and into it he put something he had taken from deep inside the long woolen fabric wrapped around his body. It was something small and long, wrapped carefully in flannel. He hopped on his horse, glanced at her, and galloped away.

She stood in the open doorway and looked down at what he left her. Her mother stood beside her, all reproach gone, two kindred souls bonded in womanhood, both staring in wonder at the curious gift.

Murron unwrapped the flannel.

Hidden within its folds was a dried thistle flower, the one she had given him at the graveside many years before.

15

THE NEXT DAY DAWNED CLEAR AND FOUND WILLIAM rethatching the roof of his house. Standing there on the high bracing timbers, he could see off in the distance a column of English soldiers marching through the countryside, training. He stared at them a moment, then went back to work, spreading out the long yellow strands of thatching grass. He heard a rider approach and looked down to see that it was MacClannough.

"Young Wallace—" MacClannough said.

"Sir, I know it was strange of me to invite Murron to ride last night. I assure you, I—"

"My daughter is another matter. I came to fetch you to a meeting."

"What kind of meeting would that be, sir?"

"The secret kind."

There was a pause then of barely two seconds, yet it seemed long to both of them. "I'll get my horse," William said.

They rode together deep into the hills and reached a cave tucked in a corner sheltered by trees and shadow.

They looked to be sure they weren't watched, and then dismounted, leading their horses with them as they entered.

The inside of the cave was very dark, but as William and MacClannough got in, someone struck a match, then lit a candle. Its flame illuminated twenty men, farmers of the shire.

"You all know William Wallace," MacClannough told them.

They did. Among the men were Hamish and Campbell, his father, who seemed to be the leader here. "We risk our lives bringing you here, because we are willing to risk our lives for the son of Malcolm Wallace. You understand?" Campbell asked him.

William nodded. He knew rebels when he saw them.

"Every day, they send in more troops. Our country becomes an English playground, a place to harvest our sons as soldiers and our daughters as whores," Campbell explained.

"That's a bit too vivid, Campbell!" MacClannough bristled.

"Vivid but true! When Malcolm Wallace was alive, we met here for every raid." He turned his wild gray eyes on William. "Your coming back made us remember your father. And made us ask if we are still men."

William looked around the group, lastly at MacClannough.

"I came back home to raise crops. And, God willing, a family. If I can live in peace, I will," William said. He looked once more at old Campbell, then at Hamish, and walked out of the cave, leading his horse with him.

Campbell shook his head. No one else spoke. Then MacClannough followed William.

The two rode back in silence; they reached the crossroads on the ridge above the Wallace farm. As they were about to part, MacClannough stopped his horse and spoke. "If you can keep your intention to stay out of the troubles, you may court my daughter. If you break your intention, I'll kill you."

MacClannough rode away. William rode down to his farm. But along the lane, he stopped and looked for a long time at the graves of his father and brother.

16

THEY DID NOT SEE EACH OTHER AGAIN FOR TWO WEEKS. BUT when one of the MacClannoughs wed his daughter to the son of another local farmer, he sent out a runner to announce the event and invite friends to the celebration. Young Wallace was included in the circle—scarcely anyone was left out, and yet he took the invitation as a sign of acceptance by his old neighbors. So on a Saturday afternoon in late summer he found himself beside Murron, strolling through grass up to their kneetops, in a field beside the church. All the farm families had turned out, but very few of the villagers, as the bride's family, being tenants on the land of a nobleman, was not prosperous enough to invite and feed them all. Yet there was ample food and flowers for color and plenty of music, as several farmers full of spirits followed the nuptial couple about and serenaded them with bawdy songs.

William and Murron had sat on opposite sides of the aisle during the wedding, she with her family, he alone. The words of the Latin mass, mysterious to most of the congregation, had bathed the ceremony with a majesty; and Murron, who had seen so many of her friends make the solemn journey into marriage and had turned down so many offers to take the trip herself, felt the spirit of the wedding in a way she had never felt it before, as if those holy words had been

61

shaped at the dawn of time and sent down the ages specifically for her.

Then she and William had met at the door of the church as the congregation had filed out behind the bride and groom to begin the real celebration. As Murron and William came face to face, they scanned each other's features suddenly and desperately, as if afraid that in the days since they'd last met everything had changed, they'd gotten it all wrong somehow, the face that had been filling their waking thoughts and their sleeping dreams was really just like every other. But once their eyes met, they saw the same dreams, the same promise, the same gleam, like looking into the face of someone who is gazing through the door of heaven.

So now they walked side by side, their steps matched, not daring to hold hands though their knuckles brushed as they matched steps. It seemed to them that everyone was watching them. And yet that didn't seem to matter.

"Your father doesn't like me, does he?" William said, smiling.

"It's not you," she said. "He dislikes that you're a Wallace. He just says . . . the Wallaces don't seem to live for very long."

He didn't have an answer for that. His father, his brother, his grandfather . . . Death was a part of life; diseases and accidents seemed to take someone every day. But only William's mother had died in her bed of what was known as a natural cause. The men—well, with the Wallaces it seemed that death in battle was a natural cause. And yet as William walked beside Murron and looked at her auburn hair drawing in the warmth of the sunlight and her eyes absorbing the green of the grass and the blue of the sky, he wanted his hands to know nothing but the touch of her skin and the feel of a plow in his hands. He wanted life. Babies. Crops. Life! Here, forever, in peace.

And just as he drifted in the sweet flow of those vital dreams, he heard the horses. A group of riders appeared—mounted knights with banners and flying colors. At the head of the group rode an English nobleman, plumed and polished.

The wedding guests grew quiet. What could this be, the presentation of a gift? Would the noble grant the young couple a plot of land of their own? Would he give money as dowry? The bride's father had been a good tenant, helping to fill the noble's barn year after year. Surely such a surprise visit could only mean something extraordinary. The bride, a girl named Helen, with hair the color of a flaming sky, held tight to Robbie, her beloved, and watched them come.

The riders stopped in front of the bride and groom. The nobleman was gray, in his fifties. His face was plump, his cheeks red and puffy above his beard. He rose in his stirrups and announced, "I have come to claim the right of *prima noctes!* As the lord of these lands, I will bless this marriage by taking the bride into my bed on the first night of her union!"

The warm breeze rattled through the trees; the horses shook their necks in their bridles, but no one could make a sound. Yes, the noble had such a right. He owned the land; in effect he owned the people, for he could require every able-bodied man to fight in any campaign he wished for up to one month out of every twelve. Yet in recent years the right of *prima noctes* had seldom been invoked. It created hatred, it destroyed families. Perhaps that was the whole point.

Stewart, the father of the bride, lunged forward. "No, by God!" he yelled.

The knights carried short battle pikes, and they were ready for this; in an instant their pikes were pointed down at the unarmed Scots. "It is my noble right," the nobleman said quietly. "I have recently come into possession of these lands. Perhaps you have not been made sensible of late of the honors due to your lord. I am here to remind you."

The bride, Helen, felt her husband's arm go taut; even unarmed, Robbie and Stewart, his new father-in-law, were about to duck beneath the pike points, grab

63

at the horses' bridles, pull a few knights down, and kill as many as they could before they were killed themselves. But Helen was already reacting, holding Robbie tight, snatching at her father's shoulder, pulling them both back, away from the blades and the confrontation. Perhaps she thought faster, or perhaps, seeing the nobleman coming, she had already anticipated what the others there had not.

Everyone watched as she held them both close and whispered to them, frantically yet steadily. Their faces were red with fury, and they kept glancing up with eyes that blazed at the nobleman, and each time they did she whispered faster. And there was no one there that day, English or Scot, who doubted what she was telling them: that she would sooner do anything for only one night with that nobleman than lose the two of them—and God knew how many others—forever.

Then Helen stepped away from her new husband and her old father and held back tears as she allowed herself to be pulled up behind one of the horsemen. They rode away, her flaming red hair bouncing behind her, and she did not look back.

The Scots were left sickened. The bride's mother was weeping among her friends; the groom and his father-in-law stared at the ground, their jaws clenched.

And William Wallace watched it all and kept his thoughts to himself.

17

MURRON LAY SLEEPLESS UPON THE STRAW MATS OF HER bed. All night she had thought of Helen. She kept seeing Helen's eyes—those eyes refusing tears—as she stepped to the nobleman and consented to go with him. Every time she closed her own eyes, she saw Helen's.

Then Murron heard a noise, a scratching at her window. A mouse? The wind? But the scratching was persistent, and she understood; she slipped to the window and opened it to find William out in the moonlight.

"Murron!"

"Shhh!" she whispered, but he was already whispering.

"Come with me."

"I don't think my parents are asleep. They've been restless all night!"

"So am I. So are you. Come with me."

She slipped out the window and into his arms and to the ground. They ran across the grass to the trees, where William had two horses tied.

They rode, silhouettes along a ridge, as the horses' breath blew silver clouds in the moonlight.

He guided her to a grove and asked her to dismount. She followed him as he led both horses into the grove and found it open in the center—a thick ring of trees around a small grassy circle. He tied the horses to a branch, took her hand, and drew her to the far side of the circle. The trees there opened onto endless sky. A precipice! She drew back in surprise, then gasped at the beauty she saw. They were high above a loch, gleaming in the moonlight. She gripped his hand. They looked out upon together all of Scotland, the whole world below them. So beautiful, it was sacred.

"You've been here before," she said.

He nodded. "Some nights, I have dreams. Mostly dreams I don't want. I started riding at night to fill up my mind so that when I did sleep, I'd dream only of the ride and the adventure."

"Did it work? Did it stop you dreaming?"

"No. You don't choose your dreams. Your dreams choose you."

They sat down on the smooth rocks where the tree roots embraced the earth. The wind off the loch was steady and cold. Neither of them noticed it. Both seemed willing to sit there forever.

"William," she said, "I wondered so many times what had become of you. Where you had gone. What you were doing . . ." She looked out over the loch. They say no one can see the wind, but she could see it, moving over the surface of the water, making tracks where the windwaves caught the moonlight. "And if you would ever come back."

He nodded. "I've come back," he whispered. No one could have heard them, there was no other soul for miles. But it was as if he had too much voice in his throat, and all he could do was whisper.

"When you gave me the thistle . . . That you saved it . . ." She couldn't make her words come together into a whole sentence. "I understood then . . . You, too. You . . . had thought about me, too."

"Aye. Oh . . . aye."

"You've had learning. That uncle of yours, the one you went to live with—my father said he was an ecclesiastic. He must have taught you so many things."

William nodded.

"I . . . I don't even know how to read."

"You can learn. I can teach you."

She was silent for a moment, knowing he had just opened the door to the inner room of his life. "But,

66

William, you've been out into the bigger world. I've never been far from home. No farther than this spot right here, right now."

He stared off, beyond the distant mountains. "Murron, I've traveled in my body only as far as the home of my uncle Argyle and his shire. But he has shown my mind worlds I never dreamed of. I want to share those worlds with you."

He was looking at her now.

She took his hands in hers. "William, there are scars on your hands. You've done more than study."

"Aye. I have fought. And I have hated. I know it is in me to hate and to kill. But I've learned something else away from my home. And that is that we must always have a home, somewhere inside us. I don't know how to explain this to you, I wish I could. When I lost my father and John, it hurt my heart so much. I wished I had them back; I wished the pain would go away. I thought I might die of grief alone; I wanted to bring that grief to the people who had brought it to me." His words were coming fast now. Slow to get started, they had become impossible to stop. "But later I came to realize something. My father and his father had not fought and died so I could become filled with hate. They fought for me to be free to love. They fought because *they* loved! They loved *me*. They wanted me to have a free life. A family. Respect from others, for others. Respect of myself. I had to stop hating and start loving." He squeezed her hands so tight. He reached with trembling fingers and combed her wind-blown hair away from her face, so he could see it .ully. "But that was easy. I thought of you."

They kissed—so long and hard that they tumbled off the rocks. They rolled on the soft heather between the trees and devoured each other.

"I want . . . to marry you!" he said, gasping.

"I . . . accept your proposal!" she gasped back.

"I'm not just saying it!"

"Nor I!"

"But I won't give you up to any nobleman."

That caused her to stop. "You scare me."

"I don't want to scare you. I want to be yours, and you mine. Every night like this one," William said.

"This night is too beautiful to have again."

"I will be with you, like this. Forever. And I will never share you with any man."

And all of their fears and all of their sorrows became but old dry logs in one great bonfire of love.

18

ONE MONTH LATER, MURRON SLIPPED OUT OF HER WINDOW and ran silently across the soft ground to the distant line of Calendonia trees, where a horse stood tethered and waiting. She fetched a bundle hidden in the crook of one of the trees, loosed the horse, and led it further from the house. When she was sure she was far enough away that her mother and father would not hear the hoofbeats, she mounted and rode off.

At the base of the precipice beside the mountain loch stood the ruins of an ancient church. Two horses were already tethered outside when she rode up. Peaks of the stone walls that once had supported a roof now caught yellow flecks of candlelight from within the windowless shell. Murron tied her horse beside the other two and, carrying her bundle, pushed herself through the crack of the old door, its hinges rusted in place.

Up by the altar, lit by three candles, knelt William in prayer. He turned to look at her as she made her way in, and with a smile he lifted his eyes to heaven as if to thank God that she had finally arrived. Beside the candles stood Uncle Argyle.

Murron had seen the old man only once, when she

was but a child and he had appeared as such an imposing, commanding figure. Now, in the candle-light of the church, with the stars bright in the unobstructed sky above their heads, he seemed no less a manifestation of the awesome hand of God. His hair was all gray but still long and wild. His shoulders were broad, like William's, though perhaps the old man had grown a bit thicker around the middle. Yet it was a sign of wisdom and prosperity that any man could live so long and have enough to eat through every season. Argyle's face still bore the same fearsome expression she remembered, enhanced by the wild bushiness of his eyebrows, the aggressive jut of his chin, the fierce squint of his eyes. But when he moved down the aisle to her and lifted his great hand and touched it to her hair, she felt not only blessed but loved.

She stepped into the confessional booth, still intact at the back of the church, as Uncle Argyle returned to William, who resumed his prayers.

Murron emerged; she had changed into the wedding dress she had made from the cloth she bought. William rose from his knees and watched her float down the aisle, and on his face was an expression that said his whole life was worth this moment.

Together, the two lovers turned to Uncle Argyle.

The old man cleared his throat and said, "You have come to pledge each to the other before Almighty God. You have brought symbols of your vows to each other?"

From within the folds of his fresh woolen wrappings William withdrew a strip of cloth woven into the checked pattern distinctive to his family. He passed the cloth to Uncle Argyle, who held it at both ends and lifted it up toward the star-cluttered sky and stretched it out before the universe's Creator. He prayed in silence; William would later explain to Murron that Uncle Argyle sometimes prayed with no words at all, feeling those silent prayers were the purest. Not yet knowing that, she watched the old man in this holy moment and felt as if her heart was being held up to heaven to float there as pure and timeless as a star.

Argyle lowered the cloth and fixed his fierce eyes upon William. "William, do you swear on all that is eternal that you will love Murron with all your heart for all your life?"

"Aye. Oh, Aye."

"Then tell her."

"Murron, I will love you with all my heart for all my life."

"And Murron," Uncle Argyle said, "will you pledge the same?"

"William," she said softly, "I will love you with all my heart for all my life."

"Face each other, and stretch out your arms," Uncle Argyle commanded.

They obeyed, turning toward each other, and each reaching out with the right hand to grasp the other's arm almost to the elbow, bringing their inner wrists together, where Uncle Argyle wrapped the strip of tartan and tied it in a knot.

"Have you brought any other signs of your love that you wish now to give?"

With her left hand Murron reached into the bodice of her dress and withdrew a handmade handkerchief, embroidered with a thistle to look like the one she first gave him those many years ago. She watched William's face for his reaction. The lower edges of his eyes lit in yellow as tears of love caught the candlelight.

Uncle Argyle's voice was husky as he lifted his hand and said, "May the Lord bless thee and keep thee. May the Lord cause His face to shine upon thee. May the Lord lift high His countenance upon thee and give thee peace, both now and forever."

The lovers kissed.

Argyle blew out two of the candles and, lifting the third, moved down the aisle with William and Murron behind him, gazing into each other's eyes. At the door Argyle blew out the last candle and, with a

70

grand grunt of effort, forced his way through the opening there and out into the darkness.

William and Murron, their right wrists still bound together by the strip of tartan, tried to negotiate the narrow opening together and laughed at their awkwardness, as he first tried to let her precede him and she was wedged by her right arm trailing across her body; she backed out so he could go ahead of her and he trapped himself the same way. Finally, giggling like giddy children, he squeezed out with his back toward the darkness and his right arm trailing to her and she edged out facing the opposite direction.

So Murron saw them first. Then Will, turning, saw them too: a dozen of the neighbor farmers in their finest Highland dress, one of them—old Campbell, with Hamish by his side—carrying bagpipes.

Murron felt William's arm stiffen alongside hers; his face looked pale, even for someone in moonlight. All this had been meant to be the holiest secret; she had been so vigilant in keeping this from her parents, carefully stealing away to embroider the handkerchief in private so they would never grow curious or suspicious. She loved them dearly, trusted them completely, but for their sake and hers, she would keep the secret of this marriage from them until the pregnancy that she prayed would come soon had begun to show, and then she would be free from the threat of *prima noctes*. Now here were men from all over the valley! How did this happen? William would never have let the secret slip; he had fetched Uncle Argyle all the way from—

Then she saw William looking at Uncle Argyle; it must have been he who told these men!

And Murron was right. William stared at his uncle, and Argyle stared back, his face full of admission but showing no guilt. The farmers were smirking, even enjoying William and Murron's surprise. They were the same men, most of them, that William and Uncle Argyle had seen that midnight long ago, gathered around the graves of William's family, playing the forbidden pipes in farewell to their friends. William held them in esteem, even affection; but Murron knew, instinctively knew from the silence at the center of William's soul and the stiffness of his powerful arm, that he was not given to letting his secrets out.

Old Campbell began to play the pipes. The notes were clear and beautiful, drifting up to mingle with the stars. But still William frowned.

Uncle Argyle saw this displeasure in William's face and moved close to him. "A marriage needs the pipes," Argyle said, "and the knowledge of some others to seal the pact not only with God but with man."

"But . . . ," William said, "we discussed why this must be in secret."

"And it is in secret still," Argyle said. William frowned at him again, but Argyle was unshaken. "You must know who to trust. Yes, a secret is worthless if not kept—but it is equally worthless if it doesn't find another worthy of trust to share its load. These men stayed faithful to you and to the memory of your father for all these years. At any time they could have traded the story of your father's death for a share of those lands that would then be forfeit. Here, now, you are trusting them with the secret of your love, a secret even greater than life, for if you know what a man values even more than life, you own that man's life." Argyle wrapped his still strong arms around William and drew him to his chest, speaking even through the embrace. "I have taught you everything I know, but this much you must learn on your own: know whom to trust. Not everyone you trust can be loved; not everyone you love can be trusted. But your life is full when you find that place to share your secrets. That is my wedding gift to you."

Argyle rode away and held back the tears of farewell. William and Murron rode the path to the top of the precipice, where, in the shelter of the grove, they spent their honeymoon.

72

Still sweaty from their lovemaking, they rode to her house and reached it just before dawn. He stayed with the horses in the shadows of the Caledonia trees and watched her as she ran across the grass, growing bright with the coming dawn, and slipped soundlessly through the window of her parents' home.

He wanted to linger and watch her there forever. But the sun was just below the mountaintops. He lifted his hand. He didn't know if she saw him, but she waved just before she closed the window.

William rode away alone, leading her horse behind him.

19

FOR SIX WEEKS THEY STOLE TIME WHENEVER THEY COULD; and yet the long nights of the coming winter were never long enough. When the moon was down or hidden behind clouds, they went to his home—their home—and shared moments—literally but moments —beside the hearth. And in those stolen moments William Wallace understood his uncle's old truth that shared warmth was greater warmth. On other nights, when the sky opened and the moon sailed high and proud, they rode to the grove and celebrated again in the newness of their love.

Days they pretended—or thought they did—that the flowering romance everyone had witnessed had wilted before it bloomed. On church days they never spoke; on market days they passed on the road and William would nod, once for her whole family, and never speak her name. Murron thought it was remotely possible that her mother knew that something far greater was going on, but she was certain her father was completely in the dark. In fact they had been aware of every time Murron had slipped out the window. They had known, and in their hearts, they had approved.

The farmers they—or rather Uncle Argyle—had entrusted with their secret kept it far better than they. They pretended not to notice the unnaturalness of the community's most desirable bachelor refusing to even look in the direction of its most beautiful maiden. But they never elbowed each other about it, never whispered and hid smiles. And they always pretended not to see it when William and Murron passed each other in the crowded streets of the village and exchanged words without ever crossing glances.

Such a moment occurred as Murron moved through the village of Lanark on a market day. It was a pleasant, sunny morning; the air was alive with the music of flutes and the laughter of children entertained by a juggler. English soldiers were there, too; they admired Murron as she walked among stalls of dangling birds, piles of farm vegetables, woven wool laid out on planks. She stopped to admire a cart full of fresh flowers. When she looked up she saw William on the opposite side of the cart, seeming to study the rose petals spread before him and never looking to the beautiful face beyond them. "I've missed you," he said toward the flowers.

"Shush!" She lifted a whole red rose and smelled it. Putting it down again, she whispered, "It's only been a day."

"It's been forever."

"Aye. To me as well."

"Tonight then."

"My mother is suspicious already! Not tonight!"

"Then when?"

"Tonight!"

She hurried away from him, leaving him smiling.

Drunken English soldiers were standing by an ale cask, and they spotted Murron moving through the fair, glowing, beautiful. The soldiers smirked at each other; as Murron passed, one of them grabbed her wrist.

"Where are you going, *lass?*" the soldier asked.

"Let go," she said.

A second drunken soldier piped up. "Why don't you marry my friend here? Then I'll take the first night!" The laughter of his friends encouraged him; he pulled Murron into his arms; she shoved him away with surprising strength, and he staggered back to the greater laughter of his friends. For a moment Murron thought they would let it go at that—and then one of them grabbed her from behind, spun her around, and kissed her hard on the lips.

She broke free and slapped him—hard and sharp. It knocked the grin off his toothless mouth. The first soldier she pushed now threw her down against sacks of grain, and they were all over her, pinning her down, ripping her clothes, a full-scale public gang rape. As the townspeople tried to move in, the three soldiers waiting their turn at Murron pulled their knives, and the townspeople backed off.

The soldier pinning Murron to the ground, his breath hot with the stench of ale, growled into her face, "Bitch, who do you think you are?" He jammed his mouth down against hers for a long, awful time.

But then he tried to pull back, his scream muffled; she was biting off the end of his tongue! He pulled away, clawing at his mangled mouth. Now his thoughts of rape were forgotten; he pulled back his huge fist to crush it against her face . . .

But the hand was caught—by William! He jabbed the soldier's elbow in a direction it was never meant to bend. The soldier, his mouth already bloody, howled in new agony, but William still wouldn't let him go; he swung the soldier by his rubbery arm into his comrades.

Two of the soldiers leapt forward, swinging their short swords; William ducked and knocked their ale cask into their knees, then lifted the whole table where they were sitting and rammed it into the faces of two more attackers.

"William!" Murron yelled.

Her shout was too late to warn him; as he was facing one soldier with a knife, another grabbed his neck from behind. But William's strength was great and his adrenalin greater; as the soldier in front stabbed, William whirled and the knife sunk into the soldier holding him. William snatched a leg from the shattered table and crushed the stabber's skull. All the rapists, the whole gang of them, were bleeding on the ground.

"William Wallace! William Wallace!" a woman in the marketplace yelled.

But there was no time for celebration. One of the fallen soldiers had begun to scream out. "Rebels! Rebels! Help!"

More soldiers heard the call and came running. But the village folk who had cowered before the brandished weapons of the rapists had been transformed by the sight of a single Scot decimating the whole gang. A woman shoved a broom across the shins of the first new soldier to run up, tripping him onto his chin; others in the crowd bunched together to delay the other reinforcements. "Run, William! Run!" the woman with the broom yelled.

But William was gripping Murron. "Are you all right?"

"Go, William! Get away!" she pleaded.

Two new soldiers fell on William. Murron plunged her thumb into the eye of one and raked her fingernails across the face of the other; William spun and crushed their heads together like pecans and grabbed at the loose traces of the horse that pulled the flower cart. "Take the horse!" he said.

"You take it!"

"They'll chase me! Then you take the horse! I'll meet you at the grove!" He darted off through the crowd as Hesselrig, the magistrate, and more of his garrison arrived. They seemed to swarm in from every direction, dozens of them! None stopped to ask what had happened, they instinctively gave chase to the blood-splattered Scot who ran the instant they appeared. William weaved through the narrow streets of the village, knocking over baskets, jumping carts, scrambling over low rooftops as the soldiers stumbled after him, and the townspeople blocked their way.

Murron saw that all the soldiers had gone after William; she was clear! She darted toward the cart horse, but someone grabbed her leg. It was the soldier with the bloody mouth, whose tongue she had bitten off, whose arm William had broken. With his good hand, he had gotten her ankle in a death grip.

She couldn't get free. She stumbled and tried to kick him, and still he held on with his one hand. Grotesquely, through his mangled mouth, he shouted at the others. "Stop this one! She's with him!"

Two soldiers heard him and started back. Frantically, Murron stomped her free foot against the soldier's face and finally broke free. She jumped on the horse, kicked its flanks, and the horse ran.

William, hopping from roof to roof across the narrow streets of the village, saw her escaping. He slipped down into an empty alley, scrambled low across a deserted stall, and ran for the brush of the river.

Murron galloped the horse down the narrow twisting lanes. Free! But the town wasn't made for a steeplechase. As she looked back to be sure William had made it, the low hanging sign of a tavern caught her and raked her off the horse.

William reached the edge of the town and slipped into the trees by the river; the magistrate and his soldiers were running every which way, but they had lost him. Smiling at the thought that Murron had made it, too, William headed deeper into the trees.

At that moment Murron's head was clearing; she was in one piece, nothing broken! She started to get up, but the soldiers' pikes appeared over her, and then the face of Hesselrig came into view. It was red with too much exertion after too much drink. He was furious, and he was leering. "So this is the little whore he was fighting for," he said.

At the grove above the precipice, William moved into the shelter of the trees, expecting to see Murron. She was not there. He spoke her name softly, thinking she must be hiding: "Murron . . ." He listened and heard only the rustling of the wind through the treetops.

"Murron!" he yelled.

Nothing except the wind.

20

INSIDE THE ROYAL MAGISTRATE'S HEADQUARTERS, MURron was tied in a seated position on the floor, an oak staff behind her elbows, her mouth stuffed with burlap and bound with cord. Soldiers stood at the doors and windows; Hesselrig stood over her. Her eyes were frightened, and yet they were defiant. *How can she look at me that way?* the magistrate wondered. *Just a girl . . . Doesn't she fear us at all?* He thought about what she was seeing. He was himself an English soldier, promoted through the ranks to become an officer; he had led men in battle, the scars that marked his face and hands testified that he had spilled much blood—his own, and that of many enemies—on his way to what he wanted. *Don't I look serious?* he asked himself. *Don't I frighten her?*

His corporal entered. "Nothing," the corporal said, shaking his head.

From outside they heard drunken shouting. "English! English!" They looked outside and saw the village drunk weaving in the shadows, calling out to them. "Not so strong, huh? One Scot buggers six of you!"

One of the English soldiers standing guard outside threw a stone at the drunk; it clattered across the paving stones of the square, and the drunk chuckled and staggered off into the darkness.

The soldiers inside were edgy. One of them grabbed Murron by the hair and jerked her head back. "I'll show you what an Englishman can do—"

"Leave her! I want her unmarked," Hesselrig ordered.

The corporal moved closer to him and spoke in a low voice. "Our informants tell us his name is William Wallace. Has a farm out in the valley. I say we burn it."

"Not his farm. I want him," Hesselrig said.

"But how, if we can't find him?" the corporal wondered. None of Hesselrig's other subordinates would have pressed him this way, but the magistrate and his second-in-command were veterans in this ugly business of suppression. "You know how these people are. Once he's into the hill country, we can look for our whole lives and never find a trace of him."

But Hesselrig, his attention wandering back to Murron, had noticed something peeking out at the top edge of her dress. He reached down to her, slid his finger to the bare skin below her throat, and fished out the strip of tartan tied around her neck and concealed beneath her smock. She squirmed as if to bite or kick him, but trussed up as she was, she could move but little.

Hesselrig untied the strip of cloth and held it up, so the corporal could see it better. "These Highlanders, they weave this cloth into special patterns. They give them as . . ." And then it hit him. He looked down at Murron with a smile of pleasant surprise. "You're married! Aren't you, girl."

Hesselrig looked from Murron to the cloth to Murron to the corporal. "We make him come to us," Hesselrig said.

At the head of his entire garrison, Hesselrig led Murron, her arms still bound behind her, into the village square. His soldiers tied her to one of the posts of the central well that served the whole village. The townspeople didn't want to be near the soldiers, but they hung on the fringes of the square, too curious to pull away.

Hesselrig looked all around at them and shouted to the people. "An assault on the king's soldiers is the same as assaulting the king!" he shouted.

He looked down at Murron, her mouth bound, her eyes defiant.

"So under the authority of my king—and yours—I exercise his rightful power!"

He pulled his dagger from his belt, and as calmly as a man might sign his name in a letter to a stranger, he drew the blade across Murron's throat.

Her eyes sprang open like a doe's; she tried to cough. Blood wept from the gash across her throat. In but a moment, she sagged dead.

The townspeople were struck dumb. Even some of the soldiers gaped in mute horror.

Hesselrig turned calmly to his men. "Now," he said. "Let this scrapper come to me."

William slid through the shadows and reached the barn at the Campbell farm. He slipped inside, and there he found a half-dozen men, gathered in the narrow light of a shielded lantern; among them were Campbell and Hamish, who spotted William first, and cried out, "William!"

William moved into the light; he was scratched and bruised, worn from running, sick with worry. And the sight of these men gathered there did nothing to soothe his fears. "Have you seen Murron?" he asked them. His friends stared at him mutely. "She got away! I saw her! I saw her!" William insisted. When still they said nothing, he turned to dash out the door again, but Hamish was ready for that, and he and another stout fellow gripped William's arms, as old Campbell closed in and laid a hand on his shoulder.

"We heard a rumor. Only a rumor!" Campbell said. "We've sent a man to—"

But then he was interrupted by the sound of a horse galloping up. Campbell peered through a crack in the wall and saw their rider returning. "That's him!" Campbell said.

They pushed the doors and the rider, Liam Little, galloped in. He was pale; he started to speak, then faltered as he saw William.

"What is it? What?!" William pleaded.

"Tell us, man!" Campbell ordered.

"The magistrate . . . he tied her to a post in the town square," Little said. His face was already red from the hard riding, but now it grew more flushed as he worked to get the next words out. Finally he added, "And cut her throat."

William dragged his holders across the barn and pulled Little to the ground. "You're lying!" William shouted.

But when William saw the bloodshot horror in Little's eyes, he knew the story was true.

Outside that barn were stars, above a Scottish valley, where grew heather and purple thistles, and waters of crystal streams tumbled into depthless lochs. But on that night, as William Wallace's cries of grief tore from within that barn and across that empty valley, the stars stopped singing, the thistles faded, the brooks ceased their laughter, and the once-beautiful lochs, at least for him, became but great puddles of tears.

21

THE MEN INSIDE THE BARN HAD WRESTLED WILLIAM DOWN
to a seat on the hay. Hamish stood close and kept an
eye on him. Campbell mumbled with a knot of friends
in the corner.

"Has MacClannough heard?" Campbell wondered
to Little.

"He must've. The villagers went running, as if they
could get away from the sight of it," Little said.

"We'll see to him," Campbell said. "But first we've
got to hide young Wallace." He moved over to William and spoke softly, gently. "Laddie . . . we've got
to get you someplace safe. The soldiers'll be comin'."

William said nothing; but Hamish said, "Let 'em
come."

"You bite your tongue!" his father snapped. "We'll
strike back, but not now!" He turned back to William
again, leaned down to him, lowered his voice. "William, it's . . . awful. But like the loss of your father
and brother, the pain will shrink in time."

William stared. Campbell patted him, then said to
Hamish, "Get him up to the cave. We'll—"

William darted before Campbell could react and
jumped to Little's horse. He was already up onto its
back before Hamish could grab the reins in a grip that
no man or horse could have broken. "Not yet, William!" Hamish boomed. "That's what the magistrate
wants! He killed her to have you!" For Hamish,
though the strongest man there, was not a mere brute,
he was also his clever father's son.

"Then he shall have me," William said.

William stared down at Hamish. Hamish stared up

82

at William and still held the reins of the horse. But something passed between them in their looks.

Hamish let go.

William wheeled the horse instantly and galloped out, breaking right through the latch of the door.

Campbell slapped his son hard and shouted, "You let him go!"

"Because I'm going, too," Hamish said quietly.

"And I," Stewart joined in.

"And I," Little said.

"I'll get the bloody weapons," Campbell said.

William rode to town, alone on the galloping horse. Tears for Murron spilled from his eyes and tore across his face, pushed by the wind. He made one stop, at his farmhouse, and from a spot beneath the thatch of his roof, he removed the broadsword that had once belonged to his father.

All through the valley, the farmers who had been in the barn streamed after him, along every road, path, and trail that lead into the village. At every farmhouse they shouted, "The magistrate's murdered Murron MacClannough! And William Wallace is on his way to town!"

At a barrier across the main road into the center of Lanark Village were twenty professional soldiers, entrenched, fully armed with bows, pikes, swords. Their senses were alert; they knew the danger. Then one of them heard a horse's snort and peered out into the moonlit darkness.

There, at the far turning of the road, just over a bow shot away, sat William Wallace upon his horse. He had stopped, rock still. He was staring at them, all twenty of them, and he sat there all alone, and yet there was absolutely no fear in his face. The soldier knew the look of fear—even the bravest men had it before battle—but this was a different look, and the soldier had seen it before, but only rarely. It was the face of a man readying himself for slaughter—not his own, but that of others.

He saw Wallace lift his broadsword. Its great flat edge caught the moonlight. It looked huge. It was huge—nearly five feet long. It would take an expert to use such a sword; a strong man, with balance and timing, could swing it so its massive blade could cut through anything.

Wallace leaned forward to spur the horse, then heard a shout.

"Wait!" Hamish shouted.

Hamish, Campbell, and four others rode up.

Again William and Hamish exchanged a look. "All right," Hamish said. "Now we're ready."

William raised his sword. He screamed and charged.

His horse pounded toward the barricade, closer and closer to the English soldiers, their eyes grown wide and white with fear. For a moment they seemed to freeze; then half of them stood, raising bows. Not all at once, but like the sharp spattering of hail upon a stone fence, their bowstrings twanged.

The arrows cut through the air, toward William. They sliced the air around his head, they tore his clothes, but none caught his flesh; almost all were fired high in haste, and there was no time for a second volley. He charged through them, his horse leaping the barrier as William simultaneously swung the broadsword. The soldier who had first seen William and judged his heart for battle by the stillness of his face now saw that he was not just good with the sword, he was an expert and more. The stroke was smooth, appearing effortless and unhurried, and the tip, at the end of a huge arc, whistled faster than the arrows. The blade bit through the corporal's helmet and took off the upper half of his head.

The soldiers tried to rally to shoot him in the back as his horse leaped over them—one of them had sighted William's back—but the other Scots crashed into them. William's charge had mesmerized them; they had forgotten about the others. Now, as all fights become, it turned into a melee, the soldiers trying to rely on their training while the Scots gave themselves to wild fury. Old Campbell took an arrow through the shoulder but kept hacking with his sword. Hamish battered down two men with a huge ax. Still it was but a few against more than twenty, and no force in battle is greater than the confidence that one's own side will prevail. The soldiers, overcoming their first urge to flee, saw their advantage in numbers and had just begun to swarm over their outnumbered attackers when more Scots arrived. Carrying hoes, hay scythes, and hammers, they charged into the backs of the soldiers and overwhelmed them.

William raced on through the village, spurring his horse, dodging obstacles in the narrow streets—chickens, carts, barrels. Soldiers popped up: the first he galloped straight over; the next he cut down with a forward stroke, and another he chopped down on his left side with a backhand. With each swing of his broadsword, a man died.

A village woman shouted from her doorway, "William Wallace! Go, William! Go!" He galloped on, his farmer neighbors and people from the village following in his wake.

Hesselrig heard the approaching shouts. He and thirty more of his men were barricaded around the village square. The sounds were not comforting; they heard the panicked cries of English soldiers and the frenzied screams of the Scots drawing nearer. He called out to his men, "Don't look so surprised! We knew he'd bring friends! They're no match for professional soldiers!"

They saw Wallace gallop into sight, then suddenly stop and rein his horse into a side street.

Hesselrig and his men didn't like this: Where did he go? Which way would he come from? And then they heard the horses and saw the other Scots at the top of the main street. The soldiers unleashed a volley of arrows in their direction.

They were fitting a second volley of arrows to their bowstrings when Wallace ran in—on foot—and cut down two soldiers. At the same time the other Scots were charging. The startled soldiers broke and ran in every direction.

Hesselrig, abandoned, ran too, breaking for the darkness of a narrow lane. William saw him go and pursued him, not hurrying, not wishing to hurry, moving steadily now as if he had all the time in the world and nothing could stop him.

Not far along a twisting lane, the bulky magistrate faltered. He turned to fight, and William slashed away his sword.

"No! I beg you . . . mercy!" Hesselrig pleaded.

William stunned him with a blow from the butt of his sword.

All around the village center, it was a scene of mayhem. A panic is never pretty, but there are times in battle when the routed soldiers are allowed to flee. This was not one of those times. The Scots were killing with a vengeance. But when they saw William dragging Hesselrig back down the street, they broke off pursuing the English soldiers and stopped to watch. Pulling Hesselrig by the hair, William hauled him back into the village square, hurled him against the well, stood over him with heaving lungs and wild eyes, and stared at Murron's murderer.

"Please. Mercy!" the magistrate begged.

William's eyes shifted, his gaze falling on a stain: Murron's blood in a dark dry splash by the wall of the well; the blotch of death dripped down onto the dirt of the street. William turned back to Hesselrig, jerked back the magistrate's head, and drew the length of the broadsword across his throat.

The other Scots were silenced by what they had just seen and done. On old Campbell's face was a look of reverence and awe.

"Say grace to God, lads. We've just seen the coming of the Messiah," Campbell proclaimed.

The English soldiers had seen it, too. One soldier, hidden on the roof of a house, seized the moment and slid down and ran for his life.

William staggered a few steps and collapsed to his knees. There in the dirt beside the well he saw a familiar checked pattern, and with trembling fingers, he lifted the strip of tartan, filthy now with blood and dirt, that he had given Murron on their wedding day.

He seemed deaf to the sounds around him; for not just the Scottish farmers but the townspeople, too, had begun a strange hi-lo chant. "Wal—lace. Wal—lace. *Wal—lace! Wal—lace! WAL—LACE!*

The cry the Scots made in Lanark in June of 1296 was the ancient Highland chant of war. William's wild eyes slowly regained their focus. He looked at the blood of Murron; he looked at the blood of the Englishmen on the sword his father had left him.

22

IN THE AFTERMATH OF THE BATTLE, THE FARMERS HAD withdrawn to Campbell's house. A dozen men were there. William sat on the floor, his back against the wall, staring at nothing and saying nothing; he had not spoken since he had spurred the horse out of the barn on his way to Lanark. Old Campbell lay by the hearth surrounded by several men who tended his shoulder wound, under Campbell's own direction. "First take that jug of whiskey off the table," he told them. "No, don't drink it, ye fool, pour it into the wound. Aye, straight in! I know it seems a waste of good whiskey, but indulge me!"

The arrow had plugged into the meat of his shoulder and had been an awful chore to get out. Yet it was not the wound itself that Campbell knew could take his life, but the possible infection afterward. Campbell's friends did as he instructed. "Now," he said, "use the poker." They took a glowing poker from the fire and ran it through Campbell's shoulder, where the arrow went. There was a terrible sizzle, and the farmers grimaced at the very sound of it. Old Campbell's jaws clinched and his eyes watered, but all he said then was, "Ah. Now that'll get your attention, lads." Then he looked down at his left hand. His thumb was missing. "Well, bloody hell, look at this!" he said. "Now it's nothing but a flyswatter."

As Campbell supervised the cleaning and cauterizing of this second wound, Hamish moved over and put a hand on William's shoulder. "You've fought back, William," he said.

"But I didn't bring her back."

There were noises outside. A whiskerless lad, one of the sentries Campbell had scattered along the approaches to the farm, burst into the house. "Somebody's comin', I think they're soldiers!" he sang out.

The men scrambled for their weapons and rushed to protect the entrances while they looked out every window, searching for the safest route of escape. But Liam Little came in just after the lad and said, "Nay, 'tis not soldiers! 'Tis MacGregor from the next valley!"

The farmers moved to the door, opened it, and found twenty more farmers with torches and weapons, dressed in battle tartans. Campbell had made it to his feet as if he'd never been wounded and shook hands with MacGregor as easily as if welcoming him to dinner.

MacGregor was a man Campbell's age, darker of hair and grayer of beard. He was short and powerful, and at least three of the men behind him were his own sons. "We heard about what happened," MacGregor said. "And we don't want ya thinkin' ya can have your fun without us."

A smile spread across Campbell's face. "Just like a MacGregor to invite himself to a party."

MacGregor grinned back, but then his gaze shifted; William had moved up behind Campbell.

William looked out to the earnest young faces glowing in the torchlight. Then he gazed around at the faces of the others gathered inside the house. Then to MacGregor he said, "Go home. Some of us are in this, I can't help that now. But you can help yourselves. Go home."

"We won't have homes to go to soon enough," MacGregor said. "Word of what you did at Lanark has spread through the whole valley, and the English garrison at the castle will be comin' through to burn us all out."

They looked to Wallace—all of them did. And it seemed, at least to Hamish, that his eyes seemed to change temperature. Before they had been warm and soft with grief, but now they turned steely, like a blade left overnight on the heather and covered with winter frost.

The castle of Lord Bottoms stood along the river an hour's ride upstream from Lanark. Its stone walls were barely taller than a large man, but Lord Bottoms, master of the castle, took far more comfort in the presence of the two dozen English soldiers who endorsed his ownership of these dominions and augmented his own personal bodyguard of like number. It was Lord Bottoms who had taken the bride Helen to his bed upon the claim of the right of *prima noctes,* indulging not only his appetite for fair young women but also that for more lands, for he understood Longshanks's desire to dominate these people. He equally understood the certainty of Longshanks's displeasure should an act of rebellion such as the one just occurring at Lanark go unpunished.

So it was that in the courtyard within his castle walls Lord Bottoms was personally directing furious military preparations. Armorers pounded breastplates, honed spears, and ground swords in a shower of sparks; kitchen servants bustled about preparing rations for travel. And through all this Bottoms was shouting orders. "Gather the horses! Align the infantry!" He snatched the arm of a man running past. "Ride to the lord governor in Stirling. Tell him that before sunset tonight we will find this rebel Wallace and hang him—and twice as many Scotsmen as good men they killed! Go!" Bottoms heaved himself up onto his own horse and shouted, "Form for march!"

The troops scrambled from every doorway and out into the courtyard. At the same time, the man Bottoms had dispatched as messenger tugged a horse to the gate and nodded for the keepers to open it. As they pulled the windlasses to wind up the chains that lifted the gate, he mounted the horse. The moment the gate was high enough he spurred the animal, galloped outside—and rode squarely into a spear that impaled him.

Wallace and his Scots, hidden just outside the gate, came pouring through the gate before its keepers could react; they were knocked to the ground and the ambushers had control of the entrance. A whole band of them streamed through. The English soldiers were taken completely by surprise. Bottoms sat on his horse and gawked around in confusion as the troop he had thought of as so powerful suddenly broke up all around him. Many of his men still hadn't taken their weapons from the grinders; they found themselves beaten to the earth, or they knelt there on their own in surrender. Bottoms tried to shout orders: "Stop them . . . Don't let . . . Align . . ."

Scots dragged Lord Bottoms off his horse: One drove his spear at the lord's heart when Wallace's broadsword rang in and deflected the blow.

"On your way somewhere, m'lord?" Wallace asked.

The Scots, with the fortress already theirs, laughed in victory.

"Murdering bloody bandit!" Lord Bottoms spat.

Wallace's sword jumped and stopped a whisker from the lord's eyeball. "My name is William Wallace. I am no bandit who hides his face. I am a free man of Scotland. We are all free men of Scotland!"

The Scots cheered, drunk with the new taste of victory.

"Find this man a horse," William said.

Stewart, father of the abused bride, was sputtering. "This is the lord who took my daughter on her wedding night!" he said.

William looked evenly at Stewart. "Yes. And now he would have killed this whole county if we'd let him. Now give him a horse."

A spearman extended the reins of the lord's thoroughbred.

"Not this horse. That one." Wallace pointed to a bony nag hitched next to a glue pot. Then he glared at Bottoms. "Today we will spare you and every man who has yielded. Go back to England. Tell them Scotland's daughters and her sons are yours no more. Tell them . . . Scotland is free." As the Scots cheered, Wallace threw Bottoms onto the nag's back and slapped the horse's rear. It shambled away, followed by a handful of survivors, as the Scots chanted . . .

"Wal—lace, Wal—lace, Wal—lace!"

Into a flat patch of ground, not far from the Calendonia trees where Murron and William had met for their secret nights together, they dug the hole for her body. A carver from the village had made her a stone marker bearing the name Murron McClannough. Beneath her name he had chiseled the outline of a thistle into the stone.

It was sleeting on the day they buried her, as if the tears of heaven had frozen on their way to the earth. Bagpipes wailed like banshees as Murron's body, wrapped in burial canvas, was lowered into the earth under the gaze of her mother and father, her neighbors, and William Wallace. Her mother was crying loudly, her father wept in silence, and William knelt at the graveside, hiding within his closed fist the wedding cloth she had embroidered for him.

He stared at the chiseled thistle in unspeakable grief as the village priest sprinkled in dirt and holy water and the gravediggers filled the hole.

When others began to drift away, William stayed. When he looked up, he saw Murron's father, old MacClannough, still there, broken in grief. The old man's eyes stared at Wallace from across the grave of his daughter, then at last he, too, drifted away.

Alone, William reached into the tartan that wrapped his chest and withdrew the strip of cloth he had given her. He placed it above her heart and pressed it with his fingers deep into the dirt. Then he put the embroidered handkerchief inside his woolen wrap, next to his heart, stood slowly, and walked away.

23

IN THE ROYAL PALACE DOWN IN LONDON IT WAS A VERY different kind of day, sunny, even warm. Prince Edward was in his garden, playing a medieval version of croquet with his friend Peter. The princess, ignored by her husband but expected to be at all times attentive to his interests, sat watching. But Nicolette was at her side, and together they could talk, always being careful not to be so loud as to be a distraction or so quiet as to cause suspicion, for whenever they whispered, Edward seemed to think they were discussing him.

That morning Nicolette had juicy gossip she was eager to share. As Edward and Peter strolled and chatted down by the far wickets, Nicolette leaned closer to Isabella and said, "I've just heard the most romantic tale. It just happened up in Scotland. It is wrenching—a great tragedy!" She said this in the gravest French, and yet her dark eyes danced in dramatic delight as if she was relating the occurrences of a play. "Some village girl, exquisitely beautiful— and I say this because the man who told me the story remarked on how beautiful he had heard she was, and you know how men are, they never comment on beauty unless it is great—she was in her home village when she was attacked by a soldier. They say she attacked the soldier first, but even the English officials here do not believe that. They know she was being raped, they even admit that they encourage it. And—"

"How can you know that?" Isabella interrupted.

"I do know!" Nicolette insisted, pretending to be surprised and even offended that Isabella should question the accuracy of her gossip. "I know it to be true! I have my sources, they would not lie to me—for they know I would see through it."

"Hmp! No English *official,* as you put it, would ever admit that rape was encouraged."

"You demonstrate how silly you are and how little you know about men or anything else that goes on in a royal court! Of course they would not admit such a thing to each other. Never ever to another man of any rank. But to me, under certain circumstances, they would tell everything they know. In fact it is almost impossible to keep them from telling everything they know, even when I would rather not know it!"

"Go on with the tale. You're boring me with your boasting," Isabella said, but she was far from bored by either the tale or Nicolette's brags.

"Where was I? Oh, yes. The village girl. Exquisitely beautiful—did I say that? She was being attacked by an English soldier. And her lover, a Scottish

93

tribesman—have you ever seen a Scottish tribes-man?" Nicolette interrupted herself.

"No. Have you?"

"Well of course! There were some of them in France, mercenaries. I saw them when I was visiting my uncle in Normandy. They are big men with wild hair and calm eyes. My uncle pointed them out to me. He had given a band of them shelter when they had fled across the channel to avoid capture."

"And they fought for money?"

"My uncle said they fought because they loved fighting. He only gave them money because he didn't want them fighting for someone else."

"Get back to your story, I beg you."

"Ah yes. The girl. Exqui—"

"Exquisitely beautiful, I know! You said it already!"

"Exquisitely. And she was being raped when her lover happened along . . . But no, I don't think he simply happened along, I think he must have been staying close to her, watching over her—don't you think so? If she was so beautiful, and they were so in love, that is what he would have done. Yes, I'm sure of it. What do you think?"

"I think you are making up this whole story, and I am sure now that I am bored with it, for you are a bad poet."

"Oh. So I am making it all up, is that what you think?"

"It is obvious. What happens, a man fights for a woman? How unusual, how remarkable! Oh, I forget, you said it was a tragedy. So they were both killed, I suppose, and lived happily ever after." Isabella dismissed any other conclusion of the tale by taking an apple from the silver bowl beside her and biting off an unladylike mouthful.

"No," Nicolette said haughtily. "In fact only one of them was killed." She looked off across the flat green lawn and pretended to be entirely finished with the narrative, but she knew she had her friend hooked now.

"Which one?" the princess asked after a very short pause.

Nicolette spun back to her, delighted to spill out the rest. "The girl. She was killed—but not during the rape! The tribesman—I think in Scotland they call them clans, not tribes—he fought the soldiers, all of them, very many! Then he ran, thinking his lover had escaped by another direction. But she was captured by the sheriff. And the sheriff . . . perhaps he loved the girl himself, perhaps he was jealous, who will ever know? But he killed the girl."

"No!" Isabella said, believing it all.

"Yes. Cut her throat in the town square. When her lover learned of this, he attacked the entire garrison. Rode in alone! Or they say alone, but then they say others came with him at some point, I don't know, it all gets confusing here. Maybe the others came later. But what I know for sure—and this is the reason I know the story at all—is that news of this event has spread all over Scotland. It is like every Scot felt the girl's pain and her lover's rage. And her lover—his name is Wales-es or . . . no, it is Wallace—his name has spread with the news. Like fire across a field of parched grass. The English are sending up more troops to catch him and hang him. I have heard that the king may even send—"

And at that moment their conversation was interrupted by the arrival of the king himself. Longshanks strode into the garden followed by advisors who could barely keep up with the gait of his long legs and marched straight through the prince's game, furiously kicking aside the balls and wickets. "You play games here?" Longshanks shouted at his son. "Scottish rebels have routed Lord Bottoms!"

Prince Edward glanced first to his friend as if to draw strength there, then lifted his chin in a show of calm. "I heard. This Wallace is a bandit, nothing more," Edward said to his father.

Longshanks slapped his son, knocked him down among the colored balls and wickets. Isabella and

Nicolette had already jumped to their feet at the arrival of the king, and now they both gasped. Even some of the advisors who had come with the king turned pale at this public abuse of the prince.

But Longshanks's temper was something none of them had the least inclination to confront. The king was red faced, screaming. "You weak little coward! Stand up! Stand up!" Longshanks jerked his son to his feet. Peter, the prince's friend, had flinched with the first blow and now tried to move to the prince's side, but Edward lifted a white hand and warned him away.

Longshanks's eyes were leaping from his head. "I go to France to press our rights there! I leave you here to handle this little rebellion, do you understand? *Do you?!*" He had grabbed his son by the throat. It must have happened before, for Edward seemed less frightened than angry. Although the veins popped out in his neck, he glared at his father with matching hatred.

"And turn yourself into a man," Longshanks spat, and with that he shoved his son away, turned, and left as abruptly as he had come.

Now everyone left in the garden hurried to the prince's side. Peter reached him first as did other of their male friends who had been watching the game from the opposite side of the garden. Isabella reached him, too, and, forgetting all pretense of royal calm, seized his hand in concern.

"Are you all right?" she asked, breathless. For the first time since coming to England, she felt something for her new husband, wanted to comfort him, hated the king for his sake.

Edward seemed startled by her presence beside him. Bright with humiliation, he shouted, "Get away from me!"

Isabella was confused. "I just . . . I was afraid you," she stammered.

He slapped her. A quick sharp blow, smacking across her face. She staggered but recovered her balance. In that eternal instant just after the blow, when everything she had ever assumed about her future was changing forever, she felt her own pride stiffen and made a point of remaining standing and not falling down as her husband had. Nicolette jumped forward and seized her arm; her other attendants rushed to her from their mats in the shade, but Isabella shook off Nicolette's arm and raised a hand to her other attendants to show she needed no assistance. Her left cheek burning red, her eyes icy, she curtsied slowly to her husband. "I only wished to be of help, my most noble lord," Isabella said in a flat, low voice.

"I will settle the Scottish problem!" Edward snapped in the direction of his own retinue of young men, who seemed by their stiff postures to be wishing their clothes looked less festive and more military. "Go to Lord Pickering. Tell him to send the cavalry out to suppress these rebels. I want this Wallace found and hanged!"

The frightened aides scurried away. The prince, suddenly finding himself at a loss for what to do, followed after them with Peter by his side.

Now, at last, Isabella rose from her curtsey. With her first step she staggered, and Nicolette snatched her arm to steady her. "You're dizzy!" Nicolette erupted and added a vile epithet in French.

"Shh!" Isabella said. "I am unhurt."

They walked toward the door of the palace arm in arm. Under her breath so that none but Isabella could hear, Nicolette said, "I hope your husband goes after the Scotsman himself. This Wallace will kill him for certain."

97

24

A BIT NORTH OF ITS GEOGRAPHIC CENTER, BRITAIN IS pierced by two jagged slashes of water that dart inland, one from the east and the other from the west, cutting the island nearly in half. The bottleneck of land that remains is a beautiful rolling plain, broken here and there by sudden promontories that jut into the north Atlantic sky. This land is the doorway to Scotland, and Stirling Castle was its gatekeeper. Rising on the noblest of the promontories, its stony battlements gazed out for miles in all directions, daring all comers.

Safe within the walls of this castle sat Lord Pickering, head of the English army in Scotland. He was in the great room with his generals, discussing the deployment of their forces, when he received the royal messenger. Reading the note the prince had sent him, Pickering replied to the messenger, "Please report that I have already sent out the cavalry. And assure the prince that I shall catch Wallace one way or another."

The messenger left as Pickering burned the message.

At the same time, at another castle not far away, Robert the Bruce lay in bed with a young Nordic beauty. She was drowsy; the lids hung heavily over her vacant blue eyes. But the lovemaking had not defused the restlessness of Robert's spirit. He lay on his stomach, turned away from her on the bed. She stirred and kissed his neck, but he didn't respond.

"I wanted to please you," she said.

He seemed not to have heard her, then at last he

muttered, "You did." But he was numb as she nuzzled him again. She sagged back, and he still stared away, lost in thought.

But then he became aware of her and realized her feelings were hurt. He tried to explain what he'd been thinking. "In Lanark Village," he said, "the king's soldiers killed a girl. Her lover fought his way through the soldiers and killed the magistrate."

The blond beauty he'd spent all night and most of the morning with just looked at him blankly.

"He rebelled. He *rebelled!*" Robert insisted. "He acted. He fought! Was it rage? Pride? Love? Whatever it was, he has more of it than I."

The blue eyes only appeared vacant; Robert's young lover understood exactly what he was saying. She turned away from him. "You might have lied," she said toward her pillow.

Robert heard the hurt in her voice. He knew there was no way to explain it away, to make her believe even for a moment that he cared about her or anything else in his life with the kind of passion he'd just been marveling at. "I'm too arrogant to lie," Robert said at last.

He rose, pulled back the curtains, and squinted at the sunlight. Late morning. It was time.

He dressed in fresh clothes and left her there in his bed with an empty kiss that she welcomed with an empty smile.

He moved grimly up a dark castle staircase. He followed a servant who carried a candle against the gloom. They reached a door, which the servant unlocked. Young Robert took the candle and entered the room, the light from the tallow and wick barely penetrating the darkness.

Robert willed himself forward and placed the candle on a table in the center of the room. There was a shuffle in the dark; then, as if floating out of the black waters of a murky pool, came a face drifting into the candlelight. The boundaries of the face—the tip of the nose, the point of the chin, the bottoms of the ears,

99

the mounds of the cheeks—were eaten away. A leper. Robert the Bruce, the Elder—Robert's father.

The younger Bruce had steeled himself for the sight, and now he did not look away. His father, isolated in his disfiguration, looked back at him with the eyes of the condemned. And yet there was no pity there for himself or anyone else. The elder Bruce enjoyed these visits from his son; the chance to advise, counsel, direct—to plot his son's ascension to the throne of Scotland—it was now all he had.

"Father, an armed rebellion has begun," young Robert said.

"Under whom?"

"A commoner named William Wallace took the English at Lanark, and now people flock to him."

"A commoner? So no one leads Scotland."

The old man paused to ponder, and young Robert waited in heavy silence, broken only by the sputtering of the tallow in the candleflame. The elder Bruce lifted his yellow eyes and pointed a half finger at his son.

"You will embrace this rebellion," he said in his dusty voice. "Support it from our lands in the north. I will gain English favor by condemning it and ordering it opposed from our lands in the south. Whichever way the tide runs, we will rise."

But young Robert did not get up immediately to carry out his father's wishes as he usually did. He kept his seat and struggled to find the right words for something that, at the time, he would have said held only the mildest interest for him; and yet his mind could not let it go. "This Wallace," Robert said. "He doesn't even have a knighthood. But he fights with passion, and he is clever. He inspires men."

"And you wish to charge off and fight as he did," his father said.

"It is time!" young Bruce found himself saying with unexpected energy.

But his father was not surprised; it was almost as if he'd been wondering when such emotion would

100

spring out of his son. He shot back, "It is time to survive! Listen to me! You are the 17th Robert Bruce. The sixteen before you have passed you land and title because we ride both sides of every road. Press your case to the nobles. They will choose who rules Scotland."

"They do nothing but talk!" Robert said.

"Rightly so! They are as rich in English titles and lands as they are in Scottish! Just as we are! You admire this man, this William Wallace. Uncompromising men are easy to admire. He has courage. So does a dog. It is exactly the ability to compromise that makes a man noble. And you must understand this: Edward Longshanks is the most ruthless king ever to sit on the throne of England, and none of us, and nothing of Scotland, will survive unless we are as ruthless, more ruthless, than he."

Young Bruce rose heavily and moved to the door. But his father's voice reached out and caught him there.

"Robert . . . look at me. I wish the world were different, and courage and conviction alone were enough. They are not. Even with my nose and ears falling from my head, I can face this fact. So must you."

With a last long look at his father, Robert left him and climbed alone down the passageway of stone stairs that led back to his own rooms.

25

THE NEXT DAY TROOPS RODE THROUGH THE SCOTTISH countryside. They questioned civilians, threatening to pull down their houses and burn their fields, but none seemed to know anything; most claimed never to have heard of anyone named William Wallace, even in Lanarkshire, where he had lived. But when a pillar of dark smoke rose from the valley in which the Wallace farm lay, the other farmers and the villagers of the shire came out of their homes and stared at it in reverential silence.

When night came, and the villagers huddled behind barred doors, and even the rabbits of the heather seemed afraid to stir from their burrows, William Wallace and Hamish Campbell rode through the darkness along the trail that connected their childhood homes. When they reached the Wallace farm, a half moon was just peeking from behind the broken clouds, and in its light they saw the destruction.

The house in which William had been born, where his mother died, where he had known the carefree days of childhood and the happy camaraderie with his father and brother—that house had been torn down. Not one stone remained atop another; the English had made a point of that. Its timbers had been stacked and burned. The outbuildings had received the same treatment.

William looked at it all, and there was not a ripple of reaction in his face. Hamish looked for some sadness, some anger, some emotion of any kind, and saw none. This made the big redhead uneasy. He had sworn to himself that he would stay by William's side no matter where that took them, and he would protect his friend even when—especially when—his friend's pain was so great that he no longer gave any thought to his own safety. Hamish was particularly intent that he never again let William plunge off alone as he had at Lanark. So William's stony silence frightened him.

But the deadness in William's face was only an illusion. That face changed when they came upon the plots of the Wallace family graves.

The graves had been dug up, the bones scattered and ridden over by horses, so that only chalky splotches, gray on the earth in the thin moonlight, remained. Even the headstones that once marked the graves had been upended and set into the ground upside down as if to point the way for the wandering spirits of the dead to find their way to hell.

When William saw this, his face was no longer stiff. It came alive; though it scarcely seemed to move, all of it changed. It was a look so fierce that Hamish could smell the hatred. He had seen Scots hate before, but this was different. The look that had been on William's face when he attacked and killed the garrison at Lanark was suddenly there again, and what struck Hamish was that the hatred seemed to have grown.

That made Hamish happy. It meant they were going to kill something.

But then he had a realization—and before he could say anything to William about it, his friend had already reined and spurred his horse. Hamish cursed himself and spurred his own horse in pursuit. Why did William always have to think a half second quicker?

In the Calendonia trees sprinkled on the gently sloping hillside where Murron lay buried, the moonlight lay in flat puddles on the top sides of the leaves. The undersides of the leaves were black shadow. So were the back faces of rocks, the far sides of the tree trunks, even the depressed places of the uneven earth. Everywhere you looked was ambush.

Hamish and William lay flat to the ground on the edge of the hilltop above the entire valley. They could see no details from this distance, could barely make out the light pile of neatly placed stones that mounded Murron's grave. They had ridden an extra half hour to come into the valley from this direction and the last ten minutes of that in stealthy silence. But now Hamish whispered, "You sure they're down there?"

William answered nothing. He had already told Hamish exactly what he planned to do, and while Hamish was sure that William's eyes could penetrate the shadows no better than his own, it was unsettling to the big redhead that William seemed to see the soldiers lurking there, had already seen them in his mind, before they even left their horses behind and crawled the rest of the way to this spot to peer down into the valley on their bellies.

"William . . . I wish you wouldn't ask me to do this," Hamish said.

"The earth will still be soft for quick digging. You've got to help me. I won't have the strength," William said.

"But I—" Hamish started to protest.

William had already crawled off into the darkness. Hamish swore under his breath and crawled after him.

At the edge of the Highland graveyard, between the treeline and the graves themselves, was a rill in the earth from which underbrush sprang. This underbrush had been thickened by cuttings brought in from the forest beyond, and beneath this added camouflage lay four English soldiers. When they had first taken their places here, just as darkness fell, the promised reward for the head of William Wallace had made them alert and optimistic. Then they had grown edgy from the long vigil in a dark graveyard; now they were drowsy. But they perked up at the first sound of muffled hoofbeats.

They reached for their weapons—short swords smeared with dirt so that no gleam of moonlight could betray their position; they knew that to catch this William Wallace they would have to be crafty. Barely breathing, they lifted their heads to peer toward the stack of new stones in the center of the graveyard. They saw the lone rider moving up the valley, keeping close to the shadows, guiding his horse in a quick quiet trot rather than a louder gallop but stopping every twenty yards or so to listen and scan the shadows.

Three of the soldiers in the underbrush were new recruits, first-timers in Scotland; they now blessed the sergeant who had led them there, concocting this whole ambush. The sergeant knew these Highlanders!

He had positioned his corporal and four more men at the far side of the graveyard, so that even if Wallace escaped their first charge, he would run directly into their spears.

The soldiers in the underbrush worked themselves into crouching postures, ready to spring as soon as the rider dismounted. They strained to make out the face of the horseman as he neared the grave . . . and they stopped listening.

By the time they heard the hoofbeats on the soft earth behind them, it was too late. It didn't make sense. They couldn't make out their direction, then they whirled, their eyes bugging, as a cloaked figure galloped in from the woods behind them. The figure was swirling fire! He hurled burning torches into the clustered soldiers and the clustered brush. The four soldiers tried to scatter from the flame, and the rider—William Wallace—cut them down with his massive broadsword.

Meanwhile, Hamish had reached Murron's grave and was digging frantically. The stones he had scattered with a few kicks of his huge feet and a swat or two of his massive hands. The new dirt parted easily and he began to free the shrouded body from the shallow earth. He cringed, not with the effort but from the very idea of what he was doing.

Hamish could feel a charge coming. William had plotted the entire English ambush in his mind and had already warned him exactly where the soldiers would be. And now sure enough they came, more soldiers rushing in from behind the rocks at the far side of the graveyard. Hamish didn't even look at them coming, he just struggled to get the shrouded body out of the ground. Wallace charged the soldiers and drove them back. One he rode over, another he hacked, but the others scrambled back in their shock and confusion as the ambushers became the ambushed.

William galloped to Hamish and jumped down beside him.

"I'll take her," William said.

He had ignored a charging soldier; Hamish cut the man down just as he reached William's back.

William clutched the body to his chest and climbed into the saddle, a tremendous physical feat that he seemed not to feel at all. Hamish ran and bounded into the saddle of his own horse, wheeled, and drove back two more soldiers with the slash of his own broadsword. Then he galloped after William.

William rode through the moonlight as he clutched Murron's shrouded body to his chest. Hamish rode behind, protecting against any pursuit.

At the grove on the precipice, William dismounted and stretched Murron's body gently on the ground. Hamish dismounted, too, with the spade he had used to dig up the old grave. He lifted his eyes to William's face and saw the moonlight shining in the tears at the edges of his eyes. "I'll wait . . . back there," Hamish said.

"Hamish, I . . . thank . . ." William stammered.

Hamish put a hand on his friend's shoulder, then quietly led the horses away.

William started to dig.

Later in the grove William sat looking at the new grave covered with leaves, completely hidden. He touched his hand to the earth.

Hamish was waiting by the stream as William came out of the grove. There was nothing to say. They mounted their horses and rode away.

26

WILLIAM SAT CROSS-LEGGED BESIDE A SMALL HOT FIRE OF dry peat and wet twigs. It had rained through all of that day and most of the previous night, and the woolens he and his men wore were soaked through; this made them wet but warm, for the woven cloth was an even better insulator when it thickened with moisture. Most of the men in the encampment were drowsy; the rain spattering on the canopy of trees above them was like a lullaby to the tired Highlanders.

But they had placed sentries at the perimeter of their camp; old Campbell had seen to that. Now he was lovingly honing broadswords to razor edges as he shared a whiskey jug with Hamish, who sat beside the fire next to William and looked from time to time at the darkness all around, like a dog sniffing for danger.

For the last hour William had been staring, not at the glowing embers of the fire as Scots sharing whiskey were inclined to do but into the smoke rising above it, as if he saw in its twists and curls some action unfolding there. But now he picked up a stick from the pile gathered to feed the fire, and brushing away the broken leaves that matted the forest floor, he began to scratch on the wet ground. It wasn't writing; Hamish couldn't read, but he knew letters when he saw them. These were patterns: squares, triangles, circles. Finally Hamish demanded, "What're ya doin'?"

"Thinking," William replied.

"Does it hurt?"

"What do we do when Longshanks sends his whole northern army against us?"

Old Campbell stopped what he was doing and sat

down beside the fire. "Aye," he said. "I've studied on the question myself. They have heavy cavalry. Armored horses that shake the very ground. We have spears and broadswords."

"They'll ride right over our formations," Hamish said.

"Uncle Argyle and I used to talk about it," William said. "No army in history has ever been able to stand before a charge of armored horse. No infantry has ever had the courage. And if they did stand, it wouldn't be courage but foolishness. Without a barrier of fortifications, the horses are unstoppable. And if we are outnumbered, as we surely will be, then giving up maneuver by hiding behind earthworks is equally stupid, for the king's archers would kill us all."

"So we fight the Highland way," old Campbell said. "Attack and run. Retreat into the hill country. Burn everything as we go. Leave nothing behind us for Longshanks's army to eat."

"And leave nothing behind worth fighting for," William said. "What if we could win a victory? What if we could stand against the king's whole army with an army of Scots?"

"Did your uncle tell you to think such things?" old Campbell wondered, peering at William from beneath a thicket of red bushy brows.

"He mused upon it," William answered.

"And what did he conclude?" old Campbell demanded.

"That we would be slaughtered," William said, smiling.

Old Campbell, satisfied, took a long pull at the whiskey jug.

But William was staring up at treetops stretching into the night sky like spikes to skewer the stars.

"We have carpenters among the men that have joined us?" William asked.

Hamish shrugged; sure, they must have.

"I want them to make a hundred spears. Fourteen feet long."

108

"Fourteen?" Hamish began.

But before he could question William further, they were interrupted by a cry from the sentries: "Volunteers coming in!"

They looked to see a half-dozen new volunteers being led in, blindfolded. William stood, flanked by Hamish and old Campbell. Ever since the action at Lanark, they had been receiving volunteers, who came to them through the old clan networks of Scottish resistance. More and more young men had been trying to join them as the story of William Wallace's revolt was told and retold. Handling so many would-be rebels was becoming a problem for the secret network of trusted men in each village, who supplied William and his roving band with food, shelter, and information as they darted from place to place to stay ahead of the pursuit of the soldiers and the potential betrayal of any Scot who might be tempted by the ever-increasing reward money to sell information of Wallace's whereabouts to the English. Old Campbell had set up the security procedures; any man wishing to join Wallace's band had to be known to the trusted villager who vouched for him. This was not foolproof, of course; men who could be counted on to stand beside you in a fight or face torture without blurting your name to a captor might not be the best judges of character. The singleness of heart that made some men instinctively loyal made them blind to duplicity in others. Old Campbell knew there could be flaws in his network; William knew it, too.

So they looked over the volunteers the sentries brought in. All looked fit; none looked so well fed that his sympathies might be suspect. Finally old Campbell gave a nod, and the sentries removed the blindfolds.

As the new recruits saw William Wallace for the first time, their faces glowed like the firelight. He was dirty like the others, his hair wet and tangled with leaves, his arms scratched, his skin pale from hiding by day and raiding by night. But they saw the fire inside him.

They recognized it. It was what they had come to follow. They rushed to him.

One of them, a tall slender man with the thick accent of western Scotland, fell upon his knees at William's feet. "William Wallace!" the new recruit said, almost weeping with joy. "I have come to fight and die for you!"

"Stand up, man. I'm not the pope," William said.

"I am Faudron!" the new man spouted. "My sword is yours! And—and I bring you this tartan—"

He reached into his cloak, but before he could produce whatever he had there, both Hamish and Campbell had drawn their swords and put the points to his neck.

"We checked them for arms," the sentry told them.

Carefully, Faudron pulled out a beautiful tartan scarf and stretched it out to William. "It's your family tartan! My wife wove it with her own hands."

William looked down at the checked cloth—newer, more deeply colored, but the same design as the strip of cloth he had given Murron. For a moment all of William's thoughts drained from his mind; his head felt like a bell struck by a phantom hammer, ringing with the echoes of his lost love. He stood mute as Faudron untied the tattered old woolen cloth that William had used for so long to keep the rain off the back of his neck and then urged the new one around his shoulders in replacement. Finally William found his voice. "Thank your wife for me," he said to Faudron, and the new man seemed moved to see the gift so fondly accepted.

Then a new voice broke in. *"Him?* That can't be William Wallace! *I'm* prettier than this man!"

They all looked at a slender, handsome young speaker, who spoke with the lilt of Ireland. He seemed to be talking not to any of them but to himself. The Irishman paused for a moment, frowned as if hearing instructions he could scarcely believe, and then burst forth again as if in reluctant compliance: "All right,

Father, I'll ask him!" The Irishman stared suddenly at William and demanded, "If I risk my neck for you, will I get a chance to kill Englishmen?"

"Is your poppa a ghost, or do you converse with God Almighty?" Hamish asked, scowling.

"In order to find his equal, an Irishman is forced to talk to God!" the newcomer declared. Then, apparently hearing more instructions unperceived by everyone else, he shouted, "Yes, Father!" Turning back to William, he announced, "The Almighty says don't change the subject, just answer the fookin' question."

"Insane Irish—" Campbell said.

The newcomer whipped a dagger from his sleeve, and with a speed that surprised everyone, he put the blade against Campbell's throat. "Smart enough to get a dagger past your guards, old man," the Irishman said. But then he froze as he felt the steel of a broadsword against his own neck. Not daring to twitch, for the edge of the sword was already biting into his flesh and the sword had slipped from its scabbard with such speed it was frightening, the Irishman's eyes traced the steel into the hard, hungry hand of William Wallace. Behind the sword's hilt, Wallace was smiling.

"That's my friend, Irishman!" Wallace said. "And the answer's yes. You fight for me, you kill the English."

"Excellent!" the Irishman said, lifting his dagger away from old Campbell's throat and stepping back from him. "Stephen is my name. I'm the most wanted man on the Emerald Isle. Except I'm not on the Emerald Isle, of course, more's the pity."

"A common thief," Hamish said in disgust.

"A patriot!" Stephen protested.

"Give me your dagger," Wallace said and stretched his hand out for it. The Irishman stared back at him. "Now."

The Irishman shrugged and handed the blade over, handle first. Wallace shook his head and moved back

111

to the fire. "When you prove you can last through the cold and the hunger and the lack of sleep, we'll give you a chance to prove you can fight as well as you talk," he said, and the sentries took the newcomers to find their own spaces.

27

A COLUMN OF ENGLISH LIGHT CAVALRY—A HUNDRED riders—moved in ordered formation across a field of bluebells, lush in the Scottish summer. At the head of the column was English Lord Dolecroft, and as he rode, he twisted in his saddle to admire the precision he had maintained among his men. For three cool wet months they had pursued William Wallace and his band of rebels through the counties between Edinburgh and Glasgow. They had felt themselves so close to their enemy, they had found fires still smoldering. Only a week before they had come upon a campsight so hastily abandoned that they discovered meat cooked but uneaten and knew, here in this hungry land, just how close that meant they had come. But they had never seen their prey. Still his men maintained their discipline; they kept their horses healthy, their weapons sharp; they did not straggle. Dolecroft knew that sooner or later this would pay off. It had to.

Just as he had this thought, the scout at the head of his column gave a low whistle, and Dolecroft spun back around to see five Scots trudge out of the forest up ahead. Even at that distance Dolecroft could see they were exhausted men. They walked on wobbly legs, clearly weakened from hunger; they hadn't even lifted their eyes to see the English column. Even so, they were in a formation of their own, a huge redheaded brute at the center of a V formation, as if they were the vanguard of a larger band. Dolecroft stared, scarcely able to breathe. It was as if he could halt his men right there on the road, and the spent Scottish outlaws would march right onto the points of the English spears.

Then the Scots saw them; the big redhead staggered, spun round, snatched at the men on either side of him, and virtually hurled them back toward the forest from which they'd come. The startled Scots ran like frightened deer, and Dolecroft knew instantly that they had just made their second blunder—this one fatal—for in their surprise they were leading him straight back to their main band, possibly even to Wallace himself!

The scout was waving wildly, but it was unnecessary: every rider in the column had seen the Scots already. "After them!" Dolecroft shouted and spurred his horse.

Hamish and his men—for it was Hamish that Dolecroft had seen—changed direction, but the English scout spotted them crossing a hilltop and led the column after them.

Scrambling over rocks, tripping and falling, tumbling downhill and clawing their way up again, the emaciated Scots ran for their lives. The English horsemen galloped in pursuit, closing the gap quickly. The Scots changed direction onto rockier ground. Dolecroft shouted the order, "Patience! Mind the footing!" and his experienced riders slowed their pace so their horses could handle the harder footing without danger and still drew nearer their prey.

Hamish now made his final blunder, leading his men in panic across an open field surrounded by low hills. The Scots were boxed in; there was no escape. Dolecroft felt a passing pang of disappointment that the fleeing men had not led him to the heart of the whole band, but they could still take one or two of these harried men alive, and who could say what a little torture might reveal? Dolecroft spurred his horse on, and his whole column charged into the open field.

The English scout was the first to notice something wrong. His horse was staggering, having difficulty with the footing. "We're in a bog!" the scout shouted.

And so they were. The Scots, bounding from grassy clump to grassy clump like rabbits through a familiar field, were trotting along with surprising ease, but the horses were miring halfway up their forelegs in the soggy earth. This was not comforting to horses; it made them jittery. "Here, it's firm this way—" Dolecroft called.

But as they moved toward the firm ground, fifty Scots appeared on the crest of the hill on the far side of the bog. A grizzled redhead—old Campbell—stood at the front, and he was smiling. On the hills to the left and the right more Scots appeared; the English were boxed in the bog. Dolecroft wheeled and looked to his rear; and there stood William Wallace, his broadsword resting on his shoulder, fifty more Scots behind him.

Dolecroft scarcely had time to realize his blunder. Wallace lifted his broadsword, screamed, and led the charge. The Scots swarmed in from all directions; the English horses could barely move, the bog sucked at their hooves. Wallace's broadsword swung so fast that it blurred in steel and blood.

It was a slaughter.

When Lord Pickering, head of the English occupational army in Stirling Castle, was handed news of the disaster, he was dipping his fingertips into a bowl of berries sent to him by the king himself, who was campaigning in France. Lord Pickering read the message, and his face turned as white as the porcelain bowl. "Another ambush! My God! . . . What about our infiltrator?" he asked his assistant.

"He has already joined them, m'lord," his assistant told him.

Pickering sat back and calculated. If their infiltrator had already joined the Scottish rebels, then he was with them during the ambush. So they would trust him. He could get close to Wallace. The plan was working.

It would not be so bad to have to tell the king that he had lost so many men to ambushes and raids by these rebels if he could present to the king the head of this man that so many Scots were looking to as their savior.

Pickering felt better. He went back to his berries. After a few minutes, he called for more wine and some cheese.

28

DURING THE TIME HE HAD SPENT WITH HIS UNCLE ARGYLE, William Wallace had studied all of the terrain of Scotland. Uncle Argyle had told him that the survival of any man who fought against outrageously superior numbers would depend on that man's knowledge of the land through which he would be hunted. William had learned his lessons well. In a time when many people had never left their home village and could never find their way back to it if they were carried but ten miles away, William had crisscrossed his country with his uncle by his side, stopping here and there at the home of one of Uncle Argyle's fellow ecclesiastics to examine a new book or even at a monastery's library, riding on to discuss the knowledge gleaned from those volumes, but always, always, studying the terrain.

So it was that after the ambush of Dolecroft's cavalry, William Wallace led his men north into a deep woods, where they would find more shelter and protection. They needed rest and were laden with the booty they had taken from the English cavalry: extra weapons, clothing, food. Many of the men with Wallace, including old Campbell and his son Hamish, were experienced sheep rustlers and were familiar with the north–south trails that led across the ridge tops, but they found these forests that William led them into to be mysterious, mystical places. They did not see the trails that William saw. They didn't like the unfamiliar noises they heard when they tried to sleep. They didn't like the way the moon, especially when it was full as it was this night, seemed to be walking with them, looking down on their every move. Wallace realized their discomfort; as Uncle Argyle had told him, men will choose the familiar way, even when it appears less favorable. But they were safer here—or so William thought.

He walked along through the trackless forest, his heavy sheathed broadsword across his shoulders. They were all on foot; the horses they had taken from the cavalry were already on their way to be sold in the Highlands. William began to think of trade—another topic of discussion with Uncle Argyle. England wanted to control Scotland's trade with other countries, but there was so much Scotland could produce that traders in other places might—

One of the men close behind Wallace staggered and fell from exhaustion. The men who tried to help him could barely find the strength to lift him to his feet. Angry at himself for forgetting the fatigue of his men, Wallace said to Hamish, "Stop here and rest."

They collapsed to the leaves and loam and greedily squeezed water from sheep belly canteens.

Wallace sat down on a pad of moss and leaned back against the trunk of a tree. He tried to think, to remind himself to keep thinking, but he was so tired. He had not realized it before.

Suddenly he froze; a shaft of moonlight illuminated a cloaked woman standing twenty feet ahead of him. Something about her was familiar, and then she pulled off the hood and revealed her auburn hair, cascading in the moonlight. It was—

It couldn't be! But it was! Murron! Her pale gray eyes held him, watching in absolute peace, a half smile on her lips, as if she'd been anticipating his reaction to this surprise and had already played it out in her mind.

"Murron! Is—is it you?" William cried out.

Joy exploded on his face; he heaved himself heavily to his feet and ran to her but stopped before he touched her, as if she might evaporate. But it *was* Murron without question! Overwhelmed, he clutched her.

"I need you so much!"

She smiled at him, softly, sadly.

"Murron! I love you! I love you! Do you know it? Do you?"

"William . . .," a voice said. But it was not Murron's voice, it was someone at William's shoulder. "William!" the voice insisted. It sounded like Hamish. And Murron began to fade.

"Stay, Murron! I need you! Stay!" William pleaded.

Murron smiled softly at William, but his arms couldn't enclose her. He wept as he understood, even before he awoke. He was lying on his new tartan, in camp, as Hamish shook him. Tears were puddled in William's eyes, and Hamish didn't have to ask what he was dreaming.

William looked up into Hamish's face and saw that his friend was alarmed. "What is it?" William asked, pretending he had not slept, much less dreamed.

"A noise, William! Listen! Hounds!"

Wallace jumped up and heard the distant yipping of a dog pack. Stephen, the new Irish recruit, raced up and said, "We must run in different directions!"

"We don't split up!" Hamish said sharply.

"They used hounds on us in Ireland. It's the only way!" Stephen shot back.

"He's right, Hamish!" Wallace looked around him; old Campbell already had the men roused up. Wallace

117

darted to him and grabbed his arm. "Divide them and run!"

Wallace, Hamish, and old Campbell shoved men in different directions, then ran themselves. Wallace's group was about a dozen; they raced through the woods, dodging trees, fleeing deeper into the forest. It was hard going, but the dogs were no threat without armed handlers, and if William knew the English, they would not come into this woods without strong numbers. The run would be as hard on them as it was on the Scots, and with so many men scattering, the dogs would soon grow confused and discouraged.

They stopped and listened. The barks were getting closer.

"Split again!" William ordered.

The twelve divided into two groups of six and raced away in opposite directions.

But no matter how they ran and dodged, the barks grew nearer.

Hounds. They had to be following some scent! William looked for a stream to run along to try to mask the smell of the men from the noses of the dogs, but there was no running water near. He jumped up, grabbed a low branch, and pulled himself into a tall tree. He worked himself up the branches and peered into the woods beyond. This high in the tree the hounds sounded louder and more numerous; and through breaks in the trees, he could see the glimmer of many torches. To the English it was like a fox hunt, and William Wallace was the fox.

He scrambled to the ground where Hamish, old Campbell, and several of the others were waiting. William could see that old Campbell was ready to give up on running and make a stand here, but that was hopeless. The hounds would drag them down and the swordsmen that followed would finish what the dogs did not.

And so they ran. The barks were getting very close. Wallace could feel the rising instincts of panic. The blood beat in his ears, his breath scalded his lungs.

And the hounds were relentless. Wallace's group was down to Hamish, old Campbell, and the two new recruits: Faudron and that insane Irishman who called himself Stephen.

Suddenly William Wallace stopped running and turned on those with him.

"What is it?" Hamish said. "Come on, William, run!" The barks were getting closer and closer, but suddenly William was ignoring them.

"No matter how we go, they follow," he said. "They have our scent. That is, they have my scent."

"Run! You must not be caught!" Faudron pleaded.

But William Wallace just stood there.

"We can't stop!" the Irishman insisted.

"They've tricked us," William said.

"What's the crazy man saying, Lord?" Stephen of Ireland asked, looking toward the stars.

"The dogs have a scent. My scent. Someone must have given it to them," William said quietly.

"Who would do such a thing?" Stephen said with a wide-eyed look of Irish astonishment.

"Exactly," William said. "Who?" And he pulled out his dagger.

Back among his contingent of swordsmen and royal hunting dogs, Lord Pickering felt the excitement of the impending kill. He sensed it from the dogs; he sensed it in himself. The prey had stopped running. The dogs barked frantically; they tugged so hard at their leashes that the handlers were almost dragged along. The lead handler turned and called back, "Be ready! We have them!"

The soldiers gripped their weapons, ready to take their prisoners. Pickering had already told them he wanted Wallace alive; it was always best to make an example of rebels by allowing those who shared their sentiments to witness the execution. Now he called again, "Remember, I want Wallace a prisoner!" Only a few of his soldiers heard it; most were strung out in a long line stretching far behind the dogs, but Pickering was not too worried, for he had made sure his most experienced and reliable soldiers were in front.

The dogs, their handlers, and the lead soldiers burst into a small clearing. The dogs found a body, stabbed, his throat cut; the dogs plunged their snouts into the gore and yipped wildly. The handlers had to fight furiously to tear the dogs from their bloody prize.

Lord Pickering approached the body and looked down. It was Faudron, mangled now but identifiable, with the new scarf he had given William in place of William's own tucked into his shirt.

"Damnation! *Damnation!*" Lord Pickering bellowed, and seizing the arm of his assistant, he dragged the man over for a closer look at the body. "That is Faudron, isn't it? Isn't it?"

The assistant peered down at the bloodless face; the dogs had gotten to it, but they had left enough for the assistant to be sure who it was. "Yes, m'lord," he told Lord Pickering.

Pickering ranted. He had conceived the plan of an infiltrator, had even picked Faudron from among the likeliest candidates. This should have worked! How could Wallace have known? Hell with it, he could wonder at that later. "After him! Get them going again!" he shouted at the dog handlers.

"Their noses are drowned in new blood. They'll follow nothing now, m'lord!" the lead handler said. The dogs were milling around, barking aimlessly.

And just as the realization hit Pickering that he couldn't pursue Wallace any further, something else hit Pickering: the dagger of Stephen of Ireland, who had covered himself in a cloak and slipped in among Pickering's men. Pickering's eyes went wide, then rolled back as Stephen's dagger slid expertly through his back ribs and into his heart. As Pickering fell and his men realized what had happened, Stephen had already ran back into the trees.

The soldiers hesitated for a moment, then a captain said, "After him!"

Three men raced into the darkness of the forest in the direction Stephen ran. Suddenly they heard the whistling of a huge broadsword, and the unmistakable sound of steel cutting through bone could be heard with the faint death groans of the soldiers. Then the head of one of them came rolling out of the trees, into the clearing, to stop at the captain's feet.

The English soldiers crowded together; even the dogs whimpered and picked up the fear of the men around them. It was like they were surrounded by something superhuman and demonic.

Then Wallace's voice came booming out of the darkness; he played up the spookiness of it all. "Eeeenglishmennnnnn!" William shrieked.

The soldiers were terrified—and rightly so. They were realizing that they were lost in this forest; their leader had been murdered right under their noses. Suddenly they were not even secure in their numbers, for most of the other soldiers hadn't even reached the clearing yet.

The weird Scottish voice roared from the blackness around them: "You seek William Wallace. You have found him. Tell your masters—those of you that make it home—that when you come armed into Scotland, you come into hell!"

A pause; nothing but silence and fear. Then with a bloodcurdling yell, three wild men tore out of the darkness from different directions, their swords slashing. They cut down soldiers, and the others panicked. They ran anywhere they could. Terror spread through the forest.

Wallace, Hamish, and Stephen were left alone in the heart of the woods. They howled, barked like dogs, and snarled like wolves—and then laughed like hyenas!

"I thought I was dead when ya pulled that dagger!" Stephen said.

"No English lord would trust an Irishman!" Wallace said.

Hamish squinted down at the little Irishman, thought for a moment, and said, "Let's kill him anyway."

They laughed again until their sides hurt.

Then William Wallace's laughter leaked away. He found the tree where he had fallen asleep and stood beside it now and stared into the dark forest where he had seen Murron in his dream.

29

THE NEWS OF WALLACE'S VICTORY OVER LORD PICKERING raced across Scotland like an Atlantic gale.

It spread to Inverness, where two men were drinking in the town alehouse and one said, "William Wallace killed fifty men! Fifty if it was one!"

The same tale was exchanged by two farmers at a crossroads below Glasgow, only here it was said, "A hundred men! With his own sword! He cut through the English like—"

In the taverns of Edinburgh, the story was going: "—like Moses through the Red Sea! Hacked off two hundred heads!"

"Two hundred?!" doubted one of the listeners, still sober enough to be incredulous.

"Saw it with my own eyes," the speaker insisted.

But in the string of valleys where William Wallace had spent his boyhood, all looked absolutely normal: sleepy and peaceful. The clansmen who lived here never spoke of William Wallace. If an outsider mentioned his name, the farmers, their wives, and even their children all took on bewildered and rather dull expressions and seemed never to have heard of the man.

It was here, between the setting of the sun and the rising of the moon, that a Highlander, a runner, slipped through the inky blackness and tapped on the door of the house belonging to Stewart the farmer, who opened the door immediately and invited the man inside. But the runner did not stay; he whispered with Stewart for a moment and then ran on up the valley.

Hamish Campbell watched the runner from behind the closed doors of the barn. When he was sure he had gone, he turned and moved to the back of the barn, where the soft light of a shielded lantern glowed on twenty Highlanders, lying in the hay. Stewart had fed them well; he had found fresh clothes for some and sound weapons for others. Now most of them were asleep.

Hamish did not trouble them; he climbed the ladder into the loft, where his father and Stephen of Ireland sat cross-legged on the hay. They had been whispering for hours about the secret crafts of rebellion: how to use farm implements in battle, how to set an ambush, which kinds of moss are best to stop bleeding. The old Scot and the young Irishman had much in common. When Hamish arrived, they kept right on whispering.

Hamish moved past them to the dark corner in the very back of the barn, where he found William Wallace asleep. Hamish knelt and watched him, not wanting to disturb his friend's slumber; and yet that sleep clearly was not peaceful. William's face twitched, his body jerked, his lips moved as if they desperately needed to speak but could not make the words come.

Hamish knew what he was dreaming. Hamish, in his own way, had loved Murron, too.

There was a knock on the door of the barn in the rhythm Stewart used. Old Campbell and Stephen of Ireland broke off their talk and watched as one of the Highlanders down below opened the door to their

123

host. He moved in and moved to the ladder up to the loft as the rest of the Highlanders stirred, knowing by Stewart's hurry that their time of rest was over.

Hearing the commotion below, William awoke suddenly and gazed at Hamish with the dazed look of someone who had leaped across worlds in an instant. He stared about him and seemed to Hamish disappointed to find himself back on this side of death, where his loneliness was a physical pain. He then looked at Hamish as if nothing had happened, as if he had awakened like any other man might, and Hamish pretended the same. "What is it?" William asked, seeing Stewart mounting the top of the ladder. "What's going on?"

"A messenger has arrived," Hamish said.

Stewart looked around him at each face before he spoke. "The English are advancing an army toward Stirling," he said. "They appear to be reinforcing the one already there. It looks like a full-scale invasion."

Campbell sucked a long full breath into his massive lungs. Scotland invaded. Full-scale war. Everything he had dreaded, feared—and prayed for. "Do the nobles rally?" he asked.

"Robert the Bruce has been chased from Edinburgh! But word of the march has spread, and Highlanders are coming down on their own by the hundreds, by the thousands!" Stewart said.

And then without anyone meaning to, they all turned and looked at William Wallace.

30

STIRLING CASTLE STOOD THEN AS IT DOES NOW, PERCHED on a hill high above a grassy field cut in half by a river spanned by a bridge. Now the bridge is made of stone and steel; in June of 1297, it was made of wood.

On the seventeenth day of that month, Scottish nobles had gathered on a smaller hill overlooking the field; they wore gleaming armor, with plumes, sashes, and banners, and were attended by squires and grooms.

The mists of morning shrouded most of the field. But from the opposite side of the bridge they heard the clattering of a huge army moving forward. Lochlan, a noble with extensive holdings near Edinburgh, galloped to Mornay, who, as the representative of the strongest alliance of noble families on the field that day and a well-known ally of the imprisoned Robert the Bruce, was accepted by the other nobles as the man best accredited to discuss battlefield terms with the English commanders. Lochlan had come to the field that day expecting to negotiate, not fight, but the sheer size of the English army had his heart pounding. "It sounds like twenty thousand!" he shouted to Mornay even before he had drawn up his horse.

Mornay was calm. He too expected no battle; his voice, unlike Lochlan's, was dull with disappointment. "The scouts say it is ten."

"And we have but two!"

The business of slaughter is a cauldron of boiling emotion, and the same dark apprehensions that had begun to spatter within Lochlan's belly were likewise churning in the guts of the common Scottish soldiers who stood clustered around the small hill on the northern side of the bridge. There was an abbey on this hill, and many of the Scottish commoners on the field that morning had reason to look at the abbey and wish they'd had the privilege of selling their lives into monastic slavery of the soul rather than face the lot that was theirs that day.

Most of them owned no land, nor did they own the houses where they lived. They were allowed to inhabit the huts they called home by the good graces of the nobleman whose land they were privileged to work. The commoner then paid his liege lord a share of the harvest, the portions being determined not by the laborer's productivity or the size of the family he was trying to feed but by his station in life, a status preestablished at the moment of his birth.

But service of labor was not all the commoner owed his lord; he was also required to present himself for battle whenever and wherever his lord required. To refuse to do so was more than disgrace; it meant turning himself and his family into wanderers and beggars. Still, the Highlanders had never been known as reluctant warriors. Theirs was a beautiful, rugged, unforgiving land, lashed by furious winds and surrounded by ferocious seas. They were descendants of marauding tribes and Vikings; they believed in courage.

The arrangement of their society seemed quite normal to the common Scots on the field that day. Like all men, they drifted with the flow of their lives.

But standing on a cold hillside on a foggy morning and staring across a field where other men stand with the sole purpose of spilling your blood and brains upon the ground has a tendency to make you think in basic terms. And the Scots thought not of society but of life and death.

The English were massed below the stone battlements of the castle and the river at the base of its hill. They stood in ordered ranks: arches, pikemen, swordsmen, axmen. Behind them loomed the cavalry, line after line of mounted knights with lances. It was the biggest army, the largest assembly of humanity in any form, that the Scots had ever seen. Their weapons were new and polished. They had steel helmets, iron shoulder plates, chain mail. Even the horses wore armor.

The most protection any of the common Scots wore was a shirt of padded leather. Their weapons were old, and some were only farm implements adapted to the purpose at hand, but the edges were sharp. The Highlanders were used to making do, and they credited more the wielder of the weapon than the weapon itself.

But this day did not feel like theirs. All armies have a mood, flowing down from the man the warriors see as their leader, and the Scots knew the men who led them to that dying field cared nothing for their lives or even for the victory they might win in sacrificing them. As through the mists they saw the numbers arrayed against them, a young soldier tugged at a grizzled veteran and muttered, "So many!"

The veteran took no pains to keep his voice down. "The nobles will negotiate. If they deal, they send us home. If not, we charge. When we are all dead and they can call themselves brave, they withdraw."

The young soldier had never seen a pitched battle, but he was no coward. He had fought in numerous clan wars. Then it seemed he fought for honor. Here nothing made sense. "I didn't come to fight so they could own more lands that I could work for them!" he said.

"Nor did I. Not against these odds!" the veteran said. And then, with no other thought, he simply lowered his pike and began to walk back through the lines, heading north toward the Highlands. The younger man, surprised at first, quickly followed him.

Like a leak in an earthen dam, the desertion quickly gathered force. At first one by one and then in clumps, more of the Scots lowered their weapons and turned their faces toward home.

Seeing their army dissolve before their eyes, the nobles were powerless. If a few men or a small group failed to satisfy their obligations in battle, they could be fittingly punished, but when the whole multitude defied their noble authority . . .

"Stop!" Lochlan screamed. "Men! Do not flee! Not now! Wait until we have negotiated!"

But Mornay was scarcely surprised by what he saw. "They won't stop, and who could blame them?" he said quietly.

But suddenly they did stop. William Wallace came riding into the mob of men followed by his clan. He was striking, charismatic, his head without a helmet, his hair flowing in the wind, his powerful arms bare, his chest covered not in armor but a commoner's leather shirt. Unlike the heavy knights on their armored horses, Wallace rode a swift horse like he was born on it.

The entire Scottish army watched in fascination as Wallace and his men rode through them toward the command hill. A half dozen of the men with Wallace were also mounted. The rest ran in that Highland scurry that was as fast as a horse's trot; some of them carried on their shoulders mysterious wool-wrapped bundles so long it took three men in a line to carry each.

The deserting Scots whispered among themselves. The young soldier who, without knowing or intending to, had started it all now frowned at the veteran and wondered, "Could that be William Wallace?"

"Couldn't be. Too young. Not big enough," the veteran told him.

The common soldiers, already having broken ranks, drifted in clusters up the hill to see the confrontation. As Wallace and his mounted captains reached the nobles, Stephen of Ireland, riding beside him, laughed. "The Almighty says this must be a fashionable fight, it's drawn the finest people," Stephen said.

Lochlan and his noble friends stared at the tall,

powerful commoner before them. So this was William Wallace. Wallace stared back. "Where is thy salute?" Lochlan said, his noble pride already stinging from the defiance of the rabble.

"For presenting yourselves on this battlefield, I give you thanks," Wallace said.

"This is our army. To join it, you give homage," Lochlan demanded.

"I give homage to Scotland. And if this is your army, why does it go?!" Wallace reined his horse around to face the mob of sullen men, all ready to desert. For a long moment he said nothing, just sat on his horse and looked down in awe at this thing that had grown beyond anyone's imagination.

He glanced at his friends: Campbell, Hamish, Stephen. They had no suggestions; they were just as awed as he was.

Then a shout came from the grizzled veteran, deep within the ranks of the deserters. "We didn't come to fight for them!"

And another man called, "Home! The English are too many!"

There was a rising clamor of agreement. Wallace raised his hand, and the army fell silent. "Sons of Scotland!" he shouted. "I am William Wallace!"

"William Wallace is seven feet tall!" the young soldier called.

"Yes, I have heard!" William shouted back. "He kills men by the hundreds! And if he were here, he'd consume the English with fireballs from his eyes and bolts of lightning from his ass!"

Laughter rumbled through the Scottish ranks. It was not a noise that anyone on the battlefield had expected to hear that day. Wallace was smiling, but now the smile left his face.

"I am William Wallace. And I see a whole army of my countrymen, here in defiance of tyranny! You have come to fight as free men. And free men you are! What will you do with freedom? Will you fight?"

"Two thousand against ten?" the veteran shouted. "No! We will run—and live!"

"Yes!" Wallace shouted back. "Fight and you may die. Run and you will live at least awhile. And dying in your bed many years from now, would you be willing to trade all the days from this day to that for one chance to come back here as young men and tell our enemies that they may take our lives but they will never take our freedom?"

And the army of common Scotsmen, who only moments before had been trudging away from the battlefield, united in a shout that made the ground shudder. The sound—not the noise of many small creatures but the roar of one great one—quivered in the chest of every man and made him feel a part of something too big to control.

Down on the plain, English emissaries in all their regal finery galloped over the bridge under a banner of truce. The Scots grew silent watching them come.

The veteran, ashamed of what he had been doing five minutes before and wishing to justify his actions, pointed out to the bridge and yelled to his comrades, "Look! The English come to barter with our nobles for castles and titles. And our nobles will not be in the front of the battle!"

"No! They will not!" Wallace boomed. He dismounted and drew his sword. "But I will."

Slowly, the chant began and kept building louder and louder: "Wal—lace! *Wal—lace! WAL—LACE!*"

The bagpipers played and pulled the mob back into clan units. They lifted their weapons—spears and hoes, short swords and axes—toward the overwhelming numbers of the enemy army, and they stood.

Old Campbell, Hamish, and Stephen moved up beside William. The two Scots, father and son, were inward and quiet, but the Irishman's tongue was quick, and he said what they all were thinking: "Fine speech. Now what do we do?"

"Bring out our spearmen and set them in the field,"

Wallace said and watched his three friends gallop to the center of the front row of the Scottish battle line, where their clan had taken up a position.

Mornay rode over to Wallace bringing the horse he had dismounted and extended its reins to him, an invitation to join the prebattle talks. Wallace mounted up and rode out with the Scottish nobles to the near end of the bridge, where the English contingent was waiting.

The two groups of riders met. Cheltham, a black-bearded noble whose square face bore the scars of previous battles and who would be expected to lead the English charge should this confrontation result in actual battle, glared at Wallace. Could this fierce-looking commoner be who Cheltham thought he was? Cheltham knew the others: "Mornay. Lochlan. Inverness," he said, nodding to each.

"Cheltham," Mornay said, "this is William Wallace."

Cheltham refused to look at Wallace again. "Here are the king's terms," he said brusquely. "Lead this army off the field, and he will give you each an estate in Yorkshire, including hereditary title, from which you will pay him an annual duty of—"

"I have an offer for you," Wallace broke in.

Cheltham tried to ignore this crude interruption. "—From which you will pay the king an annual duty—"

Wallace pulled his broadsword and snapped its point to within an inch of Cheltham's throat. "I said I have an offer for you!" Wallace shouted, and Cheltham's eyes flashed in fury and disbelief at this violation of their protocol.

"You disrespect a banner of truce?!" Lochlan sputtered in similar outrage.

"From his king?" Wallace asked. "Absolutely. Here are Scotland's terms. Lower your flags and march straight to England, stopping at every Scottish home you pass to beg forgiveness for a hundred years of

131

theft, rape, and murder. Do that, and your men shall live. Do it not, and every one of you will die today."

Cheltham barked at the Scottish nobles, "You are outmatched! You haven't even any cavalry! In two centuries no army has won without it!"

"I'm not finished!" Wallace roared. "Before we let you leave, your commander must cross that bridge, stand before this army, put his head between his legs, and kiss his own ass!"

The outraged Englishman wheeled his horse around and led the rest of the negotiating contingent in a gallop back to the English battle line.

Wallace and the Scottish nobles watched them go. Mornay was the first to break their silence. "I'd say that was rather less cordial than he was used to."

"Be ready, and do exactly as I say," Wallace told them and reined his horse back to the Scottish army. The noblemen looked around at each other and then followed.

Wallace galloped to the center of the Scottish line and dismounted where his men were breaking out new fourteen-foot spears. Hamish, eyebrows raised, looked expectantly at Wallace: had he done as they planned? Wallace smiled faintly and nodded.

"I wish I could see the noble lord's face when he tells him," Hamish said.

Over on the English side of the field, within the shadow of the castle, Lord Talmadge's blood boiled from Cheltham's report. His eyes narrowing with rising fury, he glared toward his enemy and saw Wallace's spearmen taking up a position on the far side of the bridge. And at that very moment the Scots turned, lifted their kilts, and pointed their bare backsides at the English! To Talmadge it seemed they had aimed the demonstration at him personally!

"Insolent bastard! Full attack! Give no quarter! And I want this Wallace's heart brought to me on a plate!" Talmadge ordered.

Cheltham spurred his horse to form up the attack. The English army moved forward toward the bridge, so narrow that only a single file of riders could move across it at any one time. The English heavy cavalry, two hundred knights, crossed the bridge quickly and formed up on the other side of the river.

And with that one simple repositioning of his forces, Talmadge had put the Scots in the most dangerous situation they could have faced. The cavalry was his most formidable threat, the one for which no army had a counter. The Scots' only hope would have been to try to stop the riders at the narrow bridge, where, had the Scots resisted, an assault of archers and infantry would have been required to get the horsemen across. But the Scots had not even contested the maneuver! It was clear to Talmadge that Wallace was not only insolent but a fool.

Things looked terrible to the Scots themselves. And it was then that Stephen turned to Wallace and said, "The Lord tells me He can get me out of this mess. But He's pretty sure you're fooked."

Talmadge and his men stared across the river in dismay. Still the Scots were doing nothing. "Amateurs!" Talmadge spat in disgust and dismay. "They are neither wise enough to contest us or smart enough to flee! Send across the infantry!"

"M'lord, the bridge is so narrow—" Cheltham began.

"The Scots just stand in their formations! Our cavalry will ride them down like grass. Get the infantry across so they can finish the slaughter!" Talmadge demanded.

The English leaders shouted orders and kept their men moving across the bridge. Talmadge gestured for the attack flag.

The cavalry on the other side of the bridge saw the signal banners commanding their attack. They took the lances from their squires and lowered the visors of their helmets. They were proud, plumed, glimmering;

their huge horses, draped in scarlet and purple, held them high above the mortals who stood on mere earth. They looked invincible.

With a great shout, the knights charged.

To the Scots who stood and watched them come on, the noise of the horses' hooves was like thunder of a storm that no army could weather. No one on the battlefield had ever seen anyone even try. Formations of men, feeding on each other's will to fight or poisoned by each other's panic, had always scattered, for there was no known weapon for footsoldiers to resist the charge on open ground and no amount of courage to stand and face it.

And yet the Scots stood.

On and on the horses came. The rising thunder of the charge mixed with the sound of a heart hammering in every Scottish chest.

The lances lowered, an onrushing cluster of death. Closer . . . closer . . . closer.

Wallace jumped to the front of his clan. "Steady!" he shouted. "Hold . . . hold . . . *now!*"

The Scots snatched their fourteen-foot spears from the ground and snapped them up in unison, thrust forward in ranks, the first line of men bracing their spears at an angle three feet above the ground, the men behind them jabbing theirs at a five-foot level, the men behind holding theirs at seven feet.

The English knights had never seen such a formation. Their lances were useless—too short!—and it was too late to stop. The momentum that was to carry the horses smashing through the men on foot now became suicidal force; knights and horses impaled themselves on the long spears like beef on skewers.

Talmadge could see it; but worse was the sound, the scorching screams of dying men and horses, carried to him across the battlefield.

Wallace and his men now stood protected behind a literal wall of fallen chargers and knights. Wallace drew his broadsword and led his swordsmen out onto the field where they attacked the knights that were still alive. Most were off their horses; a few had managed to pull up their mounts. But the armored knights moved like turtles; the Scots swarmed around them, and the field ran with blood.

Suddenly all was quiet. Wallace lifted his huge, blood-stained sword, faced Talmadge in the distance, and bellowed, "Here I am, English coward! Come get me!!"

Talmadge was even more enraged—and his judgment was gone. "Press the infantry across!" he barked at Cheltham.

"But m'lord!"

"Press them!"

Cheltham gave a wave, and the vanguard of the English infantry began to stream onto the bridge.

Wallace smiled. He grabbed Hamish by the shoulder. "Tell Mornay to ride to the flank and cross upstream. Wait! Tell him to be sure the English see him ride away!"

Hamish hurried off with the message.

The Scottish nobles watched from their position on the abbey hill as the English infantry began moving across the little bridge. Behind them were their personal contingents of cavalry, a few dozen riders lightly armed. Having had no part in the first great shock of the battle, they felt unable or unwilling to do anything more than watch—and criticize.

"If he waits much longer, he will squander the brief advantage he gained," Lochlan was saying as Hamish galloped up.

"Ride around and ford behind them!" Hamish ordered.

The nobles did not challenge Hamish's insolence; rather they questioned the wisdom of the instruction that they knew had come from Wallace. "We should not divide our forces!" Mornay protested.

Hamish exploded. "Wallace says *do it!* And he says for you to let the English see you!"

"You listen to me, you common bastard!" Lochlan spat, but Mornay understood the strategy and put his hand on Lochlan's arm.

"They shall think we run away," Mornay said. "He has got them. He has planned everything from the first moment." He looked at Hamish. "Tell Wallace we will do it."

Mornay stood high in his stirrups, waved grandly to his men, and led them in a gallop around the back side of the hill.

Lord Talmadge saw the Scottish nobles ride off and shouted to Cheltham, "See! Every Scot with a horse is fleeing! Hurry! Hurry! Press them! Lead them yourself!"

Cheltham spurred his horse forward and herded half the English army across the river.

Wallace lifted his sword. *"FOR SCOTLAND!"*

He charged down the hill toward the soldiers massing on the north side of Stirling bridge. And the whole Scottish army followed him.

The English soldiers on the Scottish side of the bridge could not stand against the ferocity of the attack. They were outfought, outled, and outnumbered. They were thrown back toward the bridge itself, their only lifeline.

Talmadge was shocked at the butchery of his forces. It seemed impossible to him. It was a scene so horrible, so unthinkable to him that he could barely look, and yet he could not pull his eyes away. He felt his other field commanders at his shoulder, wanting instructions. It was hard to think. "Press reinforcements across!" he ordered them.

The flagmen signaled; the English infantry leaders, desperate to save their friends on the other side, tried to herd more of their footsoldiers onto the bridge, turning the already jammed passage into a plug of writhing humanity.

On the other side of the bridge, Wallace and his men were carving through the English vanguard. The Scots had already reached the bridge itself. Now everything

136

was chaos. The English footsoldiers on the bridge who tried to shove their way forward to fight were pressed back by those trying to flee the hacking Scottish blades. Talmadge's cavalry was gone. His archers, with friend and foe so tightly packed, were useless. And his infantry had a deathgrip on itself.

But Wallace and his men moved in only one direction: forward. They hacked at anything they could reach: necks, faces, backs, it didn't matter. The waters below the bridge ran red with blood.

"Use—use the archers!" Talmadge sputtered.

But the archers saw that they were useless now, and they had begun to smell the stink of panic rolling through the army; they were edging back, looking for a route to flee.

On the bridge, the Scots kept carving their way through the English soldiers—nothing could stop them. Wallace was relentless; each time he swung, a head flew or an arm. Hamish and Stephen fought beside him and swung the broadsword with both hands. Old Campbell lost his shield in the grappling; an English swordsman whacked at him and took off his left hand, but Campbell battered him to the ground with his right one and stabbed him.

The Scots reached the English side of the bridge and began to build a barrier with the dead bodies.

The English were not without courage. Cheltham, rallying the infantry blocked on the castle side of the bridge, led the desperate counterattack. The Scots made an impenetrable barrier of slashing blades, yet still Cheltham kept coming. As his men reeled back, he urged his horse into a gallop, intending to punch a hole through the Scottish barricade . . .

And Wallace stood to his full height, swung the broadsword, and hit Cheltham with a vertical slash that parted his helmet, his hair, and his brain.

Talmadge had seen enough; he wheeled his horse about and galloped away.

"Bloody coward!" his remaining general spat. But there was no time for that; he had to save the army.

"We are still five thousand!" he shouted. "Rally! Make a stand!"

The English forces below the castle were trying to form up for a second counterattack, just as Mornay and the Scottish horsemen, having forded the river high upstream, came crashing into the English flank. The English reinforcements were taken completely by surprise.

Now it was a rout.

At the bridge, Wallace saw the English soldiers in utter panic, running in every direction, and being cut down.

And the Scottish soldiers tasted something Scots had not tasted for a hundred years: victory.

Wallace looked around at the aftermath of the battle: bodies on the field, soldiers lying impaled, stacks of bodies on the bridge, the bridge slicked with blood.

Before it could all sink in, William was lifted on the shoulders of his men. And even the noblemen took up the chant, alongside the commoners . . .

"Wal—lace! *Wal—lace! WAL—LACE!*" the Scots chanted.

31

ON A FIELD IN FRANCE, THE CONTINENTAL ARMY OF Longshanks the King was encamped on a field of grass, yellow in the dry summer. Longshanks was in his command pavilion, looking at maps and deriding his generals. His campaign to dominate France had worked itself into a maddening stalemate. Some of the French nobles remained loyal to their king, saying the crown of France should be worn by a Frenchman. Other nobles accepted Longshanks's arguments that, as a Plantagenet, he *was* a Frenchman. This was not quite true, of course, but thrones were contested throughout Europe on shakier claims. Even if Longshanks was not properly in line for the French throne, his daughter-in-law was, and his future grandchildren would be. So the struggle in France, like royal wars everywhere, became a contest of bluff and bribery, with bits of fighting and military action lumped among great layers of political manuever. It was maddening for Longshanks. He felt the age in his bones. His joints ached in the cold night dampness and he had developed a persistent cough.

He took it out on his generals. "We should have been to Paris by now! Now the army will have to winter here!"

The generals had themselves grown so frustrated that they were willing to speak up in the king's presence. "Sire, we are not prepared to winter here," one of them said. "We could lose half our men to starvation and cold."

Longshanks knew this already; he accepted the realities of war and had planned accordingly. "In the spring we will move our army across from Scotland," he said.

A messenger, exhausted and mud spattered, rode up, jumped from his lathered horse, and hurried straight into the tent. He bowed sharply and handed the king a scroll. As the king read, his face, which his advisors had been noticing was a bit pale of late, took on a flush they had not seen for some time. Then slowly Longshanks lowered the scroll, and through a mouth set stiff in anger, he said, "We have no more army in Scotland."

THE
GUARDIAN

32

Inside the great hall of Edinburgh Castle, William Wallace knelt before Angus Craig, foremost of Scotland's ancient elders, who lifted a silver sword and dubbed William's shoulders. "I knight thee Sir William Wallace!" Craig declared.

William rose and faced the great hall, crowded with hundreds of new admirers as well as his old friends: Hamish, his father—with one loose sleeve, but otherwise none the worse for wear—and Stephen of Ireland, all in new clothes and armor. Their faces were clean, their bruises healed, the blood washed from their hands and hair. William had never seen them look so sparkling. They stood erect and proud among so many others who had never once fought for the positions of power their finery proclaimed.

But those others, they were Scots, too. They stood looking at William with—what was it exactly that he saw in their eyes? It was like wonder, but not that sweet awe of a child lying on his back on the summer heather and looking up at the stars. Just behind the eyes of these noblemen in their furs and the ladies in their lace was the confusion of something not quite making sense to them.

In ten minutes, when William had walked out of the room and stood at a window alone, overlooking

Scotland's ancient royal city, he would understand what this look had really meant. Those people had never seen anything like him and his friends. To the nobles, common Scottish warriors were mere brutes, but now they were confronted by something strange and baffling: a commoner who had outsmarted Scotland's enemies. This was disturbing; it shook their assumptions. Yet they freely admitted their admiration of the strategy that had won the battle. They liked to speak about it as if Strategy was a living thing unto itself, that it somehow rose up apart from the men who created it and put it into action. Maybe thinking of it this way made them more comfortable, for to admit otherwise would be to say that commoners were, if not superior, at least equal to the nobles.

William Wallace would see all that later when he had time to think about the new perspectives he had from this pinnacle of admiration. He would also see that this was a tremendous opportunity to unite both noble and common Scot in a campaign unlike any they had ever made.

But those were the thoughts of reason and reflection. Now, as he stood among the sparkle and the music of the castle, his mind did not yet weave the threads of sensation; it just took them all in.

And in the center of his chest was an emptiness.

He lifted his eyes to the rear of the hall, where the great balcony was backed by a magnificent arched window. He stared at the sunlight streaming in there, and in the center of its blinding brilliance, he imagined her familiar form: Murron, so real to him in this moment of triumph that he could almost see her, glowing like an angel, could almost speak to her, touch her.

Almost.

Wallace reached inside the ornamental chestplate the nobles of Scotland had given him, and his fingers found the cloth that Murron had embroidered with a thistle, her gift to him on their wedding day.

* * *

Less than an hour after the knighting of William Wallace, old Craig convened a meeting of Scotland's ruling nobles in the council chamber of the castle. A massive table ran across the width of the room. Aligned on either side were the two rival factions of nobles, one supporting the claim of Balliols for the vacant throne, the other, the claim of the Bruces; all of them were muttering among their allies and refusing to look at their opponents. Old Craig was in the center chair, with young Robert the Bruce on his right. Amid the murmuring of the nobles, Robert leaned over and whispered to Craig, "Do you know this William Wallace's politics?"

"No. The Balliols have spread the story that he supports them. Perhaps he does, but perhaps he does not. I sent my servants with food and help for his wounded after Stirling, and they reported back to me that Wallace's men held you in esteem."

"His men. But what of Wallace himself?"

Old Craig could barely keep from shaking his head at young Bruce's naïveté. Here he had grown up in one of Scotland's noblest families, and yet he didn't understand the enchantments of power, the human urge to imitate the influential, the seductions of syncophancy. "Wallace's men admire him with a burning fervor. They believe he is like them, they want to be like him. He carries an aura of victory, of invulnerability. The Highlanders are a headstrong, independent sort, but they are men, and they will seek to copy the one who leads them."

Craig saw that Robert still didn't quite understand his point; he made it more plainly. "Wallace's men love him. They very nearly worship him; they would die for him. They would surely hold no opinion that seemed counter to his. If Wallace's men favor you, then he surely must have some sympathies in your direction."

Robert the Bruce looked down at the table, rubbing his lip and taking this in. *Is he innocent or dull?* Craig wondered. *Or is it that he is like Wallace and believes in action more than analysis?* Then it occurred to Craig that this might be exactly what William Wallace did favor about Robert the Bruce. The Bruces were known to fight first on one side of an issue and then on another—but they were known to fight.

Whatever the state of William Wallace's sympathies, they were now crucial to the interests of every nobleman in the room. Old Craig leaned back to young Robert and whispered, "Just remember this. Wallace's weight with the commoners could unbalance everything. The Balliols will kiss his ass, so we must."

A court steward stepped in and announced with solemn formality, "Lords of Scotland: Sir William Wallace!"

The nobles on each side of the table tried to outdo each other in their acclamation as Wallace strode in, flanked by Hamish, Campbell, and Stephen, splendid in their tartans. They stopped in front of Craig at the middle of the table.

Robert the Bruce had attended the knighting ceremony for Wallace, but the Bruce had kept himself back among the crowd as he had been advised to do by his father. After the way adoration for Wallace had swept the country in the aftermath of the victory at Stirling, Bruce the Elder had told his son to observe the way people responded to him and how he carried himself in the presence of a crowd, for it was clear that this Wallace had something that could sweep up whole armies of men. Now, in these smaller surroundings, Bruce had the opportunity to study the man at close range.

Wallace stood with his feet planted as wide as his shoulders, and for a man with shoulders so broad, the posture could have looked bullying. But his face contained none of the surly arrogance of a brute. He was handsome, strikingly so; manly, calm, and self-contained—young Bruce could see why tough men like the Highlanders would follow this man into battle. It was a face women would like, with softness

146

in the pale green eyes and light playing in the blondish hair. His chin was up, his mouth set, his eyes still. And young Robert the Bruce knew, without needing to be told by his father or old Craig or anyone else, that before him stood a man who never had nor ever would subjugate himself to any other man.

Old Craig rose to his feet. "Sir William," he said. "In the name of God, we declare and appoint thee Guardian, High Protector of Scotland!"

The nobles rose; court attendants hurried to Wallace and draped a golden chain of office around his neck. The nobles applauded.

Almost before the applause died, a member of the Balliol clan, who had kept an open seat beside him, spoke up. "Sir William! Inasmuch as you and your captains hail from a region long known to support the Balliol clan, may we invite you to join us?"

The Balliols—and everyone else in the room—looked at Wallace, and old Craig secretly swore at himself for allowing the Balliols to have used such a simple mechanism as seating arrangements to align Wallace with them.

But Wallace's gaze had locked onto Robert the Bruce! It was as if two young lions had instantly recognized the leadership power of each other. And Craig realized for the first time that Wallace had never before laid eyes on the Bruce. Recognizing the colors and design of the Bruce's tunic, Wallace studied the young warrior who had not joined him at Stirling. "You are Robert the Bruce," Wallace said.

"I am," Robert replied.

"My father fought in support of yours," Wallace said, "whenever your father fought for Scotland."

"My father always fought for Scotland," young Bruce said. "He was just sometimes forced to fight against Scots who did not fight for Scotland."

"I fight for Scotland," Wallace said.

"I know," Bruce said.

The Balliols shriveled. The nobles on the Bruce side could barely keep from grinning.

Suddenly the Balliols changed their tactics. "This new success," their leader began, "is the result of all of Scotland's efforts, and now is the time to unite all of Scotland and declare a king!"

Then Mornay, who was sitting to the right of young Bruce, smiled coolly and said, "Then you are prepared to recognize our legitimate succession!"

Balliol reacted instantly. "You're the ones who won't support the true claim! I demand consideration of these documents!" With that he reached for the parchments that bore the Balliols' written case for ascendancy, the same scholarly arguments they had presented at every meeting of the council. The documents had never borne any true weight before; but clearly the Balliols were bringing them up again now in an attempt to sway Wallace with their legal legitimacy.

But if they thought William Wallace would be impressed by genealogical tables, they had badly miscalculated. He wasn't even looking at them; he was staring again at the Bruce, who suddenly felt ashamed of the bickering.

"Those were lies when they were written!" Mornay said with contempt. "Our documents prove absolutely that—"

Suddenly Wallace turned his back and walked toward the door.

All the arguments died into an abrupt silence. Then Craig called, "Sir William! Where are you going?"

Wallace turned, and his eyes swept over everyone at the table. "We have beaten the English! But they'll come back, because you won't stand together." Wallace moved back to the table and frowned at the men there as one might at a group who refused to agree that grass was green or the sky blue. Wallace's voice rose. "There is one clan in this country: Scotsmen. One class: free. One price: courage." Wallace turned again, and again he strode toward the door.

"But . . . what will you do?" Craig wanted to know.

148

Wallace stopped. "I will invade England. And defeat the English on their own ground."

The nobles had stopped breathing.

"Invade?!" Craig sputtered. "That is impossible, it—"

Wallace slung out his broadsword and moved down the length of the table, bashing the succession documents into the laps of the nobles! *"Listen to me!"* he shouted. "Longshanks understands this! This!" Wallace thrust his massive broadsword high in the air.

Some of the nobles, when they had heard Mornay's tale of Wallace arriving on the battlefield and rallying the entire army when it had already begun to desert, had doubted the story. But seeing the fire in Wallace's face, the passion in his voice, the power of his presence as he gripped the handle of the double-edged claymore and shook the steel at their faces, made them know every word had been true.

"There is a difference between us," Wallace said with quiet fervor. "You think the people of this country exist to provide you with position. I think your position exists to provide the people with freedom. And I go to make sure they have it."

Wallace banged through the door. His friends suppressed smiles and marched out behind him.

Wallace and his men were striding down the stone corridor of the castle, away from the council chamber, as Robert the Bruce ran out after them.

"Wait! Sir William! Please!" Bruce caught up with Wallace. He struggled for a moment, then took Wallace's arm and urged him to step into an alcove so that his words could be overheard by no one, even Wallace's lieutenants. "I . . . I admire what you said. But you can't talk to them that way. They are fat cowards, most of them, but we need them."

Wallace turned away, but Robert caught his arm again.

"You despise us," Robert said. "I can't blame you; I've heard what you've been through. But remember,

149

my brave friend. These men have lands, castles. Much to risk."

"And the common man who bleeds on the battle-field, does he risk less?" Wallace asked.

"No. But nobles . . . can help . . ."

But even as Robert the Bruce was struggling, Wallace was pouncing. "Nobles? What does that mean—to be noble?"

Robert found himself without a ready answer.

Wallace leaned closer and shook his fist between them, like a big brother telling a younger one to be brave. "Your title gives you claim to the throne of our country!" Wallace said. "But men don't follow titles, they follow courage! Your arm speaks louder than your tongue. Our people know you. Noble and common, they respect you. If you would lead them toward freedom, they would follow you. And so would I."

William Wallace walked away, leaving Robert the Bruce alone in the alcove of Edinburgh Castle.

33

YORKSHIRE SPREADS ACROSS ENGLAND LIKE A CROWN OF nature upon the nation's head. Lying almost at the center of the island of Britain and in the upper region of England, its rolling hills of heather, grass, and flowers and its skies of fluffy clouds prompt a dreaminess in people and have inspired a whole tradition of stories of enchantment.

At the heart of this heartland stands York. In the late thirteenth century, it was a fortress city, completely surrounded by a towering wall. The rich commerce of the lush region moved in and out of York's commanding gates in confident vitality, all under the watchful eye of the royal governor, who commanded a standing army of defenders that guaranteed the collection of the king's taxes and kept the king's peace. For as long as men believed in fortress cities, York was the stronghold not only of Yorkshire but of all of northern England.

The royal governor of medieval York was the nephew of Longshanks himself. This nephew was everything Longshanks wanted in a son, if what he truly wanted was a son to mirror his father. He was ruthless and ambitious; he reacted to threats with aggression. He knew that power and the will to use it produced rewards; it certainly had in his case, for to be the royal governor of a jewel like York was to be in possession of the king's full confidence and blessing.

And yet the first few weeks of autumn had been anything but pleasant for the governor. Word of the disaster at Stirling had spread through the countryside, such an assault on predictability and reason that hysterical thinking began to affect even his magistrates throughout the shire. Almost every day he received panicky messages of alarm; Scottish raiders were on the move, they said. Some of them reported an entire Scottish army on the march! Of course no one could pinpoint an exact location of this phantom army; reports of night marches were being made by the same kind of peasants who reported stumbling on conventions of warlocks and gatherings of the undead.

Yet as the reports persisted, the governor began to believe that the Scots might be making exploratory forays into Yorkshire. Highland Scots had raided the Lowlands for centuries, stealing cattle. It was possible that the Scottish luck at Stirling—for certainly it was only luck—had encouraged the foolhardy to raid into England itself.

Still the reports persisted from more and more reasonable sources. Mayors and magistrates began requesting troops to reassure their frightened citizen-

151

ry. The governor sent out scouts. The scouts did not return.

He sent out more scouts. One of them got back alive, shouting that the entire Scottish army was indeed on the move, led by William Wallace, in Yorkshire itself.

The governor convened his military advisors in the map room of the central tower of the fortress city. Choosing from the shire maps that lined the wall shelves, the governor had maps spread on every table, and he ordered his aides to assemble all the appeals for help they had received in recent days. They sought to find a pattern in Wallace's travel. But the written appeals for help seemed to show no direction of Wallace's movements. Their work was interrupted as the governor's captain of defenses strode in with another note and said, "M'lord, a message from your cousin, the prince. He says London has no more troops to send us."

"Doesn't he understand that every town in northern England is begging for help?!" the governor erupted and then held his tongue. He was miffed at young Edward, miffed that he had no fondness for war, miffed that in spite of this his father had given him authority to direct domestic troop movements during Longshanks's absence in France, and miffed— the truth be told—that it was Edward and not himself in line to be the next king. But the young Edward had not ascended to the throne yet, and from the rumors coming up from London, it was by no means certain that he would. Yes, Edward was Longshanks's only son, but there was horrible bitterness between them, and while heredity was supposed to be the only channel of transmission of the divine right of kings, Longshanks was a man to change history to suit his will. Wasn't he doing exactly that in Scotland? Or at least that's what he was about to do until he stumbled over this stone named William Wallace.

The governor looked back to his maps and wondered aloud, "Where will Wallace strike first?"

"I should think these smaller settlements along the border . . . ," the captain guessed.

They heard shouts from the courtyard below their tower and looked out to see a rider dismount from a lathered, mud-spattered horse. "What news?" the captain called out.

"He advances!" the rider shouted back.

The governor pushed the captain aside and barked down at the fool, "But to *what town?*"

"He comes *here!*"

34

WILLIAM WALLACE RODE AT THE HEAD OF HIS ARMY ALONG a hard, dry road through fields grown brown with the autumn and thought how ugly a thing panic was, especially among civilians. They were fleeing in terror, some toward the walled city in the distance, some away from it. It was strange to see them moving opposite ways; people were like flocks of birds and tended to flee at once and in the same direction. The fact that the civilians were colliding with each other going to and from York had to be a sign: the royal governor had already learned of the Scottish approach and had locked the gates. Those still trying to reach the city were refusing to believe they could be turned away.

But as they saw the main body of Scots on the road, the civilians fled across the farmland, leaving behind a tangle of carts for the army to shove out of the way like a plow cutting through a field.

In camp two nights before, Wallace had asked old Campbell to find him the best carpenters in their army. These men Wallace combined with a group of Highlanders handpicked for their ability to move quickly through hostile ground. He had given these men instructions and sent them off while it was still dark. Now, as they reached the last thick stand of trees before York, one of those same Highlanders ran out to him and led Wallace and his lieutenants into the woods, where they came upon a massive contraption; its wooden wheels were as tall as the carpenters who had made them, and piled above them were thick trees lashed together and covered with layers of tangled brush to screen stones and arrows away from the warriors who would push it all.

Wallace nodded his approval. The battering ram was ready.

Standing on one of the tall stone parapets flanking the entrance of his city, just as night was falling, the governor of York looked down at the people far below him, banging on the thick wooden gate and begging to be let in, and their cries made him angry. He was tempted to order his archers to shoot them. "What is wrong with those people?!" he demanded of the captain who stood next to him, surveying their defenses. "Don't they know this city cannot be taken?"

The captain saw the irony of the question as the citizens who lived outside the walls and were even now pleading and lifting their children in the air, as if showing them to the soldiers lining the parapets would soften their hearts enough to unbar the great gates and allow a few more to rush inside. A professional soldier, the captain saw the danger; the desperate citizens saw the city as secure—their cries made those already inside feel safer still—but the truth was that York was vulnerable. The governor has dispatched more than half of the city's potential defenders to the various outlying towns and hamlets that had been calling for reinforcements. Now York itself was jammed with the governor's supporters, flatterers, favorites, and hangers-on, everyone who fled to the shadow of the great city at the first whiff of trouble and who had the influence to gain admittance. But there were not enough fighting men.

The captain, who made more of Wallace's victory at Stirling than did the governor, knew it was possible that Wallace had intentionally concocted the depletion of the city's forces through a shrewdly planned campaign of raiding to draw the defenders away. Wallace was unpredictable; and these royal relatives who ran the English army, they were *too* predictable. The captain hurried off to direct the preparations for defense against a full assault, walking away even as the royal governor was talking.

"We will not allow a bandit to panic the greatest city in northern England!" the governor was saying to no one now. And then, looming out of the gray twilight, he saw them, the entire Scottish army coming at the city in a trot. Among the vanguard of foot soldiers rode William Wallace, huge broadsword strapped across his back. Behind him was the ram.

The civilians saw him, too. Their screams grew more frantic, they pounded on the gate with increased panic—and then suddenly they fled.

The captain appeared again beside the governor, and looking at those who had been shut out, running now to get as far away from the city as possible, he thought, *Do they flee because they know we won't let them in? Or is it because they no longer wish to be inside?*

Watching the Scots come on like an endless black cloud building into a relentless storm, the governor turned to the captain and asked, "Find every Scottish civilian in the city—traders, craftsmen, and their families, all of them—and bring them to me. I especially want the ones wearing the Scottish cloth. Fetch them all."

The captain did not understand the purpose of the order, but he did not challenge it, for he saw on the governor's face a look worthy of his uncle, Longshanks the King.

* * *

The battering ram, thrust by two dozen of Wallace's favorite Highlanders, picked up speed and slammed into the wooden gate of the city. With the collision, the battle was on. Flaming arrows sliced through the night; pots of boiling oil splashed down from the parapets onto the attackers who swarmed the gate.

The oil beat the first wave of Scots back, but Wallace rushed forward and grabbed the ram cart with his own hands. The attackers rallied to him and helped him slam the gate again and again. The arrows, stones, and oil from the parapets caught some men, but the ram was well designed and sheltered most. The gates, rising twenty feet high, cracked and then broke altogether; but behind it was an awful tangle of carts, broken sheds, impenetrable rubbish. Wallace grabbed a torch, threw it into the wooden tangle, and shouted, "Back! Wait for it to burn!"

Inside the city, the captain hurried into the tower room where the governor had taken refuge. "M'lord, they've breached the wall!"

"Then do as I ordered."

Outside the walls, the Scots waited, biding their time as the barrier burned. Suddenly they looked up in horror; the English were throwing the bodies of hung Scots over the wall. Men, women, even children, dangling at the ends of nooses.

The Highlanders stared in mute shock. Wallace was frozen; for a moment he was a boy again, back in MacAndrews's barn, staring up at hanged bodies he could scarcely believe were real.

His men charged forward.

"Stop!" Wallace screamed. *"Not yet! Listen to me!"* The clansmen heeded the only voice they would have obeyed at that moment. "They wish to frighten us! Or goad us into attacking too soon! But don't look away! *Look!"*

The Scots looked at the hanging bodies.

"Behold the enemy we fight!" Wallace thundered. "We will be more merciful than they have been. We will spare women, children, and priests! For all others, no mercy!"

Wallace drew his broadsword. The burning debris inside the gate collapsed and left a tunnel through the fire. Wallace screamed and led the charge.

35

WITHIN THE TAPESTRIED WALLS OF HIS LONDON APARTments, Prince Edward and his friend Peter heard a contingent of horsemen clatter into the courtyard below. They looked out the window and saw the arrival of Longshanks. They leaned back into the room, and Edward began to pace nervously.

"It is not your fault! Stand up to him," Peter urged.

Edward showed Peter the dagger he had concealed in his belt behind his back. "I will stand up to him and more."

Longshanks banged the door open and stalked in angrily, followed by two advisors. First he glared at Peter with obvious loathing, then turned his piercing stare to his own son. "What news of the north?" Longshanks said, his voice husky with anger.

"Nothing new, Majesty," Edward answered. "We have sent riders to speed any word." They had known for some time of the massacre at Stirling, but they had heard nothing for days from York. Edward had sent an angry message to his cousin, York's governor, demanding to know why no intelligence had been coming down from the north. His cousin knew Longshanks was returning to London and would be furious. Edward suspected his cousin was intentionally trying to erode the prince's relationship with the king even further.

"Our army wiped out at Stirling, and you have done nothing?!" Longshanks spat and, choking on his own bile, began to cough.

"I have ordered conscriptions. Through all of the autumn and winter we can raise a new army. And through that same winter we can starve the Scots. By next spring they will have hung this bandit Wallace themselves and will beg us to come rule over them!" Edward delivered this speech, rehearsed and revised with Peter's great care, and glanced to his friend for his approval. Peter nodded subtly and glanced back to the Longshanks.

But before the king could respond, a messenger rushed in, bowing as he entered. Seeing the king there, too, he hesitated, not knowing whether to hand the message he carried to the prince, who had dispatched him, or to the king himself. "Here, give it to me!" the prince ordered, feeling a growing sense of being in command.

The messenger handed the prince the scroll he had brought. Edward unsealed it, read the message, and nearly lost his balance. He stared around the room blankly, as if he had forgotten where he was and who these people were who stood there with him.

"What is it?" Longshanks demanded.

"Wallace has sacked York."

"Impossible," Longshanks answered. He turned on the messenger. "How dare you bring a panicky lie!"

The messenger had also brought a basket. He approached the central table with great dread, placed the basket on it, and uncovered its contents. Prince Edward was closest; he peered in, then staggered back. Longshanks moved to the sack coldly, looked in, and withdrew the severed head of his nephew, York's governor. Former governor.

Peter, seeing Edward falter, spoke up quickly. "Sire! Thy own nephew! What beast could do such a thing?!" he said.

The king seemed not to have heard. He dropped the head back into the sack, unmoved. After a moment he said, "If he can sack York, he can invade lower England."

"We would stop him!" Peter insisted.

"Edward, who is this who speaks to me as if I needed his advice?"

The prince looked up and drew himself into a defiant posture. "I have declared Peter my high counselor," he announced to his father.

Longshanks nodded as if impressed. He moved to Peter and examined the gold chain of office that the young man wore about his neck. Then Longshanks seized Peter by the throat and the waistbelt and threw him out the window, the same one Edward and Peter had looked out, six stories above the courtyard. Peter screamed, but not until he was almost to the ground.

Edward rushed toward the window in horror. He looked out at the man he had loved, the only one he had ever fully trusted, broken and bloody on the paving stones far below. He stared for a long time. Then Edward drew himself back inside the room and turned toward his father in shock and hatred and only then remembered the dagger.

He drew it and went for his father.

He stabbed at Longshanks. The old king dodged back, shouting to the advisors who jumped forward to interfere, "No, let him come!" The king smiled at the attack, parrying with his left arm, letting it be cut. His eyes burned. "You fight back at last!"

Then Longshanks unleashed his own hateful fury; he grappled with Edward, knocked the dagger away, hurled him to the floor, and began to kick his son. Again and again he kicked, exhausting his strength and his fury on the young man, broken in heart and in spirit.

Edward lay passive and bloody; Longshanks coughed up a bit of blood. He ignored it and his son's wreckage and went back to the discussion as if this fight was normal business.

"We must sue for a truce," Longshanks said, still winded but trying to hide it, as if even to be breathing hard after beating his son was an insult to his own manhood. "Failing that, we must buy him off. But who will go to him? Not I. If I came under the sword of this murderer, I would end up like my nephew. And not you. If an enemy of England saw my faggot son, he would rather be encouraged to take over this country. So whom do I send?"

Longshanks calculated.

36

AT THE CITY OF YORK, EVERYTHING HAD CHANGED. THE walls were still there, but there were no longer any gates. The streets lay deserted. The Scottish warriors who had fought since Stirling, some of them since Lanark, and had covered hundreds of miles in relentless marches, had slept in wind and rain and frost with little more than their tartans to wrap around their bodies for shelter, now found the vacant buildings of this English city to be repellent. They took what food they could find and carried it outside the walls, where they built cook fires and made their encampment beneath the stars.

Since taking the city, they had rested, letting wounds heal, mending woolens, and sharpening weapons, for they knew more battle was coming. Some busied themselves in plunder of the city's goods, but others cared nothing for that. They were Highlanders—farmers, herders of sheep. What did an English city have that they needed? York was just the first stop! They fought under William Wallace, and with Wallace leading them, they could fight into London itself!

Wallace, Hamish, and Stephen were within the late

governor's map room, poring over the finest intelligence Longshanks's royal servants could offer. They had maps of roads, harbors, trading points, wells, everything they could want to know to plan their next move. A man didn't even need to be able to read to glean the riches of the maps—everything on the parchments was portrayed with fine drawings, some of them illuminated with colored pigments. Hamish, somewhat dazzled by it all, looked up from the map he had been studying and said, "It's a banquet either way we choose. West are farms full of meat, east are towns full of drink."

Stephen piped up, "I say drink first and eat later. And as usual the Almighty agrees with me."

Wallace shook his head. "South. We attack south. Where they have Longshanks."

Campbell hurried in, so excited he could hardly get the words out. "A royal carriage comes. An entourage. They send riders under a banner of truce, asking you to meet them at a crossroad. The carriage flies the banners of Longshanks himself!"

"What if it's an ambush?" Hamish wondered.

"I hope it's an ambush," Stephen said. "I haven't killed an Englishman in five days."

Wallace buckled on his sword.

Taking six riders with him on the road and deploying Seorus and his Highlanders to scurry through the woods on either side as a screen against ambush, Wallace traveled the short distance to the designated crossroad. When they were almost there, the Scots stopped as they had planned, and Seorus went forward alone, silent as a shadow. He returned in ten minutes and reported to Wallace. "It's a pavilion tent out in the middle of the grass. Fancy. I counted ten soldiers outside and could make out one, maybe two more, in the shade inside. But no ambush. I circled the whole camp. But we'll be in the woods just in case."

Wallace and his lieutenants remounted their horses when Seorus stopped them. "One other thing. Strange. The soldiers aren't English."

"What do you mean they aren't English?" Stephen said.

"Let Seorus talk," Wallace said for the sake of Stephen more than for Seorus. Seorus was a compact, tightly muscled Highlander, leader of a band of mountain warriors who followed Wallace with fanatical devotion. Seorus, like the others he had brought down from the Highlands, was intensely loyal and intensely proud; if anyone doubted him, especially in the presence of Wallace, he tended to kill without warning.

"I mean not English in the sense that they are French," Seorus said with a slight glance toward Stephen. "French is not English. Or would you care to argue about that?"

"It just makes no sense, that's all," Stephen said.

"Seorus," Wallace broke in, "let's move."

Seorus waved for his clan to follow him, and Wallace rode ahead with the horsemen into the crossroads itself. There they found it exactly as Seorus said: a royal carriage to the side of the tent, out in the middle of a sun-drenched meadow, with nearly a dozen soldiers milling about, and not stocky Englishmen clothed in red but slender Frenchmen in royal French blue.

Wallace and his men rode in a complete circle around the tent. The soldiers watched warily, but they were disciplined and made no threatening moves. The Scots stopped thirty feet from the tent entrance.

No sound from the tent. Wallace rested his hand on the handle of his broadsword, ready.

"Longshanks! I have come!"

Servants pulled back the sides of the tent door, and a tall, slender, shapely female figure appeared. There in the shadows, she looked just like Murron! William was not the only one who noticed the resemblance; he glanced at Hamish and Campbell and saw them haunted by it, too. Was this another dream? William paled as she stepped into the morning sun. She moved toward him, her face lowered. It *was* Murron! He was dreaming again—or he was insane.

She reached him, lifted her face—and he saw the princess.

Not Murron! And yet as William saw the princess more closely, he was still shaken by the resemblance. In the way she carried herself, in her shape, in the way the regal lace framed her face as wedding lace had once framed Murron's, she haunted the empty rooms in the secret chambers of his heart.

And while the princess reminded William Wallace of everything he had loved and lost, he haunted her with everything she wanted and had never found. Tall, powerful, commanding, his shoulders thick, his hair wild, his eyes soft, even pained. A man facing the hatred of the world's most powerful king; a man who had won great battles and commanded armies, yet who looked as if he could spur his horse away right now and ride away from adoration and glory and never miss any of it. She had never seen a man like this. She had never known such a one existed.

Wallace dismounted and moved to face her. Their eyes hung on each other. She saw something that she had not seen in the face of a man in her whole life. It was grief. Whatever else they said about him, this much she knew was true: he had loved the woman he had lost; the pain of it was still etched in his face.

She surprised him by bending at the knee in a half-submissive yet proud curtsey.

"I am the Princess of Wales," she said.

"Wife of Edward, the king's son?" William asked.

She nodded; somehow she was already ashamed. "I am sorry to be a disappointment. I come as the king's servant and with his authority," the princess said.

"It's battle I want, not talk."

"But now that I am here, will you speak with a woman?" When he said nothing, she led him under the pavilion, a purple canopy shading rich carpets laid on the bare ground. Hamish, Campbell, and Stephen dismounted and followed, shouldering their way in beside the princess's guards, so they could watch Wallace's back.

Inside the Scots found more opulence than they had ever before seen, even in Edinburgh Castle. A carved, gleaming table supported a silver serving bowl full of fruit, and even the apples and oranges there seemed to sparkle as if they too had been polished. Attending the princess were a beautiful young handmaiden—Nicolette—and a thin graying nobleman in a rich tunic embroidered with the king's symbols. The royal servants had brought a throne for the princess and a lower chair for Wallace. She sat; he refused the chair. She studied him and took in his anger and his pride.

"I understand you have recently been given the rank of knight," the princess began.

"I have been given nothing. God makes men what they are."

"Did God make you the sacker of peaceful cities? The executioner of the king's nephew, my husband's own cousin?"

"York was the staging point for every invasion of my country! And as for that cousin, I regret that he had but one head to lose. To try to repel us, he hanged a hundred Scots, even women and children, from the city walls."

"That is not possible!" Isabella protested. But she knew Longshanks and knew his family. She glanced at Hamilton, the richly dressed royal crony that the king had sent with her as both advisor and informant, and Hamilton averted his eyes.

"Longshanks did far worse the last time he took a Scottish city!" Wallace said.

Wallace watched as Hamilton, his silver hair smoothly combed, his beard finely groomed in the style of the court, his white hands graceful and delicate, tilted himself toward the princess and said softly in Latin, "He is a murdering bandit. He lies."

Wallace replied in Latin, "I am no bandit! And I do not lie!"

They were startled at Wallace's fluency in the language of scholars. He saw this; it made him angrier still. "Or in French if you prefer!" he went on. *"Certainment, c'est vrai!* Ask your king to his face, and see if his eyes can convince you of the truth!"

She stared for a long moment at Wallace's eyes.

"Hamilton, leave us," Isabella said.

"M'lady—" Hamilton began.

"Leave us now," she ordered.

He reluctantly obeyed. He saw that she wanted the exchange to be private, and Wallace turned and nodded for his men to leave.

Stephen, who had been admiring the lady's beauty nonstop, leaned in and whispered to William, "Her husband's more of a queen than she is. Did you know that?" Without waiting for an answer, Stephen moved off with Hamish and Campbell.

The princess gestured to her handmaiden, and Nicolette, eyebrows lifted high in surprise, floated past Wallace, glancing back to appraise the view of him from behind and darting one last look at Isabella before moving out to stand beside the French guards by the carriage.

Wallace and the princess were left alone.

She spoke quickly as if anxious to settle their business and end the meeting. "Let us talk plainly. You invade England. You have it within your power to cause great suffering and death. But you cannot complete the conquest, and I perceive you are clever enough to know that. Yes, you have been victorious, close to your shelter and supply. But the deeper you go into England, the harder your task will be."

Wallace broke in. "We will bear the hardships to make our country free. English rule ensures our deprivation."

She forced herself on, anxious not to deviate from the approach she had planned for herself. "The king proposes that you withdraw your attack. In return he grants you heridity title, estates, and this chest with a thousand pounds of gold, which I am to pay to you personally."

"A lordship. And gold. That I should become Judas."

"Peace is made in such way."

"Slaves are made in such ways!" The sudden passion of his outburst startled everyone: the princess, those watching from outside the tent, and even, so it seemed, Wallace himself, for he turned away from her sharply and struggled to control the emotions that had leaped from him.

Isabella gripped the handles of her regal chair. Her eyes were wide as a doe's and fixed on this man who stood before her in all his power and all his pain, and she understood exactly what had caused it all. She said something in a voice so soft that not even Hamilton, standing the closest to the tent opening and straining to hear, could make it out; the only one who heard was Wallace. What she said was, "I understand you have suffered. I know . . . about your woman."

And Wallace said back to her, just as softly, "She was my wife. We married in secret because I would not share her with an English lord. They killed her to get to me." He did not even turn his face to her, and yet she was breathless in the certainty that everything he said was true. "I've never spoken of her," he went on. "I don't know why I tell you now. Except you remind me of her."

He lifted his face now, and their eyes met.

"You resemble . . ." he began. "But not just in how you look. She was strong inside, like you are. She could have been a queen herself. In another world, a sweeter, kinder world, a world of justice, she would have been." He tried to push the memories away, moving his hand as if they were physically beside him. He stared fully at the princess, and his voice took on an urgency, like pleading.

"Someday you will be a queen. So you must open your eyes," William said. "When I was seven years old I saw thirty Scottish patriots hanged in a barn, lured there by Longshanks under a flag of truce. My father and brother stood up to that savagery and lost their lives. When I grew to be a man, I tried to live in peace. I fell in love with . . ." But he could not bring himself to speak her name.

But he wanted—needed—to tell this woman who reminded him so much of Murron just how and why he had lost her. "The soldiers of your king decided they could take her, like everything else in Scotland. I fought them, but she was caught. To lure me to capture, the king's magistrate cut her throat in the square of Lanark Village."

He paused and drew in a long slow breath. Isabella watched him, her eyes burning, her arms aching to hold him. He looked at her, his eyes growing harder. "My fight is not with fortress cities. It's with one man's desire to rule another man. Tell your king that William Wallace will not be ruled. Nor will any Scot while I live."

The princess rose slowly from her chair, moved in front of him, and lowered herself to her knees. Hamilton and her other attendants saw this from a distance and were shocked. But the Princess of Wales bowed herself before the heart of this commoner.

"Sir," she said in a voice only Wallace could hear, "I leave this money as a gift. Not from the king but from myself. And not to you but to the orphans of your country."

She lifted her face. Their eyes held a moment too long.

Wallace and his captains sat on horseback at the head of their company and watched as the princess's procession left. Hamish studied Wallace's face. Wallace noticed and gave him a noncommittal shrug. As the carriage rolled away, its window curtains lifted

167

back slightly. All they saw were the princess's fingers, but they knew she looked back.

Wallace reined his horse away and rode back to camp.

37

THE LIGHT OF THE MOON SLIPPED DOWN THROUGH THE clear night air, over the charred broken timbers of York, into the barren streets of the sacked city, and onto the shoulders of William Wallace.

He walked there alone.

The bodies of the dead had all been carted away and buried, a task organized by York's monks and nuns. They had gone to the monastery and convent Wallace's men had spared and had recruited helpers from outlying villages to come back to the city and give the men who had once defended it a Christian burial. At first the villagers had been too frightened to come; they were amazed even to find the monks and nuns alive, knowing that Longshanks, when he had sacked a Scottish city near the borders, had slaughtered everyone within it, including not only the women and children but the nuns themselves. The monks and nuns of York assured them that this had not been the case with their city and that Wallace had given them a promise to allow Christian burial of the dead. Still the villagers would not come, many of them believing the nuns and monks were but ghosts or false apparitions sent by the devil to deceive them. The churchmen returned to the villages with women and children who themselves had been spared, and finally the people came out and hauled away the dead for sanctified burial.

The decapitated body of the governor was an exception. Wallace order it hacked apart and fed to the dungeon dogs.

He ordered the bodies of the Scots who had been hung from the walls to be cremated in a giant common pyre, and their ashes taken, to be spread upon Scotland.

And so York was empty, an entire city laid to ruin, and William Wallace walked among its burned-out, empty streets. Even the rats and dogs and cats had deserted the wreckage. There was nothing here but charred wood, dirty cobblestones, and moonlight. Never had William felt so alone.

He felt something unfamiliar. It was fear. Since Murron's death, he had feared nothing. Death did not frighten him; if it meant he could join Murron on the other side of life, he would welcome the passage. His dreams of her, though full of sadness, were still a comfort, a reassurance that his hopes of reunion might find fulfillment.

But something had stirred in him when he was with the princess that day, and he worried that those stirrings might keep Murron from coming to him, if only in his dreams.

Wallace walked through the streets all night long. As the black sky was turning gray with dawn, he returned to his campfire, where he found Hamish slumped in a seating position and dozing. He snorted and started as Wallace sat down beside him. Hamish had been there all night, waiting up for him, worrying about him.

He said nothing about William's absence. "Want some meat?" he asked, pointing to a joint of meat kept warm beside the fire.

William shook his head. "No word yet from Edinburgh?"

Hamish glanced over to the tent where his father lay snoring. He had hoped old Campbell would be the one to tell William. "One of the messengers got back last night, just after you went on your walk." Hamish paused, took a breath. "They're not sending any more men, William."

"They know about York? About our victory here?"

"They know."

"And still they won't support us with reinforcements?"

"They say you have heaped glory onto the throne of Scotland—whoever ends up sitting there. They had decreed more honors and glories for you—"

"As if they could decree honor!" William said bitterly. Then he tried to hold back his anger. "But no reinforcements."

"No reinforcements."

William stared at the fire.

Old Campbell stirred awake, saw William at the fire, and rose stiffly. He looked to Hamish, who nodded in answer to his father's unspoken question: yes, he had broken the news to William. Old Campbell sat down at the fire with them.

Finally William spoke. "The princess was right about one thing. We can terrorize northern England, but we can't complete a conquest, not without reinforcements."

"We can get food from the land! We can supply ourselves from England itself!" Campbell said. "All my life—do you hear me, William?—all my life I've wanted to fight *them,* the way they've fought *us,* on *their* land! Now we're here. I don't want to go back. Not till we've finished it."

Hamish said nothing. William knew Hamish's opinion differed from his father's, but they would speak of that later. William looked at old Campbell, who so often seemed like his own father, and said, "No one wants to finish this fight more than I do. And the men with us are like you, they would fight to London itself. They feel nothing can beat us. And truly I think that nothing could if we had a full army and true support. But it's not just battle that bleeds an army. It's disease. It's accident. To march from here to London we would lose more men to sprained ankles and dysentery than we lost in the taking of York. We would get to London. If I lead this army to London without reinforcements, then I lead it to slaughter."

"So what do we do?" Stephen said. He was lying near the fire, beneath his blankets. He spoke without ever opening his eyes. He may not have slept at all.

"We withdraw," William said. "But don't think this is over."

38

PRINCESS ISABELLA, HER SPINE STRAIGHT, HER HEAD LIFTED high, moved into the great hall of the London palace where Longshanks was conducting his council of war. She curtsied deeply to the king, then to her husband, Prince Edward, still marked from his beating.

"My son's loyal wife returns, unkilled by the barbarian!" Longshanks said. "So Wallace accepted our bribe?"

"No, he did not," the princess said, still standing before the council table. The king provided no chair for her; she was expected only to report and leave them to their business. The other advisors—even Hamilton, already there at the table with Longshanks —looked at her as if she was but a model, there to receive their approval of a gown.

Longshanks glanced at Hamilton and looked back to Princess Isabella. "Then why does he stay? My scouts say he has not advanced."

"He waits. For you. He says he will attack no more towns—if you are man enough to come fight him." She said this with her eyes lowered to the floor, afraid that if she looked directly at the king, he would see her defiance.

But instead of exploding in fury at Wallace's challenge, Longshanks's voice sounded strangely pleased. "He waits. And the longer he waits, the hungrier his army grows. His own nobles will not support him. He will return to Scotland. He must."

"So you will not fight him?" the princess asked.

"You may return to your embroidery," Longshanks said.

"Humbly, m'lord."

She curtsied again and turned to leave. Longshanks called, "You brought back the money, of course?"

She looked at the king. Clearly he already knew the answer with Hamilton sitting so close to him. The old crony would not even raise his eyes. Isabella knew he must have rushed in to tell the king everything he knew the moment they had arrived.

"No," she said. "I gave it to the children of this war—in token of your greatness as a king."

"Little fool," he said, half under his breath, yet not caring who else heard—even her.

She felt the words like a dagger but forced herself toward the door.

Longshanks had already begun addressing his council. Isabella, her ears burning with her own anger, was again surprised by the king's tone. She had expected —to be honest, had desired—the king to be cut by Wallace's courage. But Longshanks seemed so unconcerned. He was speaking loudly with a tone of boasting, proud of what he had done. And before she reached the door, Isabella put aside her own anger and listened to exactly what the king was saying:

"So the Welsh bowmen will not be detected, moving so far around his flank up the western coast. The main force from our armies in France can land here, on the east of Scotland."

Isabella froze at the door. Troops from Wales and France, all being sent around to attack the Scottish army from the direction it least expected?

Prince Edward spoke up. He had not uttered a word to his father since the horrible day when Longshanks had beaten him after throwing Peter from the window. But the old man seemed to be growing senile; his planning was so flawed that Edward could not resist the chance to point it out. "Welsh bowmen?" he sneered. "Your troops from France? Even if you dispatched them today, they'd take weeks to assemble!"

"I dispatched them before I sent your wife," Longshanks said.

Isabella, forgotten at the door, felt the blood go cold in her chest. Longshanks had used her for this treachery! Her earnestness, her sincerity, her very innocence, had made her the perfect tool for this deception. She had sworn to Wallace that the king desired peace, exactly as Longshanks had known she would do. Even though Wallace didn't believe it—and had Longshanks anticipated that as well?—the whole effort was to draw the Scotsman's attention away from the attacks coming at him from behind.

From that moment, any spark of loyalty Isabella of France had felt for her father-in-law, King Edward I of England, died within her heart.

Longshanks was still speaking in a loud, commanding voice. The success of his deception and the demonstration that his spirit to rule was still greater than his son's had given the old king new animation. "I want a thousand crossbows!" he commanded his generals. "If our craftsmen can't make that many, then deal with the Dutch!"

Prince Edward, still stinging and anxious to redeem any shred of pride, protested, "The weapon has been outlawed by the pope himself!"

"So the Scots will have none of them, will they? See to it!" Longshanks barked.

Isabella closed the door softly and drifted back to her rooms, her feet moving silently on the stone floors as if she no longer had any weight at all.

39

A STIFF WIND CHASED THE BROWN REMNANTS OF AUTUMN through the clattering tree branches in the English countryside. It seemed that the moment the army set off north, toward Scotland, the winter had come. A light dusting of snow swirled in the barren fields as Wallace led his army through the bitter cold of twilight back to Scotland.

Wallace, lost in thought, seemed to trust the horse to know the way home. For the first hours of the march, Hamish had ridden back in the ranks; now he nudged his horse up besides William's. Their horses walked along together for a while, Hamish saying nothing. Finally William pressed him, "What is it? What's on your mind?"

"There is some grumbling in the ranks," Hamish said quietly. "They don't like the retreat. They're saying we came all this way for nothing."

"They're saying? Or you're saying?"

"I'm with you, William. But now we're cold and hungry again as we have been for most of a year. And when my soldiers ask what for, what do I say?"

"You say we stood and dared the English to fight, and they would not." William looked over at his friend and saw Hamish's great freckled brow wrinkled in a frown above eyes that struggled to see the significance of all this and couldn't. "Hamish, half of any fight is to prove your honor to yourself. The other half is to prove your honor to your enemy. Without both, there is no victory."

Too deep for Hamish. He shook his head and smiled. "Whatever you say, William."

But William wanted Hamish to understand; it was

174

as if he needed for his friend to believe the same thing, to help him have the faith to keep going. "When our enemies understand that we deserve to be free, that's when we'll truly be free."

Hamish rubbed his nose the way a Scotsman does when he thinks the logic of an argument is just so much manure. "When our enemies are dead," he said, "that's when we'll be truly free."

William laughed deeply from his belly. "Maybe you're right, Hamish. Maybe I think too much. But I tell you this: our enemies are not the problem. Our friends back in Edinburgh, they are the problem. Men who fight each other openly may find the honor in each other and establish respect; men who pretend support but sell their souls—and try to sell yours— only make hatred."

Hamish nodded. If he had any more thoughts, he kept them to himself.

40

ISABELLA HAD JUST FINISHED A LETTER TO HER FATHER. SHE had struggled to sound happy, writing of the flower gardens she had been designing for the spring planting and the herb patch she hoped to include. Toward the end of her letter she had mentioned her trip north on the king's mission to the Scottish invaders, but she did not disclose to her father any knowledge of Longshanks's true intent.

She had dripped wax onto the final fold of her envelope and had just pressed into it the seal of her ring when there was a knock upon her door. She stopped, surprised and alerted. No one knocked at the door of her private apartments. Her servants came when she rang for them, or if they brought her a summons from the king, they called to her softly from outside the door without knocking. But who could this be?

She opened the door to find her husband, Prince Edward. Seeking to conceal her surprise, she lowered her eyes and curtsied. "My Prince," she said.

"May I come in?"

The question embarrassed both of them. "Yes. Do. Please," she said quickly. "Come and sit by the fire."

He entered quickly and found himself standing in the center of an unfamiliar room; he had not been alone with her since the night of their wedding, and now he found himself looking around at the new furnishings: a table from Bordeaux, damask wall hangings the color of a Parisian sky at twilight, a painting of a French field full of wildflowers. Turning round to face her, his eyes looked both lonely and sad. "I had not thought," he said, "how much you must miss home."

It was the first kind thing he had ever said to her. She curtsied again, slowly this time, and replied, "My home is here with you."

She moved to the hearth and the two chairs where she and Nicolette had spent so many hours sharing their thoughts. "Please, do sit," she said. "Shall I have food and drink brought?"

She was about to ring for a servant when Edward said, "No, no, no, that isn't necessary. I had just . . . dropped by, that's all."

She knew, of course, that this could not be true. Her apartments were in a far wing of the palace, and even if they were not almost strangers to each other, it would be obvious that he had come here with some purpose. Isabella studied him, there in the center of the room, lit by the feeble gray light of the narrow window. He looked unusually sallow, his features lax and translucent, as if his face had been fashioned from the smooth drippings of a candle. His lip, split from one of his father's kicks, had begun to heal but still

176

looked tender. His cheek still bore a trace of bruise. But it was his eyes that looked most painful. They were rimmed in red, and they appeared so lonely and hopeless, like those of a seawife whose husband's body has already washed up upon the shore and who stares at the horizon anyway.

Edward was alone, totally alone. She saw that. He had never trusted anyone but Peter, perhaps had never loved anyone except him, and now he was gone. Isabella felt his isolation. It was, in its way, like her own. She wanted to reach out to him, to comfort him some way, to make peace between them. She wanted to say something. She wasn't sure what, but something that would tell him she wished to trust him and have him trust her. She was just about to try when he said, "Where is Nicolette?"

"Nicolette?" Isabella tried not to hesitate. "I sent her to my castle in the north."

"The one your father owns? By the Scottish border?"

"He . . . gave it to me for my use—our use—after we were married. He told me it needed some work but was sound and had fine lands surrounding it, which could produce quite well if properly seen after. I had not thought of it for some time, but on my journey to Yorkshire I saw how beautiful the countryside was and I thought the northern castle might be an excellent project to undertake once the Scottish threat is settled. I sent Nicolette to make a survey of the property for me to determine how extensive the work might be."

She realized she was explaining too much, and she wondered if she was only imagining that Edward looked suspicious as he said, "But you think it is safe to send your lady-in-waiting with only a half-dozen French guards to protect her to a castle that is scarcely a day's ride from Scotland? When all of Wallace's army is still there?"

Isabella's mind was racing. So Edward knew where

she had sent Nicolette, even knew exactly how many of her personal bodyguard she had sent along to protect her. "I felt safe in doing so, m'lord. It was clear to me that, however great a savage this bandit Wallace is, he would not allow any action against a woman's entourage, especially one traveling beneath the banners of France, formally neutral in the conflict between Scotland and England. Even without such diplomatic protection, Wallace would have a standing order that women be left alone. He has too much pride to behave otherwise."

"You think he is an honorable man," Edward said, his eyes questioning.

"I have just said that he is a savage. But even savages have their rules." She added quickly, "I also believed the trip could serve the purposes of the king. Nicolette and such a small band will most likely travel north completely without the notice of anyone. But should it happen that Wallace ever learned of it, it would seem to him that the royal family in London has accepted his leadership of Scotland and that we anticipate a peaceful future with our neighbors to the north."

Edward nodded. He wanted to change the subject and looked around for some excuse. "That painting of the lavender fields is beautiful. Who did it for you?"

"I did it, m'Lord."

"You? I had no idea."

"Shall I call for refreshment?"

This time he did not protest, and the princess had her servants bring warm ale and bread. The prince joined her beside the fire but did not touch any of the food and made forced conversation about castle construction. He clearly had no interest in the subject. Soon he excused himself and left her alone.

She had the servants clear away the dishes they had brought, and she sat down alone by the fire and stared into the flames. And there she saw it all clearly.

Edward had not come to find a friend. In all his

178

loneliness and pain, he was not seeking an ally, either political or emotional. He had come to learn if she could be trusted. He had come to spy.

Longshanks had sent him.

The princess was glad she had sent Nicolette.

41

THE RETURN TO SCOTLAND WAS A TRIP LONG AND HARD. ON the way south to fight the enemy, the Scottish warriors had been difficult to hold back; now they were difficult to move forward. Villages along the side routes were tempting targets for many of the Highland clans that made up the Scottish army. Used to making independent decisions and feeling their obligations to the army as a whole were over, now that it was withdrawing victorious, they began to dart off at will to rustle sheep and ransack villages. No one within Wallace's inner circle, including Wallace himself, had any great desire to discourage this; the Scots had suffered so much in the past that it seemed to them only right that the English should feel the same pains. Rape was another matter; when Wallace learned of it happening, he halted the march of his army, had the offenders tried before an assembly of the clan chieftans, and hanged.

The boredom and frustration of the retreat were shattered on a cold, dull day that began like every other day on the long march home. There was a commotion at the rear of the army, guarded by a clan of wild but unbreakable Highlanders led by Seorus, a friend of old Campbell. Seorus sent a runner forward to his friend. Wondering at the message he received, Campbell sent a mounted rider back for confirmation.

In a few minutes the rider galloped back and conferred with Campbell, who then spurred his horse up to Wallace at the head of the column.

Wallace, having noticed the running and riding back and forth, had grown edgy and ready to fight. "What is it?" he asked with excitement. "Is there a force to our rear?"

"Aye," old Campbell said, frowning, "but none to attack us. It's more of those Frenchmen—but only a few. And they say there's a woman with them."

Leaving Campbell at the head of the column, Wallace took Hamish and rode to the rear.

There they found Seorus and his clansmen, who had taken the trailing position from the outset of the march home, protecting the army from any attack from the rear. Now the Highlanders had stopped and were turned to face the road along which they had just come. Barely a stone's throw down that same road was a small clump of riders in French blue. Their horses were lathered and filthy as if they had ridden long and hard, but they sat erect, doing nothing but waiting. Seeing Wallace ride up, Seorus trotted to him and said, "There's a woman with 'em."

"You walked out to see them?" Wallace asked.

"Oh, aye. The woman is dressed like they are, in a man's cape. She tried to keep her face turned from me, but I ran around among 'em like a sniffin' dog. Tried to talk to 'em. But I don't talk their language, and they don't talk mine. They just sat there on their horses and said, 'Wallace.'"

With Hamish, Seorus, and three more of the Highlanders, Wallace advanced halfway to the group of riders. Wallace and Hamish dismounted. The French guards opened their ranks, and from their midst, the smallest of their party rode forward, reached the Scots, and dismounted.

Wallace saw that it was the handmaiden who had accompanied the princess. Nicolette was tired; her pretty face was pale with fatigue and caked with the dust and sweat of her journey, and yet her dark eyes flashed with the excitement of her adventure. "I have a message for William Wallace," she said in French. "For him and him only."

"I trust these men with my life," Wallace answered.

"It is not your life alone that is at stake here."

In Gaelic, Wallace said to his men, "She has something to tell me. And she won't do it with the rest of you standing here."

Nicolette watched as Hamish and the Highlanders, keeping a sharp eye on the French escort, pulled back out of earshot. Then she glanced behind her to be sure that the guards, too, had kept their distance. Even with no one else close by, she did not speak above a whisper. "She says she's sorry for the king's cowardice."

"Who says?"

"She." Nicolette stared at Wallace. He knew exactly who she meant. "And she says something else." Nicolette paused and lowered her voice even more. "What I am telling you could get me hung. Do you understand?"

It seemed to Wallace that this girl was enjoying the drama. He nodded.

"She says the king will attack you from the rear with a combined army of English troops ferried over from France and Welsh bowmen brought up along the west coast."

Wallace listened, dead still. The girl had not exaggerated the seriousness of her secret; giving this information to an enemy of the king was treason.

Nicolette had memorized this message she was delivering, and she frowned, intent on reciting it exactly: "The recent avowals of a desire for peace were but a pretext, meant to lure you off your guard. She who sent me did not know this at the time those avowals were made—"

"So why does she tell me now?" Wallace interrupted.

Nicolette's eyes lingered on him for a long moment; her lips curled slightly, almost but not quite smiling.

"Ah, monsieur," she said, "why *does* she tell you now? That is for you to answer." The flirty and brave little handmaiden went back to her recitation. "The attack against you will come soon. There is little time to waste. You must choose your own course—whether flight or compromise. But fighting is foolish."

"Then she knows already that I am a fool."

"Please! You interrupt, monsieur, and I must tell you this exactly. Where was I? Let's see . . . Little time . . . choose your own course . . . Fighting foolish . . . Ah, yes! Here is the rest: Crossbows are coming from Holland. Overland from Dover. At least a thousand." Nicolette smiled, curtsied, and moved to her horse, holding out her hand in Wallace's direction. Taking the hint, he tossed her up onto the saddle. She nodded her thanks, then looked into Wallace's eyes one last time, as if she had been instructed to take in every detail of him to discuss with her mistress later.

"By the way," she added, "should it become known that you and I have talked, I will say that I was intercepted on my way to Castle Bonchamps, to which I have been dispatched on an architectural survey for my mistress, the castle's owner. I will say that I was interrogated, found to be peaceful, and released. I suggest you tell your men the same story—since it is true."

She reined her horse back to the French guards, who surrounded her quickly and galloped away without looking back.

Wallace watched them go and thought of her who sent them.

Then he turned and walked quickly back to join Hamish and the others. "I need Stephen," Wallace said, "as quickly as you can find him."

42

THE PRINCESS SAT AT THE WINDOW SEAT OF A PALACE room. Her fingers held half-finished embroidery; she was looking distractedly at the dark, cold winter day outside. Across the room, Longshanks was at his worktable, discussing logistics with his advisors. Edward sat sullenly at the table with them. His father had demanded that he attend but insisted that the princess be there also, telling his son it was clear he could never rule without his wife to help him. ("The woman has fire in her," Longshanks had told his advisors. "She is the only hope that my line will continue when I am gone.")

So now the prince sat, his eyes glazed and only half alive, as Longshanks stormed at his advisors. "Why am I the only one who sees how simple this is?! Our army needs food! They can't fight without it, for the Scots will burn everything, even their own food, rather than let us have it. The Vikings have fish. They lack wool. We have wool. So trade them our wool for the fish, you fools!"

None of the advisors responded. But young Edward perked up. He knew the reason the advisors were silent. They didn't wish to be the bearers of unpleasant news. Edward, on the other hand, couldn't wait. He placed his delicate hand before his mouth to hide the smirk there. "The Viking traders have just informed us that the Scots have promised to sell them wool," Edward said, "at a lower price than ours."

"The Scots have no ships to deliver wool to the Vikings!" Longshanks said.

"The Vikings provide the ships," Edward said.

"What do the Scots get from the Vikings in return for the wool?" Longshanks demanded to know.

"Lumber—for building ships," Edward said. "Apparently, someone in Scotland intends to establish it as a trading nation. And . . ."—Edward drew this out, savoring the moment—"since the Scots have never pursued trade so aggressively before, it is only reasonable to suppose the originator of this effort is some new character among their leaders. Someone like . . . William Wallace, perhaps."

Prince Edward failed to conceal his satisfaction at seeing his father bested. Longshanks flushed with anger—whether more at Wallace or at his son, it was impossible to tell.

By the window, the princess looked down at her sewing, so that no one could see her smile.

43

EASTERN SCOTLAND LAY BENEATH THE SAME GRAY, COLD sky as did London. Inside Edinburgh Castle, Wallace paced a room full of merchants, seamen, and landowners, all summoned to discuss Scotland's daily trade. Wallace told them about the arrangements with the Vikings of Norway. He spoke to them about the need to establish independence of trade and told them of the pact he had just made with the merchants of France to trade whiskey for wine.

One of the farmers laughed and said, "We don't drink wine!"

"No, but the Danes do," Wallace said. "And they will swap for pottery and tar. Some we keep. Some we trade with Spain for their sour fruits. Then all our children will have solid teeth and straight bones."

No one knew quite what to say. No one had ever discussed such matters with these men before. They were excited by the ideas and frightened, too. Suddenly they had a hundred questions about how it all would work, and they began to ask them all at once. Wallace smiled and lifted his hands to quiet them. "I don't know all the answers," he said. "We must work them out together. I only ask you to consider whether the result of new trade would be worth the effort."

They began talking with each other—farmer to merchant, merchant to seaman. Wallace watched for a moment in satisfaction and moved over to old Craig, who had seen everything from a spot beside the huge hearth. The old man was frowning. Wallace looked at him, knowing already what he wished to say. "The king will not like it," was the old man's comment.

"We don't have a king yet," Wallace said. "But when we do, he will have trade."

"I meant Longshanks," old Craig said. "This will antagonize him further."

"He is not our king. And we could not possibly make him hate us more than he already does."

Hamish moved in and whispered to Wallace, "Stephen is back."

Wallace and Hamish hurried into the stables, where they found Stephen, tattered but smiling. They clasped forearms in greeting, Wallace delighted to see his friend alive.

"Irish! You look hungry!" Wallace said.

"How should I look after a month in the saddle?"

"Did you get it?"

"Did we get it, he asks us, Father!" Stephen babbled to the Almighty. "Does he not know the scripture, 'Ask, and ye shall receive'?" He punctuated the biblical verse by brushing away some hay in the corner, uncovering a large object wrapped in hides. He pulled them back and revealed a new crossbow with a small box of bolts.

Wallace lifted and examined the instrument. He felt its heft, tried its shoulder position, tested the tension of its string, and tried its crank. When he looked back at his friends again, his face was grave. "Hamish," he said, "order the council assembled! . . . Yes, *order* it!"

44

SINCE HIS RETURN TO EDINBURGH WEEKS BEFORE, WALlace had said nothing whatsoever to the council of nobles. When they issued proclamations praising his victory at York, he sent word that he was too busy seeking alliances with foreign powers to attend the ceremonies where the proclamations were read. When the council protested—not openly, but through Craig, who tried to visit Wallace personally but got only as far as Hamish—that diplomacy was a power belonging to the council, Wallace replied—through Hamish —that as guardian, the security of Scotland was his responsibility. Hamish even reminded the council, in words that rang like William Wallace's, that in making Wallace the guardian they had asked him to swear to be faithful to the protection of Scotland, and so help him God he would be faithful now. The council knew—knew because he passed along to them copies after he had already sent the letter—that Wallace had written the king of France, proposing a military alliance with Scotland. They also knew he had written the pope; Hamish told them he had. But Wallace did not reveal to the council the text of that letter; Hamish declared he had not read it himself and that the letter had the privacy of the confessional. Such actions troubled the council, not just because Wallace took them without consulting with them but because he *thought* of such actions without their advice. A military alliance with France could save Scotland; recognition from the pope of the independence of Scotland could bring support not only from France but from other nations as well. Wallace was a man of action, and he made men of politics uncomfortable.

When he ordered them to assemble on a secluded field outside Edinburgh, they grew more troubled still. Hamish had brought not only the inner council, comprised of noble family leaders, but also all the prominent relations he could gather, especially those with battlefield experience. Wallace had told him the more the better, and Hamish had pulled together everyone within a day's ride of the capital city, more than thirty nobles. Among them was Robert the Bruce.

It was a day of unusually flat light, the entire sky a mass of slate gray clouds. The nobles stood in clumps of three or four, whispering among themselves. "What does he want with us?" young Mornay inquired of Bruce and Craig the moment he walked up to them.

Old Craig shook his head. "No one knows."

"Who does he think he is, with this order that we come?" Mornay muttered to the Bruce. "He invades England without our instructions. He writes the king of France; he writes the pope! What is he trying to do?"

"I can't say for sure," the Bruce answered his friend, "but I can tell you what he's done already. Look around you. Instead of whispering about each other, now we're all whispering about him." Both Mornay and Craig looked around and saw that what the Bruce said was true. "Maybe his most remarkable achievement is that he has brought us together."

Wallace appeared, marching up in long, powerful strides. All the nobles had been declaring to each other the questions they meant to ask him, the explanations they meant to demand, but when they saw the look on Wallace's face, they said nothing. Hamish, old Campbell, and Stephen moved along quickly behind Wallace; when he stopped and faced the noblemen,

187

the two big Scots took positions on his left and right, like lions guarding the gates of a mythical city, while Stephen wandered silently in and out among the crowd. As deterrents to physical attack, both were amazingly effective: anyone wild enough to think of assaulting Wallace hand to hand would be sobered by the sight of the massive men at his shoulders; and yet Stephen was perhaps even more unsettling, weaving among the nobles with that saintly smile on his lips and devilish fire in his eyes and making their backs crawl and itch whenever he was behind them.

Wallace said nothing at first, just looked off toward the tree more than fifty paces away, where Highlanders were setting up a Scottish spearman's shield against a bale of hay. They tucked a melon behind the shield. Then Wallace uncovered the crossbow he had brought, wrapped in the skins, and held it up for all of them to see. The nobles gazed at the strange new weapon of war, looking so scientific, with its short, powerful bow fixed rigidly on its side at right angles to its stock, complete with a trigger mechanism and a crank for drawing back the thick, strong string. They watched in stony silence as Wallace cranked the crossbow to its full cocked position, placed a bolt in its slot, and fired at the armor.

The bolt slashed through the air and punched right through the armor and the melon, leaving no doubt what it would do to a man's heart.

Old Craig turned pale. "That is why the pope outlawed the weapon! It makes war too terrible!" the old nobleman said. He wondered if this weapon, specifically forbidden by the Vatican for use in warfare, was the subject of Wallace's letter to the pope.

Wallace ignored Craig and said simply, "Longshanks ordered these from Holland. His factories are making them, too."

"How many will he have?" Mornay asked.

"We reckon over a thousand," William answered. "And this is not all. He is bringing his army over from

France to reinforce the new army he has mustered from England. In addition, he will force Welsh bowmen into service and possibly Irish conscripts as well."

"How do you know this?" Craig asked in amazement.

Again Wallace ignored him. "I brought you all here so you could see what is facing us. This weapon will be used against us. It will shoot through our schiltrons with great accuracy. Longshanks will not respect the pope's ban, not if he can use the weapon to destroy the strategy that wrecked his army at Stirling."

"It is useless to resist him!" Craig sputtered.

Wallace erupted. "No! Not useless! We can beat this! With cavalry—light, fast horsemen, like you nobles employ—we could outmaneuver their bowmen. Look at the weapon!" Wallace said, holding the crossbow up, shaking it at them. "Yes, it is accurate and powerful, but it is heavy and clumsy, too. It is one thing to fire it coldly at a target, but it's something else again to try to shoot it when you are being charged head on by Highlanders on foot and by horsemen from your flanks and rear, all screaming like berserkers!"

"You wish us to be insane?" Mornay asked.

"I wish you to be Scotsmen," Wallace said.

There was a long silence. Wallace looked at Robert the Bruce, who did not avert his gaze but still did not speak up. At last old Craig said, "With such a weapon and such a force arrayed against us, perhaps it is time to discuss other options."

"Other options?" Wallace asked. "Don't you wish at least to bring your men to the field, so you can barter a better deal from Longshanks before you cower and run?"

"Sir William!" the Bruce said, trying to deflect the storm.

"We cannot defeat the power arrayed against us!" Craig insisted through his anger.

"We can and we will!"

"Sir William!" the Bruce said with even greater vehemence.

But the storm of Wallace's anger had already begun. He shouted at Craig, at all of them. "We won at Stirling and still you quibbled! We won at York and you would not support us! If you will not stand with us now, then I say you are cowards! And if you are Scotsmen, I am ashamed to call myself one!" With that he tossed the crossbow onto the ground at their feet, like a gauntlet, daring them.

The nobles, all of them carrying swords and daggers, gripped the handles of their weapons. Hamish and his father stepped up shoulder to shoulder with Wallace, while Stephen's dagger slipped silently from his belt and snuggled against the throat of the noble nearest him.

Robert the Bruce, backed by Mornay, jumped between Wallace and the nobles. "Stop! Everyone stop! Please, Sir William! Speak with me alone! I beg you!"

Robert was the one man capable of drawing Wallace away from the confrontation; he was the only noble Wallace had any desire to listen to. They moved a dozen paces in the direction of the shield impaled by the crossbow bolt. Stephen shoved away the man he had seized, and he moved to join the Campbells in glowering at the nobles and begging them, any and all, to step forward and fight.

When the Bruce had urged Wallace far enough away that they could speak in confidence, he turned and spoke in a suppressed but passionate voice. "Sir William, please listen to me! You have achieved more than anyone dreamed. You've made all of Scotland and all of England as well stand and wonder at what you've done! But fighting these odds now"—he gestured at the shield pierced by the bolt—"this looks like rage, not courage. Peace offers its rewards! Has war become a habit you cannot break?"

The question struck deep in Wallace. For a moment

his eyes flickered away toward the juncture of the green hills with the gray sky, as if everyone he had loved and lost had just moved beyond that horizon. But when he looked back to the Bruce, his eyes were not dreamy but blazing with life. "War finds me willing," Wallace said, "I know it won't bring back all I have lost. But it can bring what none of us have ever had: a country of our own. For that we need a king. We need you."

It was the Bruce's turn to pause and swallow. "I am trying," he said.

"Then you tell me what a king is! Is he a man who believes only what others believe? Is he one who calculates the numbers for and against him but never weighs the strength in his own heart? There is strength in you. I see it. I know it."

Robert the Bruce was both moved and ashamed to hear these words from William Wallace. Seeing this, Wallace pressed him further.

"These men are like all others, they need a leader!" Wallace said. "They will never accept me, but they will you! Lead them! Lead us all."

Robert stared at Wallace. Wide-eyed, breathless, the young nobleman seemed unable to move. Finally he said, "I must . . . consult with my father."

"And I will consult with mine."

Saying that, Wallace strode back to the main group of nobles. He glared around at all of them. Then his eyes changed, showing less anger and more pity. "When Longshanks invades us again," he said in a quieter voice, "the commoners are going to fight. I don't believe I could stop them even if I wished to. When they fight, I will lead them. We need you. Even if you all come, it may not be enough, but whether all of you come or none do, we will fight. And stand or fall, live or die, whichever we do, we will do it for Scotland."

Wallace left the field, his friends behind him, never more proud than they had been at that moment.

45

ROBERT THE BRUCE DID NOT RIDE STRAIGHT BACK TO HIS castle. He took a long detour and did not explain to his personal bodyguard the reason. He rode silently in front of them, so insensible to the countryside around them that the captain of his guards wondered whether his master might even be unaware they were so far off their normal route home. But when he inquired, after passing through another crossroad, whether his lordship had intended to take the fork that led even further from their castle, the Bruce nodded and kept on riding. They stopped once in a village, where the Bruce asked directions of a tavernkeeper, and once more along a farm road, where a herdsman listened to his soft inquiries and pointed the way.

At last they reached a small valley, marred by the shells of farm buildings burned out and never rebuilt. Robert ordered his men to remain there beside the charred rubble, and he rode over the hill alone.

To Murron's grave.

At the ragged hole that once held Murron's body, Robert the Bruce dismounted and stared at the barren cavity. It gaped there like an empty eye socket, among the other, undisturbed, graves. The Bruce had heard the story of Wallace riding in through the English ambush and pulling her body from the earth to bury it in a place where no enemy could find it. So the story was true.

He held the reins of his lathered horse and lifted his eyes from the grave to its stone marker and the delicate lines of the chiseled thistle. He frowned as if this was too much to understand. He mounted up and rode away.

In the faint nimbus of the single candle, young Robert sat across from his leper father in his father's darkened room. Young Robert reported every word of the meeting at Edinburgh, even what he had said in private to William Wallace. His father had listened with his yellowed eyes wet and so droopy that it would scarcely have surprised young Robert if those eyes had fallen out of the decaying head and plopped onto the table. But finally his father had spoken, telling young Bruce what course he must take. And now the son gripped his own head as if stunned by a blow.

"This . . . cannot be the way," he said to his father.

But the old man's brain, behind those loose, weak eyes, was still as keen as ever; if anything, the endless hours he spent alone, hiding his leprosy, had only made that brain more keen. "Wallace will not survive; he cannot!" the elder Bruce said. "He can never lead this country. The nobles will not support him!"

"But, Father—"

"Everything is clear, Robert. Everything. Think of all you have told me, of everything you've seen and thought, and you will know this situation as clearly as I do. William Wallace wishes to spill every drop of blood in his body for the sake of Scotland. But that will not make us free."

Heartsick, the father reached across the table, then stayed his arm, unwilling to touch his son with his leperous hand.

"My son. Look at me. I cannot be king. You, and you alone, can rule Scotland. What I tell you, you must do—for yourself and for your country."

Young Robert held his father with his eyes and did not look away.

46

THE PLAIN OF FALKIRK LAY NOT FAR FROM STIRLING. HAD the mists not been so heavy that morning, Wallace could have looked into the distance and seen the hill where the castle stood and the smaller one opposite it, where he had rallied the Scots to victory.

Longshanks had chosen to assemble his army upon a different field, not only fleeing the ghosts of that last defeat but escaping the battlefield features of river and bridge that Wallace had used so effectively the first time.

Wallace did not like this ground. It was open and smooth and offered no natural obstacles he could use for manuever and strategy to neutralize the superior numbers of the English. He wanted to fight anywhere but here. Stirling would have suited him again, with its bridge he could seal and its river he could use to be out of the range of the arrows. When his scouts told him where the English were heading, his first thought had been to slide the Scottish army back, pull the English into a forest, a bog, a hillside, an ambush, to choose his own day and his own ground.

But the roving bands of Highland clansmen discovered the English army for themselves, and when word passed through the Scottish ranks that the enemy was close, it was more than their instincts could bear. They moved in the direction of Falkirk without ever receiving the order to march and in fact did not march at all but raced to the battlefield, each clan competing to be the first in position to fall on their hated foes and drive them from the land.

Wallace and his lieutenants rode to the highest ground they could find and looked out over the wide smooth stretch of grass that was about to become a vast killing field. Wallace was grave.

He heard the Highlanders chanting, banging their shields in high spirits. Only segments of the English army were visible through the mists, but it was clear they were there in great numbers. The Highlanders were unafraid; the more English to kill, the better.

Old Campbell looked at Wallace's grim face and said, "If we don't begin the battle soon, the clans will start it for themselves."

Wallace looked toward the crest of the next hill to his left. Mornay was there at the head of his cavalry. Of all the nobles, only Mornay had come. But he had brought nearly a hundred riders, all armed and battle-ready. "At least we have Mornay," Hamish said.

Wallace looked to the hill on his right. It was bare. He had sent a message to the Bruce asking him to anchor the right of the Scottish battle line, but he had received no reply. Seeing Wallace's face as he gazed toward the empty hill, Hamish said, "The Bruce is not coming, William."

"Mornay has come. So will the Bruce."

There was no time to send more messages, no time to argue, no time to plead. There would be no negotiations at this battle; it would all be settled with blood. Wallace peered across the field, trying to see the English positions, trying to see all the way to Longshanks and into his mind. "They will attack first," he said. "That's what I would do, before we can get set, before any of our reinforcements reach us."

Hamish wanted to argue that there would be no reinforcements, but William seemed so sure there would be, as if he could, by believing strongly enough, make the Bruce appear from the mists. Wallace began giving orders, deploying his troops. Looking to Hamish and old Campbell he said, "You lead the schiltrons into the center of the field; we can't let them charge through our middle." He turned to Stephen. "You back the spearmen with the infantry. Tell the Highlanders to charge with their broadswords against

195

anything that approaches the schiltrons." He seized a mounted messenger by the shoulder. "Tell Mornay to watch for the ranks of crossbowmen. He must charge their flanks at the first sign of them on the field. Now go!"

Everyone hurried to take their places. Wallace looked toward the bare hill, where the Bruce was to be. It was Scotland's most desperate hour. Everything was against them now. And yet if the Bruce would come, if they could stand together, noble and common, on that field, then whatever else happened would be Scotland's victory in the eyes of William Wallace.

Longshanks and his generals sat in their saddles, arrayed for battle, banners flying, pikes at attention, faceplates lowered, all ready for battle. And yet they waited. There was no hurry at all. Longshanks was anxious to see the battle begin, but he waited—precisely because he wished to see it. Until the mists lifted, he would not begin.

It was not long before the winds began to rise. Banks of fog, like low clouds, drifted before their eyes, then opened to reveal the Scots streaming into the plain before them. Longshanks studied the schiltrons that had so decimated his last army. He marveled at them. Fourteen-foot spears. Such a simple idea. Yet no one had ever tried it before. Because it took courage to stand there before the charge, stand and *believe* the idea would work when no one had ever seen it work before.

He looked across the field and in the lifting mists he saw the man who had lit the fire of faith and courage, and had spread it among his people: William Wallace, alone now on his horse, watching his army move forward.

Longshanks lifted his visor so that his voice could be heard by all around him. "Whatever else happens today, I want William Wallace. Dead or alive. But I want him."

With a wave of his royal hand, Longshanks sent his army forward.

Wallace saw Longshanks through the break in the mists, saw him stretch forth his long thin arm and wave his troops forward. Longshanks, his enemy, within sight. He could see the king's cold hatred in the slow, almost languid deliberateness of the gesture. So many men on both sides being sent to their deaths with a dispassionate wave that said, *"I am the king; it is my will that you give your lives to my purposes, so let us get on with it."*

Wallace spurred his horse down to join Stephen among the ranks of the Scottish swordsmen, behind the schiltrons. "Do you see them yet?" he called, reining to a stop beside his Irish friend.

Stephen was scanning the mists all around the edges of the field. "No, I . . . Wait, there!" Wallace looked in the direction Stephen pointed, and sure enough, Stephen was right: moving up toward the schiltrons were blocks of crossbowmen.

The bowmen were still far out of range, even with their new weapons. Stephen shouted for his men to hold their positions; the cavalry would charge them first, then the infantry, hoping to confuse the crossbowmen and diffuse their fire. With Scots bearing down on them from two directions, the Englishmen with their unfamiliar weapons would surely break and run.

But as the crossbowmen marched nearer and the stillness of impending battle descended upon the field, Wallace heard a haunting noise. "Do you hear that?" he said to Stephen.

Stephen nodded and strained harder to peer through the veil of mist. There, behind the bowmen, he saw the blocks of Longshanks's infantry, wearing kilts and marching to bagpipes. Irish troops.

Stephen of Ireland stared at the approach of his countrymen. Wallace spurred his horse up beside him. Stephen lowered his eyes, ashamed. "So that's where Longshanks got his soldiers," Stephen said. "Irishmen, willing to kill Scottish cousins for the English."

"Their families are starving, Stephen. They'll feed them however they can. If you don't want to fight them—"

"No. I'll stand with you."

Stephen raised his eyes. They were bright with tears. He drew his sword and walked to the head of the Scottish infantry. Wallace was sure he would never see him alive again.

"Hamish!" Wallace shouted toward the schiltrons. "Do you see them?"

"Aye!" Hamish shouted back. Then he called to his father, and the two Campbells stepped in front of the formations of spearmen. They gave a signal; the long pikes bristled into the air, and the formations started forward toward the enemy. Hamish glanced back at Wallace; both men knew the spearmen were the bait here. When they had discussed their strategy around the campfire the night before, Hamish had said, "As soon as we move forward, William, you must ride to the rear of the battlefield. If this feint with the schiltrons doesn't work, we'll be butchered and there is not one thing you could do about it. So at least let me know, when we try it, that if it doesn't work, you'll still be alive. For our hopes will live only as long as you do." Wallace had nodded even while feeling he could never deserve such a friend. Now, as he saw Hamish and his father lead their most loyal Highlanders into battle, William dismounted from his horse and drew his broadsword. He took a place among the Highlander swordsmen, looked back at Hamish. Hamish's blue eyes were burning bright. His brows knotted into a furious knot. Then he threw back his head and laughed.

He was still laughing as he quickened his step and marched toward the awful weapons of their enemies.

* * *

198

Wallace watched it all unfold in the slow ballet of battle, the schiltrons moving forward like great lumbering animals, the crossbowmen still as coiled serpents, waiting to strike with their deadly fangs. It was mesmerizing . . .

But the bowmen were holding their fire.

Wallace scanned the enemy lines and ran to Stephen. "Look, just there, riding in from the left!" It was the English heavy cavalry advancing as they had done at Stirling.

"They can't be that stupid to attack the schiltrons again," Stephen said.

And yet the English heavy cavalry had begun to charge, their heavy horses thundering, shaking the ground. Hamish and old Campbell saw them coming, too, and halted the schiltrons. They jabbed their spears into the earth, bracing them into their deadly trap.

"The charge is a distraction!" Wallace shouted. "Look at the crossbows!"

Hamish and Campbell could not hear him, but Stephen did, and he saw that Wallace was right. The crossbowmen had begun to run forward, intending to close the distance between themselves and their targets as everyone watched the horsemen. And even now the English knights, having learned the lessons of Stirling, were pulling up their mounts before they reached the forest of spears. The horses wheeled and raced back toward the English lines as the crossbowmen stopped, closer than they had been before, and fired their first volley.

They fired hurriedly. The hailstorm of bolts slashed through the air in unison. The bolts fell just short of the front ranks of the schiltrons.

Wallace was waving frantically to Mornay with the Scottish cavalry. Mornay was looking right toward the action, and yet he did nothing! The crossbowmen were reloading; Wallace was screaming. "Charge! Charge them!"

Mornay tugged his reins and lead his cavalry away. One by one, like a necklace of gemstones falling from a jilted lover's hand into a depthless loch, the cavalrymen vanished from the hilltop.

Wallace and Stephen watched in silence as they were abandoned.

Beneath the cluster of royal banners at the center of the English army, Longshanks and his officers saw Mornay and his cavalry melt away. The English general, surprised himself at this development, looked at Longshanks. "Mornay?" the general asked.

"For double his lands in Scotland and matching estates in England," Longshanks told him.

Wallace and Stephen looked on in agony as the crossbowmen unleashed another volley. The Scottish spearmen, bunched in a tight group, were helpless. The bolts cut through their helmets and breastplates like paper. The Highlanders who had seen Mornay ride away now looked to Wallace. With rising panic, through the wide eyes of the betrayed, they watched as he ran to his horse, leaped up onto its back—and charged alone toward the enemy.

With wild screams, Stephen and the Scottish swordsmen raced behind him.

The English heavy cavalry surged to meet them. Desperate to reach the bowmen, Wallace wove through the cavalry, first steering his horse at an angle across their line of charge, then cutting back before they could shift their heavy lances; he dodged in, slashing with his broadsword, cutting down one knight, then another. The Scottish infantry clawed in after him, dragging down the horses, hacking their riders, then running on, following Wallace.

The English bowmen were about to fire again at the schiltrons when their captain saw the Scottish charge bearing down on them. He shouted for them to redirect their fire, and their hasty volley flew.

* * *

Longshanks and his generals were watching from the English command pavilion. They had exulted as the first volley had sliced through the schiltrons; they had seen Wallace lead the counterattack into their charging cavalry; they had looked on anxiously as he met and obliterated their horsemen; but now, as the bolts of the second volley cut into the Scots, and one bolt caught Wallace, the breath caught in their throats. Longshanks grabbed a general by the arm. "We have him!" the king cried out, then watched as, far below them, Wallace wobbled on his horse, regained his balance, and kept up the charge. The corps of Scotsmen behind him had been riddled by the volley, but they ran on behind him, surging at the crossbowmen.

"My God, can nothing stop them?" the general said as he felt the king's hand upon his arm become an angry claw. They watched as the crossbowmen, their weapons virtually useless once fighting became hand to hand, tried to flee as the Scots streamed in around them, led by Wallace, looking invincible, cutting huge vicious arcs with his broadsword.

"Full assault! Hold nothing back!" Longshanks ordered. "But take Wallace alive!"

The English infantry, several thousand strong, had already surged into the battle. The general signaled and Longshanks's third wave—pike carriers, Welsh bowmen, fresh cavalry—began moving forward.

Wallace, with blood flowing from the wound in his side, fought his way into the middle of field, where English infantry were now overrunning the schiltron. He hacked men down left and right, reached the Scottish center, and found Hamish bent over another soldier. Wallace jumped from his saddle, bashed away the ax that an English footsoldier was swinging at Hamish's back, and cut the soldier down.

"Hamish! Ham—" William shouted. And then Wallace saw that Hamish was holding his father, fallen in battle. For a moment Wallace, like Hamish, was frozen at the sight. They had seen old Campbell fight on through all sorts of wounds, the loss of fingers, a hand, an arm, but now he had a gaping wound across his stomach. He was trying to push his son to make him leave him; he was finished.

Wallace's arrival had stiffened the clansmen in the schiltron, and Stephen's reinforcements were running up. The Scots were making a stand. Wallace had but a few seconds; he knelt beside Campbell. "Hamish, the horse!" Together Wallace and Hamish lifted old Campbell onto the saddle of his horse, and Wallace shouted at Hamish, "Get him away! Now. *Now!*"

Hamish obeyed, jumping onto the horse and galloping back toward the rear.

Wallace snatched up the broadsword from the ground where he had thrown it to help Campbell; he looked about him. All around were fallen Highlanders, men he had fought beside at Stirling, some who had joined him at Lanark. Dead now or dying.

Wallace screamed. No words, just a cry of fury. He held his sword high, and his men rallied.

The two infantries, Scottish and English, slammed together. For a few moments the momentum of battle wobbled like a giddy drunkard with one foot in the air having just stepped from a hot tavern into an icy wind. The English footmen were young, terrified, and far from home; and even those who had served in the French campaigns had never seen fighting like this. The Scots had won at Stirling and at York; they were outnumbered now, but they had been outnumbered before; and they were fighting alongside William Wallace. They became the frozen wind, hurling the drunkard back in search of shelter.

"Damn them!" Longshanks screamed. And even as he saw his infantry beaten back, he saw the mists shifting again, drifting in to mask the battle before him. This was awful; Longshanks still had the force of numbers; his other corps were still attacking. The last thing he wanted was a gray cloud to cloak the field. He turned to the knight behind him, a nobleman with light cavalry held as a last reserve. "Go," he ordered.

"Wallace is their heart! Take him!" When the knight hesitated, the king shouted, "See, our reserves are attacking—our archers, fresh infantry! The battle is ours! But Wallace must not escape! All I have promised I will double, just bring him to me!"

The knight spurred his horse forward.

Wallace, through the broken banks of mist, saw them coming. "A charge! Form up! Form up!" he shouted to his men. The Scots pulled up spears and hastily formed another schiltron. The spears bristled out, ready. The English horsemen thundered in. But before the spears impaled the horses, another flight of crossbow bolts cut down half the Scots.

Still Wallace fought back, meeting the English charge. The Scots held their own. The knight who had led the English charge and had already cut his way through several Highlanders tried to ride over Wallace. Wallace knocked the knight's lance aside, and though the horse slammed into him, Wallace grabbed the man's leg and dragged him from the saddle.

The rider rolled to his feet. Wallace struggled up to meet him—and came face to face with Robert the Bruce.

The shock and recognition stunned Wallace. In that moment, when he looked at the Bruce's guilt-ridden face, he understood everything: the betrayal, the hopelessness of Scotland.

Bruce stared back at Wallace and saw a look of shock and despair that he would never forget, no matter how many lifetimes he might live.

Bruce snatched his sword from the ground, where it had fallen. He feinted; Wallace didn't respond. Bruce battered at Wallace's sword as if its use would give him absolution. "Fight me! Fight me!" Robert shouted.

But Wallace could only stagger back. Bruce's voice grew ragged as he screamed. "Fight me!"

All around, the battle had decayed; the Scots were being slaughtered. Men were streaming in; Wallace would be cut down at any second—but suddenly Stephen came through on Robert's horse! He hit Robert from behind, knocked him onto his chest, and dragged Wallace onto the horse. He could not pull him onto the saddle without help, and Wallace gave him none. It was as if the knot of hope that held his strength in place had suddenly slipped and left him feeble. Stephen held his limp body with one hand and spurred the horse, half carrying, half dragging Wallace from the field.

Robert the Bruce lifted his face. He saw Wallace escaping. All around him were the dying Scots. The Bruce lowered his eyes to the earth, muddy with the blood of his countrymen.

47

THE RAYS OF THE DYING SUN SOAKED THE LEADEN MISTS like blood upon tarnished armor as remnants of the defeated army straggled along the roads, moving north, away from Falkirk. William Wallace stumbled blindly forward, supported by Stephen on one side, and trying, in turn, to support Hamish, who carried his huge father like a child within his arms. No one knew how long it had been since the battle ended; it was as if the world had stopped turning then, with the dying doomed to stagger on forever, away from those already dead.

Old Campbell's eyes came open and rolled up toward Hamish. "Son . . . ," he said, "I want to die on the ground."

They stopped, and William and Stephen tried to help Hamish lower his father to the earth. But as they tilted him to prop him against a fallen tree, old Campbell grabbed at something that started to fall from the wound in his stomach. For so long he had seemed oblivious to pain, but now it scorched his face. Then, as he had always done before, he willed it away. "Whew," he said. "That'll clear your head."

His chin drooped upon his great chest, and he took a huge breath, finding strength from somewhere. His head came up again, and he looked around at each face. "Good-bye, boys," he said.

"No. You're going to live," Hamish tried to tell him.

"I don't think I can do without one of those," old Campbell said, glancing down at where his hand was restraining some organ from sliding out of his wound, "whatever it is."

Hamish was too grief stricken to speak.

William wanted to touch Campbell, even raised his hand, looking for a place to rest it, but every spot on the old man's body seemed sore. Then William saw that old Campbell was looking at him with eyes that were steady and soft, the same way they had looked when old Campbell had brought him the news of the deaths of William's father and brother. They looked at each other without speaking, then William said, "You . . . were like my father."

Old Campbell rallied one more time and said, "And glad to die like him . . . so you could be the men you are. All of ya."

His last three words were to Hamish. The old man let go of his guts and reached his bloody hand to his son. Hamish took it, and his father died in peace.

48

AT SUNSET THE NEXT DAY, WILLIAM WALLACE, STILL
bloody and in his battered armor, walked into the
council chamber of Edinburgh Castle. Hamish and
Stephen, the filth and gore of battle still upon them,
strode in behind him and stood at his back as Wallace
removed the chain of office from beneath his breastplate and laid it onto the table in front of Craig and
the other nobles.

Wallace turned without a word and walked from the
room. Hamish and Stephen lingered just long enough
to see the satisfaction on the nobles' face and followed
William out. They moved out into the hallway after
Wallace—but he was gone.

"William!" Hamish called out.

No answer; they moved to the great stone staircase.
"William!" Stephen called down.

But there was no answer. They headed downstairs.
At the bottom of the staircase, they looked in both
directions but saw no sign of Wallace. Both men were
troubled; there were men here who would have been
happy to plunge a dagger into their friend's back, and
they meant to be watching it. Without a word, Stephen and Hamish split up and moved off to search for
him.

Several minutes later, Hamish moved into the
stables, just as Stephen wandered in from the opposite
side. A groom was there, currying the horses.

"Have you seen Wallace?" Hamish asked.

"Just now took his horse and left," the groom told
them.

Hamish and William moved to the door of the

stables and looked out. A gray rain was falling in sheets.

Hamish and Stephen sat down on the wet hay and watched the rain. They watched for a long time. Then Hamish stood slowly and reached for his saddle.

"He'll come back," Stephen said. "Surely he will."

"No. He won't."

"Where will you go?"

"Back to my farm till they come to hang me. You?"

Stephen shook his head. He had no idea.

Even when Hamish rode away, Stephen was still sitting at the door, staring out at the rain.

49

WALLACE RODE THROUGH THE STORM. THE FALLING RAIN lashed his face and beat upon his hair, yet he did pull up a fold of his tartan to shield and warm his head but rode on like a man insane—or dead already.

He was going nowhere. He rode slowly. Sometimes the horse would stop when the drops of rain were stinging and they had moved beneath the cover of a tree. The horse would wait, expecting the rain would stop, but after awhile the waiting became tedious, and he would move on.

They moved through villages, passing common people taking shelter from the rain. They came to their doorways and looked out at the specter of this rider in battlefield dress, all tattered and marked from the fighting, with wounds still seeping blood into their bandages.

Wallace looked at them. They stared back, their faces showing no recognition. Did they know who he was? He gazed around at them, the people for whom he fought. They seemed to find him disturbing, this battered man riding in the rain. Mothers pulled their curious children back from the doorways, and men watched him like guard dogs, ready to growl should he turn their way to ask for bread or a place by their fire.

He rode on.

He came to the place where he'd been going all along without knowing it: the grove of trees where Murron lay buried.

He dismounted then and fell to his knees beside the secret grave. The rain fell on his face like tears. But he had no tears of his own. The cold, the icy rain, the wounds, nothing seemed to touch him. With his fingertips he carefully drew her embroidered cloth from beneath his leather battle shirt. Hanging in his trembling hands, filthy with the grime and gore of battle, the handkerchief she had made for him looked impossibly white, something from a better, purer world.

Rain fell that day in London, too, and thunder rumbled through the sky, its dark roar penetrating even the thick walls of the palace and reaching its innermost rooms. Snug by a massive fire in its central audience chamber were Longshanks; his son, Edward; and the king's closest advisors. On the far side of the room, away from the fire, the princess stood at the window and listened to the rain pounding against the wooden shutters.

She heard Hamilton telling the king, "Their nobles have sworn allegiance, m'lord. Every last one."

Longshanks savored the victory—and gloated to his son. "Now we kill two birds at one stroke. We must eliminate Scotland's capacity to make war against us, and we must renew our campaign for the French throne. So we recruit from Scotland for our armies in France."

"The Scots will fight for us?" Edward sputtered. "Surely you cannot believe they could be reliable—"

"What choice do they have? Now they must serve us or starve."

But Edward hated the amused curl of his father's lip and the tone of his voice that seemed to dare his son to find any flaw in his logic. And Edward was afraid of his father no longer. Longshanks could beat him to death if he wished; that no longer mattered to Edward. And yet Edward knew his father would never do that—not because of love but pride. Edward would succeed him for better or worse; Longshanks would have no other son. If he should lose this one, there would be no more Plantagenets on the throne of England. Edward's disregard for any physical threat from his father made him safe—but only bodily. Longshanks's desire to crush what he saw as his son's arrogance had only increased. And the prince was fighting back. "They fought for Wallace even when they were starving," he said. "They died for him. They won't fight for us."

"No," Longshanks said, shaking his gray mane like an angry old lion, "you are wrong. They did not fight for Wallace. They fought for the idea that he would bring them victory. Now that idea has been destroyed. There is nothing unique about the Scots; they are like all people in their desire to align themselves with the strong and not the weak. This idea, this dream, that Wallace was leading them to glory will make them even more likely than ever before to follow us, precisely because we are strong."

"But if we have not caught Wallace—" Edward began.

"He is gone!" Longshanks shouted. "Finished! Dead! If he has not yet bled to death or had his throat cut for him, he will not survive the winter! It is very cold—is it not, our flower?" He turned and smiled at the princess, standing far from the fire, at the cold draft of the window.

Everyone in the room was silent. Even Edward thought, *The cruel bastard knows she thought Wallace was a better man than any she had met in London. He enjoys this, seeing her illusions shattered as well.* And Edward himself, though he had never thought himself capable of feeling jealousy over any of Isabella's affections, felt a sliver of satisfaction. When she had returned from her meeting with Wallace, she had glowed, and neither the king nor the prince had failed to notice it. When she had heard of Wallace's defeat at Falkirk—Edward had taken the time to inform her of it personally—she had paled.

Now she stood on the far side of the room and heard the king's question but didn't turn around. She pushed open the shutters and stared outside at the wet snowflakes now swirling among the raindrops. Her breath fogged the air, and her eyes were as wet as the rain.

Inside the Bruce's darkened chamber, the elder Bruce, his decaying features sagging from his face, stared across the table at his son. "I am the one who is rotting," the old man said. "But I think your face looks graver than mine."

"He was so brave. With courage alone he nearly won," Robert said, his voice distant and tired.

"So more men were slaughtered uselessly!"

"He broke because of me. I saw it. He lost all will to fight."

"We must have alliance with England to prevail here," the elder Bruce said, pleading for his son to understand. "You achieved that! You saved your family, increased your lands! You—"

"Lands? Titles? What has this to do with that?"

"Everything."

"Nothing!" Robert stood so suddenly his chair flew backward against the stone wall of his father's dark chamber; the old leper sat so still that any visitor peeking in upon this private meeting might have thought the father's skin was melting like sooted wax in the flame of the candle.

Young Robert paced back and forth in the square

210

chamber. But he could find no words to open his heart, to let it spill out its hurt and anger. The leper spoke gently, "What I have asked of you is not easy. A king's choices never are. But in time you will have all the power in Scotland."

And suddenly young Robert exploded. "You understand nothing, Father! You say I own lands, title, men . . . power! And you would have me own more. Men fight for me because if they do not, I turn them off my land and starve their wives and children! Those men who bled the ground red at Falkirk, they fought for William Wallace, and he fights for something I'll never have! And I took it from him in my betrayal. I saw it in his face on the battlefield, and it tears at me still!"

Robert shuddered; and yet he felt a strange feeling rising in him, a new strength that frightened him, threatening to overwhelm him, even as it struggled with his old weakness.

"All men betray!" his father was saying. "All lose heart. It is exactly why we make the choices we make."

"I don't want to lose heart! I want to believe as he does!"

"My son . . ."

"No!!!" Robert shouted, his voice like a dagger to his father's core. He spun to the door and looked back. "I will never be on the wrong side again."

He opened the door, not with the impulse of an anger that would fade but the slow calm of a man who had turned from a path he never meant to walk again. The leper did not look up, and he knew that his son did not look back.

For a long time after young Robert had gone, his father sat in his chamber and stared at the slowly dancing flame of the candle.

BRAVE
HEARTS

50

KING PHILIP IV OF FRANCE DID NOT CONSIDER HIMSELF A decisive man. He never expressed this opinion publicly, of course; kings are expected to demonstrate some deference to God—claiming, as they do, that their right to rule flows from Him and thus they are closer to the Almighty than are other mortals—but they can never compare themselves to other men, much less do so unfavorably.

But Philip knew his history and was aware that kings are judged—when they are dead, and appraisal is allowed—by their victories. Conflicts that remain unresolved throughout their reigns seem testaments to the limits of their abilities, and Philip had known nothing but struggle.

At the age of seventeen he came to a throne that had been held by kings who, in retrospect, seemed to have been all powerful. They ruled the Holy Roman Empire, that political manifestation of the Catholic dream that all Christendom should be united under one temporal head, elected by the pope and his cardinals. But Philip seemed born into squabbling. His throne was attacked from within and from without. Longshanks, across the channel, claimed that he should rule both England and France, and Philip was forced to spend almost all of his time forging alliance among his own nobles to resist Longshanks's diplo-

215

macy and armies. And in moments when Philip found breathing room from that problem, his energies were drawn to the perils of the Holy Catholic Church itself; the Vatican had fallen into so much corruption and contention that Philip would eventually be forced, in the year 1309, to move the papacy to Avignon, and the world would have not one infallible pontiff but two, each of whom consigned the other to hell.

The demands of the throne were complicated, and Philip managed the best he could. Faced with hundreds of difficult decisions that, once made, only seemed to result in the need to make other decisions, he began to consider himself indecisive. If he could truly *decide* something, he thought, then he wouldn't be forced to keep deciding again and again. If he could somehow make things simpler, then he might achieve a name like Charles I, who had become known as Charlemagne—Charles the Great—or Louis IX, who had been canonized as Saint Louis.

Philip IV was known as Philip the Fair.

It was midafternoon on a fine Parisian day when this handsome, dark-haired king of France was hoping he could conclude his business soon enough to stroll among his gardens while the sun was still up, that Deroux, one of his many advisors, entered the palace audience chamber wearing a worried look. This was not unusual; all his advisors were forever looking troubled. The king only noted the weighty expression because he had been working since dawn and had thought the stream of troublesome matters being brought before him had finally dried up for the day. This last advisor waited his turn as Philip waded through the deliberations at his usual steady pace; but when at last the king turned to him and said, "Yes, Deroux," the man seemed unprepared to respond.

"Sire . . . ," he said at last, "we have a . . . a . . ."

"A problem, Deroux?"

"A visitor, sire. A man who says he is William Wallace."

William Wallace. King Philip knew in an instant

216

why Deroux had been hesitating. That name had caused head scratching and uncertainty in the French court since the first time it was spoken, just after the Battle of Stirling, where an English army more powerful than the ones that had been bedeviling France had been driven from Scotland in a single day. An unknown commoner? A military genius? A legendary figure who had taken an army away from the nobles who owned it and then led it to victory? Some of Philip's advisors doubted this Wallace actually existed.

Then they had received a letter from him. It was written in clear, forceful French, strictly correct if a bit academic. The letter petitioned the French king and his court to enter pacts of defense and trade. It made no mention of their common enemy but pointed out in a direct fashion the benefits to both countries of such an alliance. King Philip had often thought how advantageous it would be to utilize the military and economic potential of Longshanks's northern neighbors; it was obvious to him that Longshanks's efforts to crush the Scots were meant to prevent just such a possibility.

But nothing was ever simple. Philip's advisors had told their king that it might not be prudent to respond to Wallace's letter favorably; perhaps it was dangerous to respond at all. The Scottish nobles were distrustful and divided. Did this Wallace possess the authority to create alliances? If so, how long would his ability last?

The French stalled. The royal court studied and debated. By that time Wallace had been defeated at Falkirk, and Philip's advisors felt vindicated in their caution. Now here he was, in France, presenting himself, requesting an audience with the king himself.

"He just arrives, asking for an audience?" Philip asked Deroux. It was considered a breach of protocol for anyone, no matter how prominent, to request a royal audience simply by arriving; one was expected to make arrangements through carefully worked out channels.

"Yes, sire."

"How long has he been here?"

"Since this morning." Philip then understood the delay. Deroux didn't want to grant the audience and didn't want to deny it either. It was clear he even doubted for a time whether the visitor was in fact the legendary Scotsman. The king saw other advisors, men he had already dismissed for the day, filtering back into the room; Deroux must have solicited their advice, and they wanted to see the outcome.

"Send him in," Philip ordered.

Deroux waved to the guard at the door, and he admitted William Wallace. King Philip saw immediately the reason for Deroux's reluctance and the evidence of how wrong he had been to doubt this man was who he claimed to be. The warrior before them was ragged and scarred. His clothes were plain. If not for his stature, the obvious power in his arms, the breadth of his shoulders, and the handsomeness of his face, scarred though it was, he would have passed for a simple commoner. But he could not conceal the force within him; it was in his posture, his stride; he was a man who would yield to nothing. His facial expression was frightening in that it looked dead. But his eyes were not. They burned. The man nodded to the king—no bow, just a simple tilt of his head.

"Sir William," the king acknowledged.

"Thank you for receiving me," Wallace said in decent though heavily accented French.

He stood there in a long awkward silence, the king and two dozen of his richly attired gentlemen of the court all gazing at the warrior with the wild hair and the wilder eyes. And then the king surprised everyone. "It looks like a fine evening," he said, glancing out toward his gardens. "Come and walk with me."

They moved along the raked gravel of the garden, surrounded by high manicured hedges. The flower beds were barren, spaded up and lying fallow for new plantings, and yet it was a calming place, all quiet and serene. Wallace took long slow steps, his gaze lowered, his thoughts seemingly distant. The king studied him as they walked. "You seek asylum," Philip supposed.

"No," Wallace said. "I did not come to hide. I came to fight."

Several of the royal advisors, among them Deroux, were trailing along behind. They pretended to be enjoying the stroll but were straining to catch every word, and now they looked all around at each other.

"To fight for me?" King Philip asked.

"If I say that, you'll know I lie. I respect you as an enemy of my enemy, but I am not here to become your subject."

"So you hate Longshanks that much that you would fight him anywhere you can."

"I love my country so much that I will fight for it, even when it does not fight for itself."

They had come to a stone bench. The king stopped and motioned for Wallace to take a seat beside him. This caused some confusion among the advisors, who had to stop ten paces back and pretend they were keenly interested in patterns of the gravel walkway. The king smiled and said to Wallace, "You know there is a price on your head. Well, of course, you do. But I heard that with interest, for it proved you were real and not just a fanciful concoction of your countrymen. Longshanks would not offer money for a phantom. You can, I hope, understand the doubts we had about you. We heard such tales here. That you had killed a hundred men with your own sword at Stirling. That you had the English commander flayed and his hide turned into a belt three feet long . . ." The king shook his head and shrugged.

"That was a lie," Wallace said. "It was four feet long."

The king burst out laughing. Wallace smiled himself —and to the king the Scot's face seemed surprised at what it was doing, as if the feeling of a smile was unfamiliar.

"Where have you been, Sir William?" the king asked. "Hiding?"

Wallace nodded. "But not from them. Let my enemies find me. Let them come on—anywhere, everywhere, I am ready. But yes, I have been hiding. From myself."

"And now you wish to fight again."

"I do," Wallace said.

"Your Majesty . . . ," Deroux said, stepping forward, "could we please take a moment to confer?"

"There is no need to confer, Monsieur Deroux. Arrange lodgings for our visitor. Provide him with money. No," he added quickly, for he saw Wallace glower, "not as a mercenary, but to secure proper food, rest, and weapons, for my generals should be at their best to do their best."

"Your . . . generals, sire?"

"You heard me, Deroux," said Philip the Fair.

51

PARIS IN THE YEAR 1300 WAS ALREADY A GREAT CITY, A place of trade and knowledge, an object of pride to the French, a people never considered to be lacking in their opinion of themselves or their sensitivity to the opinion of others about them. Their city possessed large inns serving fine food, and it was in the best of these that William Wallace was to be found that night, sitting alone in a corner by the fire, dining upon a joint of roasted meat presented by the inn's owner, who took special pains to provide for this guest in the knowledge that he was extending the hospitality of the king himself.

No one within the inn knew the identity of the visitor; they knew he was a Scot by his accent, and it was apparent from his stature and the scars visible upon his face and hands that he must be a warrior. Many other Scots had come across to serve as mercenaries; it was assumed by the other men eating and drinking at the inn that night that this man must be a mercenary himself—and one of extreme proficiency if the king was seeing to his keep. So the innkeeper's other patrons—aristocrats all, for this was one of Paris's finest establishments—kept their distance and watched with a mixture of curiosity and vague suspicion as the strange visitor sat silently in his corner, chewing his supper and staring into the flames of the fire.

The subdued atmosphere of the inn's tavern room was instantly dispelled by Claude de Bouchard, whose voice flew through the doors several moments before his body did. "Where is he?" he shouted, already drunk. "Is he hiding? Let me look at him!" Bouchard stomped in, his boot heels heavy upon the plank floor, and everyone, except Wallace, turned to look at him. Bouchard was a tall, slender man with the prominent, straight nose of Gallic nobility and luxurious black hair falling in curls to his shoulders. He was a nephew of the king and wore the rich blue sash belt that designated him as a general in the king's army. Everyone knew him and no one cared for him, but all tried to show him deference; the king had a great many relatives, but no one thought it a good idea to offend any of them.

Bouchard was frequently loud and drunk, and this night he was exceptionally so. "A general, they tell me!" he bellowed. "Ha! Someone who will give us advice? Is that his purpose? Where is—"

Then his reddened eyes fell upon Wallace, who still had not looked up at him. Bouchard seemed to find something in Wallace's presence or appearance to be terribly amusing. He began to laugh and glance around at the others as if to see if everyone else got the joke. "This?" he chuckled. "This is someone who will teach the men of France how to do battle?"

"Please, Claude . . . ," one of the other aristocrats said quietly, moving to Bouchard and placing a hand on his shoulder. "The king—"

Bouchard threw the man's hand off. "The king invites him to join us, yes, I know!" He staggered to Wallace's table and bumped into it before he could stop himself. "Are you the man?" he demanded.

Still Wallace did not look at him.

The aristocrat who had attempted to head Bouchard off now tried once again, laughing and saying, "Come, Claude, you are drunk, so drink with us some more."

"I am not drunk!" Bouchard screamed. Wallace's refusal to acknowledge him was making him even more furious. "Look at me! Look at me!"

Wallace lifted his eyes. It should have frightened Bouchard; it frightened everyone else in the room. But Bouchard only made a face, pursing his lips and blowing out his cheeks in a look of mock ferocity. "So you are William Wallace!" the Frenchman bellowed. "The military genius! The one who is so smart he gets his entire army slaughtered! Yes, yes, you have much to teach us!"

Slowly, Wallace looked down again at his food.

"Don't look away from me! I am a true general of France!" This statement might have found several to dispute it, solely among those present; the presence of the king's relatives, along with the sons, nephews, and cousins of France's other noble families, among the army's leadership had not helped them drive the English from their territory. Generals like Bouchard were present at banquets and not on battlefields. "Do you hear me! I command you to look!" He snatched Wallace's shoulder with one hand and with the other withdrew the jeweled dagger he carried in the blue sash at his waist. He thrust the blade against Wallace's throat. "You insolent common bastard. You think you can ignore me? I will teach you to fight! I will—"

Those were his last words.

52

PHILIP THE FAIR WAS UNABLE TO KEEP HIS MIND ON WHAT his advisors were saying. He had tried to listen; for days and days he had tried. But now there was just so much droning on and on. Every day he would say to them, "What should I do with William Wallace?" and every day the talk would begin, so that he no longer heard individual words or arguments or could remember which side of the issue anyone took, since all of them seemed to take both sides all the time.

Whenever they moved on to the other business of the kingdom, Philip kept thinking about Wallace locked away in his prison for the killing of a royal relative. And even Philip could not think clearly anymore.

Today it became too much for him. In the middle of a discussion about building roads—at least that had been the topic when the king last heard what his advisors were saying—he stood abruptly, walked to the center of the room, and ordered everyone out. "Go. Now. All of you!" he said loudly and forcefully. "Yes, yes, everyone! All of you out!" After a brief moment of surprise, for their king never behaved rashly, the advisors obeyed quickly, streaming toward the door. Herding them like a sheep dog chasing the flock into its pen, the king drove them on with, "Leave me alone! I am not to be disturbed! Shut the door!"

And with the closing of the door, and its heavy wooden sound echoing through the royal audience chamber, the king found himself in blessed solitude.

He did not know what to do next; it was so seldom that he found himself all alone. He was uncomfortable standing there in the center of the great room, with no one telling him what to do next. So he began to pace from door to window and back again. At first he thought of nothing, just listened to the sound of his heels upon the polished stone floor; then he began to turn the problem over in his head: what must he do with William Wallace?

Then he heard the door opening. Philip was pacing toward the window when he heard the latch clattering, and he could scarcely believe the sound. His normally even temperament began to erupt; he whirled and had already started shouting, "What is this? Did you not understand—" when he saw her. "Isabella!"

"Greetings to you, great king!" The Princess of Wales, Philip of France's niece, sank in a respectful curtsey, but her face was radiant, and the king himself was glowing with the unexpected joy of seeing her. He hurried to her, seized her hands, pulled her up, and kissed her cheeks.

"I had no idea you were coming!" he said, searching his scattered thoughts for the possibility that his aides could have mentioned such a thing, and he had failed to note it, as if that were possible.

"Nor did I," Isabella said.

"But how . . . ?"

"I came without sending word. Since France is my country, too, and I have my own French guards to escort me, it didn't seem necessary. The only trouble I had was getting through this last door. You have some gentlemen out there who seemed to think that entry was quite impossible."

The king threw back his head and laughed. "Impossible for everyone but you!" He loved this beautiful young woman who stood before him, the daughter of his youth. He had reared her in the customary way, with nursemaids and tutors and all the traditional remoteness of king to female child. But she had always stirred up in him feelings that had made painful her betrothal and marriage to a foreign prince. The sight of her now brought back memories of summer days in the country when no court counselors rained schemes and questions and advice upon his head, and he had time to watch lovely girls becoming women right before his eyes, strolling across flowered lawns and in and out of the shade of spreading trees, during those languid seasons when the young aristocrats of France visited one estate after another with no other purpose than to enjoy life and to get to know their peers. Isabella had made him proud even then. She was never intimidated by him or anyone else; if she wished to speak, she spoke; if she wished to dance, she danced; if she wished to ride, she rode; and it was that spirit that made her more than beautiful and made him proud.

And look at her now! She had been traveling for days, and he could see that she was tired, but her eyes were keen, she was full of purpose.

"We'll have food, wine," he said and started toward the door to call his servants.

"In a little while," she said. "We'll visit at dinner if you can find the time to dine with me."

"We'll dine together every night. We'll make a month of banquets!" But then the cloud of reality passed over his face. "That is, if your visit is official, and we can behave with the open hospitality of diplomacy. If it is unofficial, you are just as welcome." He did not add that too much formal attention paid to her, though she was his own daughter, could be a political embarrassment for them both. Obviously she knew that, to have come so quickly and quietly. The soldiers of France and England were battling each other, but both kings maintained the public pretense of keeping the conflict at arm's length, blaming belligerent nobles with unruly private armies for the clashes that took place in the constant struggle for territory and power. This was a kind of royal insurance; the kings could negotiate without loss of face or capitulate without the actual loss of one or the other's head.

"My visit is official," Isabella said. "But it is not to be public."

"Then come," Philip said, leading her to the great table. "Come and sit down." They settled into the deep chairs, Philip at the head of the huge expanse of polished plank, and Isabella at his right hand. He poured her wine from the flask in front of him. She nodded her thanks but did not drink.

"I have been sent," she said. "We have heard in London that you have a . . . certain visitor."

He was pouring a drink of wine for himself; he stopped before his cup was full and set the flask down. "I do, yes. William Wallace."

"You appear irritable."

"No, it is not at you. I am unsettled that news travels so fast, especially to a court where I am—an adversary."

"My father-in-law has many ears listening for word of this man who visits you. Is he . . . comfortable?"

"I believe so, yes. His room has blankets and a bed . . ."

"And bars?"

"Yes."

"Then it is also true that he killed Bouchard?"

"It is true."

"Bouchard was a pompous, cruel, evil ass."

"Did you come to tell me what I already know?"

"Let us see if I can indeed tell you what you already know," Isabella said. She paused to lick her lips, and Philip noticed that something about all this was making her nervous. Not this royal audience; she was his daughter, and would soon be a queen herself. And not this mission she'd been sent on; clearly she had already thought out what she wished to say. But *something* was making her mouth dry.

She said, "You have in custody a man of singular circumstance. He is not a king, yet he is everything to his country. But he has fled that country and has come to you because your enemy is his enemy. He is alone and abandoned, but you, because you have met him, know that his strength does not depend on the number of those around him."

"You have met him, too," Philip broke in. "We heard rumors of your being sent to bribe him, but I wasn't sure it was true until now."

"I met him," she said, going on quickly. "I brought him the king's offer of wealth and titles, and he refused it all. Now he has come to you. It is obvious that he came of his own free will, for it is unlikely you could have sought him out yourself, in that the full power of the English throne was never able to root him out, even in Britain itself, with huge sums of money offered as reward for his capture."

"You are doing well so far, do go on."

"I am no judge of military tactics, but anyone can judge the results of his leadership, achieving victories no one else thought possible. Apart from his ability to inspire his followers, Wallace is indisputably a brilliant military strategist. He lost at Falkirk because he was betrayed. You know this. It is why you wished to use him. You did wish to use him, did you not?"

The king nodded, smiling at the keenness of her mind.

"You did. This caused Bouchard to be jealous. I know nothing of the fight itself, only that Bouchard was killed. But knowing Bouchard . . . as well as Wallace," she added almost reluctantly, "it is clear that Bouchard was the aggressor. Is this correct?"

"Bouchard forced the fight—if you could call it that. He drew a dagger and threatened Wallace with it. Wallace ignored the dagger—as if he knew Bouchard lacked the will to use it, or perhaps it was because Wallace cared nothing if he died. Whichever it was, he reached up, snatched Bouchard by the hair, and snapped his neck with a single jerk. There were many witnesses in the tavern and all of them gave the same account."

"Exactly so," said the princess, who seemed to the king to have flushed when he confirmed the Scotsman's innocence. "But still you have a problem. Bouchard was a relative. Even if most of our aristocrats despised him, even if his own family hated him, he was still a royal relative. For you to release the man who killed him—a foreigner, no less—would infuriate many of those who support you in your fragile alliance against Longshanks. But you will not execute Wallace, for you will not have the blood of an innocent man upon your soul. It vexes you even to have him in prison, but you can find no other alternative. Of course you could send him to Longshanks and even receive compensation for doing so."

"You have been sent to convince me to do just that."

"Yes," Isabella said. "Exactly. Of course, no Frenchman could stand to see his king lick the hand of Longshanks. And yet Longshanks believes you will do just that if he sweetens that hand with gold. No wonder the French and the English do not get along."

Philip wanted to ask her to say more on that subject; she could not be happy in her adopted home. But he knew she would reveal nothing voluntarily, so instead he asked her, "Do you have a suggestion for me on how I might escape this dilemma?"

"Send him to the pope."

Philip was struck dumb by the genius of the idea. His mouth silently echoed the words: *the pope*. The one judge on all the earth to whom he could send Wallace without offending anyone. He would even be doing Wallace a favor, for the Scotsman had told him, when they had talked in the garden, that only two monarchs could help Scotland now, and they were the king of France and the holy father of Rome. Philip, with enormous influence in Rome, could give Wallace the letters necessary to obtain a papal audience, and Wallace would certainly take the oath that he would go.

Philip looked at Isabella and smiled. "I hope we are always friends," he said. "I would hate to be your enemy."

"We will always be friends," she said. She found herself wanting to lean to her father and embrace him warmly, not with the studied formality she had been

228

trained to observe but with real feeling. She had never taken such a physical liberty with him. If she had had such an impulse in the days before she had left France, she would have obeyed the urge. But living in the English court had taught her restraint.

"You've just done me a great favor, Isabella," the king said, perhaps feeling the same regret that she had. "Is there anything I can do for you?"

"I think there is nothing else that can be done for me," she said.

"Would you care to see the man you have just helped free from prison? After all, he'll be leaving tomorrow."

Everything in Isabella wanted to say yes. *Bring him here, let me go to him. Yes. Yes!*

"He is barely more than a stranger to me," she said at last. "I am here in the service of justice, nothing more."

The next day she stood on a tower walkway and watched as a contingent of four guards, with a cloaked figure riding between them, journeyed off toward Rome. They had begun some distance from the French royal palace, since the dungeon where Wallace was imprisoned was not on the castle grounds, but she saw them as they topped a low hill, and she knew the cloaked figure was William Wallace.

She said a prayer for him, that God would protect him with all His saints and angels. She prayed He would bless the visit with the pope.

And after she said amen, she cursed herself for not taking the chance to see him one more time.

53

BECAUSE HE WAS ACCOMPANIED BY REPRESENTATIVES OF the king of France, William Wallace was admitted to the Vatican. He was informed, in Latin, the universal language, that he would be granted an audience with the pope—that very day. He was provided clean clothes—though the ones he had been given at the start of his journey were new—and was allowed to wash and make himself presentable for his holiness, who would be seeing him in less than an hour.

Wallace asked for a place to pray.

He was shown a tiny chapel that seemed to have been excavated from the stone walls. It was lit with many candles below a carving of Jesus on the cross. There was barely room to kneel. It was perfect.

There William Wallace prayed. It was a prayer without words; he had no words for what he felt. What a journey it had been that had brought him to this place. From a Scottish valley to a great city already more than a thousand years old. That morning he and his escorts had passed the ruins of a colosseum where Christians had fought lions for the amusement of kings. He had fought kings for—for what? For the pleasure of God? To try to burn away his grief? For revenge? Or because he had no choice?

On his knees in that chapel, he prayed with his soul. He let his thoughts float away and tried to place his heart before the throne of God. He did not expect to know God's will. Uncle Argyle had taught him the Old Testament belief in the fear of God: that the Almighty was a mystery, but His revelations were all around us.

To William Wallace, Murron was a revelation, a gift of God. His family, his friends, Scotland itself, all were blessings. And all had been taken away. For what? He did not know, and as long as he breathed, he would not know.

But maybe the pain had a purpose, and the loss of everything was meant to drive him here, where he could ask the pope to intervene on behalf of Scotland. The pope had the power; he could declare that the innocents of Scotland were under his protection; he could decree that he would evaluate all claims to the Scottish throne and would make a judgment himself as to who should sit upon it and could forbid Longshanks to meddle; he could enforce his decisions with the threat of excommunication, and maybe the whole problem could be settled with no more blood, no more killing.

That was the prayer of William Wallace's heart in the Vatican that day. What happened to him didn't matter; it never had mattered. If he had to be punished in this life or the next for fighting to be free, he would accept it. Whatever the pope wanted to do to him for the battles he'd fought, the cities he'd burned, it was all right; he'd even accept the consequences for killing Bouchard—as long as the pope would listen to his plea for Scotland.

He wished he had been a better man with a heart less full of fire. But God had given him that heart and had brought him here to pray it and to speak it.

A voice behind him said, "His Holiness will see you now."

William Wallace's lips whispered, "Amen."

The priests brought him into a large room and told him to kneel upon the cushions there. Wallace did as they instructed. The room was hung with tapestries and lit with candles; the air was thick with the scent of the hot tallow, but Wallace noticed no other details.

The pope entered; he was standing before his visitor with his hand outstretched almost before Wallace knew he was there. Wallace pressed his lips against the ring nestled in the soft flesh of the pope's plump fingers and then, for the first time, looked up at the pontiff's face.

It was a round face atop a round body, made to look even more corpulent by the pure white vestments. The pope appeared tired, or perhaps it was impatient. Even as he was allowing his hand to be kissed, he had tilted his head toward the priest-counselor at his side, who held the letters King Philip had sent and was whispering rapidly into the pontiff's ear. The pope left his hand hanging before Wallace as he listened, then, the whispering concluded, he made the sign of the cross above Wallace's head.

As the pope's languid eyes fell upon him, Wallace said with reverence, "Holy Father, thank you for receiving me."

The pope nodded quickly.

"I have come to ask—"

"Your father knows all your needs before you ask him," the pope broke in. Wallace, taught at Uncle Argyle's knee, recognized the words of Jesus from the gospels. The words in the New Testament referred to the Father in heaven; the words from the pope clearly meant the father in the Vatican, the one with the advisors and the letters from the king. "Your sins are forgiven you," the pope said. "Go in peace."

He turned away and began to walk from the room.

"But—Your Holiness!"

The priests turned, shocked at their visitor's insolence. They were more surprised still as Wallace stood. "You are in the presence of His Holiness!" one of them reminded the Scot.

Wallace lowered his head. "I mean every respect, every obedience. But it was not my sins—not mine alone—that I came to remove. It was those against my country."

The priests glared at him, and one of them turned again to the door, most likely to fetch the guards, but the pope raised his hand and stopped him.

"I wrote you," Wallace said. "When I was

232

Scotland's guardian, I wrote. I begged for help. I am no longer the guardian, but I beg again." Everyone was staring at him, including the pontiff, and Wallace plunged on. "You could endorse our rights, you could forbid our enemies to attack us, you could—you could—" He tried to think of all that the pope could do. "You control the Knights Templar. They are warriors who are sworn to fight for justice and the protection of the innocents, and I swear to you that the children of Scotland need such champions. If you—If . . ."

The pope was gazing at him in bewilderment. He turned as if he had not heard and walked out.

"So you were forgiven for Bouchard's death," said the captain of the French guards who had brought Wallace to Rome. On the trip they had become friends, for they treated Wallace not as a prisoner but as an ally. Now he was waiting for Wallace, and as he emerged from the inner chambers of the Vatican, the captain clapped the Scot on the back. "You're free."

Wallace lifted his head and stared at the Frenchman. He could not yet have been told what happened inside; he must have known all along that the letters contained the request that Wallace be pardoned. But that was the only request made and the only petition the pope was willing to consider. "You knew," Wallace said. "All this time on the trail, when I hoped and planned and dreamed of finding help here, you knew I would find none."

"My mission," the captain said, "was like the letters, conducted with the secrecy of the confessional. And now I am to take you home."

"Home?"

"To France. We will release you before we reach Paris, and you will be free to go wherever you wish. I am also to provide you with money, as I did on the journey here, so that you will not be without comfort wherever you wish to go."

233

"Is that another gift of your king?"

"Don't be bitter toward our king, my friend. He arranged for you to be free."

"But he knew all along the pope would not help me."

"Perhaps. The pope is elected by cardinals. The cardinals are controlled by kings, who war against each other, and—"

"Stop. I don't want to hear any more explanations."

The French captain nodded. "I have no antidote for your disappointment," he said. He led Wallace out to where the other guards held their horses, already packed for the trip back to France. But as they stepped into their saddles, he said quietly, so that only Wallace could hear, "Well, perhaps just one. The instructions for your care on this journey came not from a king . . . but from a princess."

And saying nothing more, the captain turned his horse and led his company back the way they had come.

54

WITHIN HIS NEW CASTLE OVERLOOKING THE RICH LANDS HE now controlled, at the edge of a beautiful loch teeming with fish, surrounded by towering mountains dusted with snow, Mornay lay in what for him now masqueraded as sleep. It had been years since he had passed a night in peaceful slumber. He was now lord of everything as far as he could see; he had directed that an opulent bedchamber be constructed in his new castle, and he had fashioned it for comfort. But even the great fireplace had been unable to drive the chill from his bones, and the tapestries and floor coverings, instead of providing the feeling of soft embrace he so desired, seemed to heighten his sense of being cramped and smothered.

He blamed these unpleasant sensations on many things. His builders had erected a drafty structure— let them deny to their graves, but they were at fault. His cooks were preparing the food in such a way that it sapped his strength—though they had grown fat, eating what he found untasteful. He suspected his friends, his physician, even his priest, of plotting against him.

He had always been a suspicious man, but he had slept well—until that day at Falkirk, when he had led his cavalry off the battlefield, leaving Wallace and his Highlanders to their fate. But Mornay refused to account for his sleeplessness in this way. "No!" he insisted, sometimes saying the word out loud when he was all alone or moaning it as he rolled about his bed as he did right now—he was not troubled by what he had done. Nor did it worry him that Wallace had never been caught. He had not been caught because he was dead, his body lost forever in some god-forsaken forest where he had dropped in starvation never to rise again or down some isolated gorge where he had fallen, breaking his stubborn skull, or out upon some moor where the birds had stripped the flesh from his bones. The phantom bands of marauders who raided the borderlands in the years since Falkirk were but lawless Highlanders, doing what the Highlanders always had done; they were not led by William Wallace, as the village wags all liked to say. "No!" Mornay was not afraid of Wallace. He was gone, never to return.

Except in Mornay's dreams, where every night Wallace did return. Then Mornay saw his face on the field at Falkirk, though on the day of the actual battle he had been too far away to see Wallace's features when Mornay led his men away. Yet now Mornay could see that face staring at him, the eyes unblinking, burning through him right into his soul. He was alive in those dreams! He would never go away!

Tonight Mornay had a new dream. Wallace was

riding toward him. Tonight it was Mornay on foot, surrounded by his enemies, with Wallace riding—and not away, but toward him . . . closer . . . closer!

Mornay awoke, sweating though still cold. He rubbed his face, looked about him to assure himself he was still within his castle and its safety, and rolled over to burrow back beneath the furs of his bed. But then he heard a noise and sat up. He heard hoofbeats. And not outside his castle but within! It was not possible. He pressed his hands to his face, squeezed his head, felt the bristle of his beard against his palms to drive out what had to be the lingering echo of his dream.

Still he heard the sound. Hoofbeats! They were growing louder, the clatter of hoof on stone, rising up the spiraling stairway of his bedchamber tower. He heard shouts, too, screams from below. The human noises did not alarm him; they seemed real, human, comforting. But what were these hoofbeats that could not exist?

Then silence; it seemed to hang outside his doorway. Mornay stared at that door. Had it all been a nightmare after all?

Then the door exploded inward, propelled by the hooves of a rearing horse.

Into the bedroom rode William Wallace.

The shouts of Mornay's guards, pursuing him up the stairway, flew in with Wallace like leaves blown through the open door. The guards were close behind, but Wallace seemed not to heed them. He looked at Mornay sitting straight up with the covers pulled up against his chest.

Wallace drew the broadsword from the scabbard at his back. Mornay never moved or spoke. His eyelids did not twitch, his eyes seemed not to see. Wallace's sword cut through his neck in one stroke.

For a moment the guards at the door froze as Mornay had. But there was no retreat for them, as other guards, the castle's entire garrison, was flowing up the stairs behind them in pursuit of the intruder.

They gathered in the corridor just outside the bedroom door. They had William Wallace trapped! That he had ridden over the sentries into the courtyard, up the stairs—it was shocking, it had taken them all by surprise. But now he could go nowhere, could not manuever within this room. They had him! A single coordinated rush and they could finish him. The king's reward would be theirs!

Wallace snatched a pelt from the bed, threw it over his horse's eyes, and kicked the animal's flanks. The horse jumped forward, blind, and crashed through the shutters and out the window.

Horse and rider plunged down, down. Past the sheer walls of the castle, past its natural stone foundation, and into the loch.

High above its surface, Mornay's guards and the castle servants clustered at the windows and looked down in awe. They could scarcely believe the feat; as they watched the water returning to its rest, they found themselves praying in silence that he would live through the fall; surely he could not! And yet he had made the jump so quickly, as if he'd planned it all along. He must have planned to die, for the water remained quiet.

But there he was! Wallace and the horse surfaced. They swam to the shore of the loch.

The guards and servants of Mornay's castle were cheering from the battlements as Wallace reached the shore, drew his horse to his feet, jumped upon his back, and rode away.

55

MORNAY DEAD BY THE HAND OF WALLACE! THE NEWS OF it burned through the Scottish countryside. So fast did word travel that by the time Craig heard of it, traveled to Mornay's castle and then on to the Bruce's, in every village he passed, he heard drunken chanting: "Wal—lace! Wal—lace! Wal—lace!"

Craig found the young Bruce walking the battlements of his own castle, hearing the same chant, coming up to him from the tavern of the village at the base of the castle hill. The Bruce snapped around the moment he saw Craig and said before Craig could greet him, "Is it true about Mornay?"

Craig nodded, his face drawn and tight. "I had to go see for myself. The tales about Wallace, they're so fantastical—he's here, he's there, he materializes out of darkness, he rides horses up castle towers—no one could believe such stories! But . . . this one is no rumor. It must have been Wallace himself. He rode up the stairway—and not up the outside of the tower wall, as some of the wags suggest! But Mornay is dead, cut down with one stroke."

Craig handed him the blood-stained nightshirt Mornay had worn. The Bruce took it with eager hands, and Craig was surprised to observe that he seemed to admire rather than to fear Wallace's apparent return.

"And he rode through the window? My God!" Bruce said. Looking up and noticing the disturbance on Craig's face, Bruce turned away and stepped to the wall overlooking the village, from which the cries of *Wal—lace! Wal—lace!* still rang up to them. "Don't you see?" Robert said. "Those people down there, chanting his name, they take him as a hero. And a hero he is. But he's not magic. He's real. Don't you see? He's real!"

Craig most emphatically did not see. What could be young Bruce's point? What could he possibly see in Wallace that filled him with excitement rather than dread? It was almost as if, in Wallace, young Bruce had found something—and in discovering it in Wallace had discovered it also in himself! But what was it? Craig was baffled, even angry at Bruce, who seemed drunk, frivolous, insane!

Trying to explain, as if he knew Craig's thoughts, Bruce said, "He *planned* what he did! Think about it! He didn't ride into Mornay's castle like a madman, with no—well, yes, I mean he did ride in like a madman, like a man possessed of demons, which he is but—he has his angels, too!" Bruce's words were tumbling, trying to keep up with his thoughts, but both were coming too fast. "What I mean—What I mean is—he has his passion and his pain, he lives with it all, he uses it all, he is willing to give up his life, and that is why he would think of an action that the rest of us could never imagine. We think first of our own preservation. He plans for his preservation, but that is not his goal."

"I don't—I have no idea what you are trying to say."

"He rode out the window. Forced the horse through. Must have blinded it some way, yes?"

Craig nodded, surprised at Bruce's perception. "Yes. The guards said he threw a pelt from the bed over the horse's eyes to trick the animal into doing something so insane."

"But it was not insane! It was the sanest thing he could do! By calling him insane, you deny his courage—a madman is without fear and thus without bravery. But Wallace! He rode into Mornay's castle, right through the spears of his guard's, into Mornay's bedchamber, and took his life and rode out the window as he had planned to do before he ever rode into the castle!" Bruce had turned to Craig and now grabbed his shoulder. "He is a man—like you and me. If we say he is not, that he is more or less, than we—then we are saying we can never be like him. But we can be. We must be."

Robert the Bruce turned back to the battlement. Craig stared at him for a long time, as the wind blew chilly against their faces and carried the sound of Wallace's name up from the village. He had grown bored with young Bruce's raptures. There were facts to be dealt with, and old Craig wanted those made clear. "So the sum of it all," Craig said, "is that you believe Mornay's killer was definitely Wallace, and—"

Robert laughed. "Of *course* it was William Wallace! Who else could it have been?"

"—and that this was not an act of wild irrationality but a carefully planned and executed act of reprisal."

"Yes, yes, yes . . . ," Bruce said as if the whole conversation had become tedious to him.

"Then . . . ," Craig persisted, "if he came for Mornay that way—"

"You understand me at last," Bruce said in a tired, dry voice. "He's coming for everybody. You. Me. All of us. He'll kill us all. Exactly as he should."

Bruce handed Mornay's nightshirt back to Craig and added, "Go show the others. Tell them to run or pray. Though I doubt either will do them any good."

Nicolette was in bed when she heard the news—but she was not alone. It was well over an hour before she could excuse herself from the gentleman who shared with her the tidings and could carry them to the princess.

She burst into Isabella's apartments and could scarcely wait to start spouting all she had been told until she had shut the door safely behind her. But then turning round, she saw the princess upon her knees beside the bed in an attitude of prayer, her hands stretched out before her, her face upon the covers. "Isabella?" Nicolette asked, moving forward.

The princess lifted her head. Tears were flowing from her eyes, and her mouth was smiling.

She had heard already.

56

LONGSHANKS AND EDWARD WERE IN THE ROYAL GARDENS, resplendent with the spring. Longshanks pulled a new flower and crushed it in his yellowed hand. "His legend grows! It will be worse than before!"

"You let Wallace escape your whole army. You cannot blame me for this," Edward shot back.

Longshanks glowered at his son, then saw the princess crossing the grass toward them in quick, determined steps. These days everything about the woman struck Longshanks as decisive. He approved of her in a way he had never approved of his son.

"Good day to you, m'lords," the princess greeted them.

"You mock us with a smile?" Edward said.

"I am cheerful with a plan to soothe your miseries. All of England shudders with the news of renewed rebellion," she said.

"Wallace's followers," Edward said, wanting to dismiss her. He had come to despise the way his father listened carefully to everything she said and only poured derision on whatever sprang from his mouth.

Isabella's response was prompt, almost curt. "Wallace himself. If you wish to pretend a ghost rallies new volunteers in every Scottish town, I leave you to your hauntings. However, if you wish to take him, I know a way."

241

Edward snickered, but his wife was steel.

"I have faced him. Have you?" she demanded.

Prince Edward's eyes flared, but Longshanks lifted a hand before him. "Let her speak," the king commanded.

"He will fight you forever. But what does he fight for? Freedom first and peace. So grant them," the princess explained.

"The little cow is insane—" Edward argued to his father.

But Isabella went on as if he was not there. "Grant, as you do everything else, with treachery. Offer him a truce to discuss terms, and send me to my castle at Locharmbie as your emissary. He trusts me. Pick thirty of your finest assassins for me to take along." She looked from king to prince back to king. "And I will set the meeting and the ambush."

Longshanks studied her. Her eyes were steely; she would not look away. "You see, my delicate son?" Longshanks said. "I have picked you a queen."

57

THE PRINCESS'S FORTRESS IN THE ENGLISH NORTHERN BORDERlands was a small, picturesque castle clinging to the coastal rocks of eastern Britain. Its walls were rough and considered ancient, even in the year 1305. They would never had withstood the battering of the great seige towers that kings like Longshanks had brought into fashion. Its moat was shallow and fringed with moss; ducks and the petals of wildflowers floated in its once-forbidding waters. But Isabella could stand atop its bannered keep and look across the sea channel toward France.

Yet she was not thinking of France as her entourage

moved through the gates and they closed behind her. She stepped out of the carriage and moved into the castle's great hall, where there stood thirty killers. Isabella stopped and stood before them, studying their faces. Many had been in the army, where they had acquired personal reputations for exacting the king's vengeance with particular enthusiasm; others were private assassins and had never belonged to any organization apart from the bloodthirsty brotherhood they shared with those around them. The princess, allowed by Longshanks to have complete discretion in all details of the plot against Wallace, had given the king's advisors specific criteria for how these men should be chosen, and as she looked around her, she saw that her directives had been faithfully followed.

The corps was led by Longshanks's chief assassin, a cutthroat with a mangled eye. He tilted his huge head toward her in what was meant to pass as a bow of respect and said, "We came in small groups, so the rebels would not suspect."

"And you have reached Wallace's men?" the princess asked.

"We tell the villagers, and the traitors pass it on. All that's left is for you to say where the ambush will take place."

"Where . . . ," the princess mused. "Where. Yes, I have been thinking about that."

58

WALLACE SAT IN THE GROVE OF TREES WHERE MURRON WAS buried. The sun, dappling through the budded trees, was warm upon his shoulders. He had not eaten for longer than he could remember and was aware that he must, but it was only a thought in a corner of his brain, not a need like this was, to be here and drink in the silence of Murron's memory.

He needed to dream of her. She had not been in his dreams for many nights. He missed her there.

He heard a rustle behind him and spun around, drawing the broadsword instinctively, before he saw—

Hamish and Stephen!

Hamish started forward, then lurched to a stop, unsure if he had done the right thing in coming here to William's holy, secret place and bringing Stephen along as well. But his fears flew away as Wallace moved up and threw his arms around both of his friends.

They spent that night in the old secret cave, where their fathers had come to plan their own raids, with no more support than they had now. They felt at home within the dark stone walls; rain was falling outside, but it was dry inside the cave, with a campfire that smoldered at its entrance, so that the smoke stayed out and the heat drifted in. They shared a fine meal—lamb that Hamish had brought and a cask of ale provided by Stephen and his close associate, the Almighty. William told them about France and his visit with the pope. His friends listened in silence. He left out details of the princess but told them of his efforts—and disappointments—to enlist outside help for Scotland. He concluded, "So that is all. There is no one outside to help us."

Still Hamish and Stephen said nothing. They stared at the fire and poked their boots with sticks; they listened to the rain fall; they sat with William and would have been content to stay that way forever.

At last Wallace said, "Thanks for the food and the drink. And for bringing 'em yourselves."

"We're not leaving," Hamish said.

"No. Somebody has to stay alive," Wallace said.

"We've already talked about it," Hamish said, glancing at Stephen, who nodded and grinned.

"We don't want to stay alive if we can't fight beside ya," the Irishman said. "And there's many more like us! Though we hardly need 'em. With you, Hamish, me, and the Almighty, we've got everybody outnumbered." From a hidden pocket of his cloak he pulled a jug of whiskey. He took a swig and handed it to Hamish, who took a chug and passed the whiskey along to Wallace, who declined, but smiled for the first time in many weeks.

"There is . . . one thing, William," Hamish said. "Longshanks is offering a truce. He has dispatched his daughter-in-law as his emissary, and she has sent word that she wishes to meet you."

Wallace's green eyes were fixed on Hamish, whose red brows furrowed like a pensive sunset. He knew William was wondering why he had taken so long to mention this—but the details were just so troubling! "The instructions were passed along to us with great care," Hamish said. "The man who told me was told by her messengers that he must remember the invitation exactly."

"Yes?" William said, growing impatient. "Go on."

"Well . . . she says she knows you would not wish to discuss a truce in her castle at Locharmbie, since that would not seem secure to you. Therefore she proposes that you meet here in a neutral, common place, where you can discuss the truce in absolute safety."

"And what is this place?" Wallace asked, wondering why Hamish was so troubled by it.

"It . . . it's a barn."

59

THE BARN STOOD IN A FLAT CLEARING BORDERED ON THREE sides by a thick forest of fir trees and on the other by the abandoned farm whose other buildings had already been cleared away. The barn itself looked sturdy, its stone side walls still sound, its timbers supporting a thickly thatched roof in fresh repair.

Wallace, Hamish, and Stephen rode in from the farm side. They stopped for a long moment and surveyed the barn and the woods around it; night was falling, and all was quiet. Before the main door of the barn stood two men dressed in the blue fleur-de-lis tunics of the French guards who had accompanied the princess on her last mission of truce. A white flag sagged from a pole thrust into the roof thatch, and the sight of it, hanging above a barn in peaceful summons, seemed to give Wallace a chill. But in full view of the barn, he handed Hamish his sword and rode forward.

Within the dark shadows of the barn, the assassins waited, their killing knives ready. Their leader was peering out a crack in the wooden planking above the stone side walls. "It's William Wallace, sure!" he whispered sharply to the others. "And . . . he's given up his sword! Be ready!"

They positioned themselves along the side walls, backing and squatting into the deepest shadows and clustering around both doors and even the single window so that nothing could come in from any direction without encountering a swarm of blades.

Outside the barn, Wallace and his two friends dismounted, tied their horses to a scrub tree, and moved toward the door. The two men in the blue tunics nodded to him, and Wallace said, "You first."

They hesitated only a moment and did not argue, proceeding through the door.

Wallace, instead of entering, grabbed the heavy bar and sealed the door! At this motion, Scots sprung from the woods in all directions.

The assassins inside had prepared for everything but this. The back door was blocked just as the front had been before they realized the ambush was being turned on them. Then when the window was chocked full of dead wood and all was suddenly dark inside, they began to panic.

But the Scots outside, scrambling up from their hiding places among the trees, did not notice the shouting from within the barn and the pounding on its doors. They placed tinder-dry brush and pitch against the barn and set it on fire. In moments the entire barn was blazing. The Scots stood back and watched the barn burn, their faces lit by the flames. After a while, there were no more screams from within.

From her castle, the princess saw the burning off in the distance, like a bonfire. She stood in a window of the old keep, staring out at the far-off glow. And then she saw, on a near hillside, silhouetted against the night and the fire, a rider.

He sat there, motionless in his saddle, looking up at the castle.

Isabella ran from her room, up one staircase, then another, and still another, and still another, until she stood on the pinnacle of the castle, so that she, too, was silhouetted, backed by the rising moon, praying that he could see her.

The lone rider was William Wallace.

On the northern side of the castle, the land fell away sharply from the castle's rocky foundations, and it was on that side of the compound that the stables stood. Beside them, built into the outer wall, was a cottage, intended as living quarters for the chief groom. But no groom was in residence since the princess had not yet stocked her stables, and it was in a window of this cottage that she placed a candle, backed by a brass reflector, that burned into the night like a tiny beacon.

For two hours the princess sat alone beside that candle, wondering if her signal was going to work. It was a twenty-foot climb, hand over hand up the mortared stones, to reach the cottage's window; she knew that would not deter him if he was going to come.

At last she heard the faint noise outside. She drew back from the window and waited.

He reached the safety of the window cove and knelt on the ledge. He looked through the window and saw her inside.

For a long, long moment the two of them looked at each other. Then in one more quick movement he pressed his shoulders through the window opening and was inside.

They faced each other in the faint glow of the candle.

"A meeting in a barn. It had to be a trap. And only you would know I would be aware of it," he said.

"It does me good to see you," she told him.

"I am much diminished since we met."

She wanted to say something—to tell him that, yes, he looked hungrier, wilder, than he had looked before and that the very sight of him made her heart pound in her chest and her face burn, but instead she looked away and muttered, "There will be a new shipment of supplies coming north next month. Food and weapons. They will trav—"

"No. Stop. I didn't come here for that."

"Then why did you come?"

"Why did you?"

"Because of the way you're looking at me now. The same way . . . as when we met."

He turned his face away. She moved to him, touched his cheek gently, and pulled his face toward her again. "I know," she said. "You looked at me . . . and saw her."

He twisted suddenly back toward the window. He was leaving.

"You must forgive me what I feel!" she said. "No man has ever looked at me as you did."

He stopped and looked back to her.

"You have . . . you have a husband," he said.

"I have taken vows. More than one. I've vowed faithfulness to my husband and sworn to give him a son. And I cannot keep both promises."

Slowly, he began to realize just what she was asking of him, and an unexpected smile played at his lips. Her smile lit up also. "You understand," she said. "Consider, before you laugh and say no. You will never own a throne, though you deserve one. But just as the sun will rise tomorrow, some man will rule England. And what if his veins ran not with the blood of Longshanks but with that of a true king?"

"I cannot love you for the sake of revenge," he said quietly.

"No. But can you love me for the sake of all you loved and lost? Or simply love me . . . because I love you?"

Slowly, he reached to the candleflame and pinched it out.

60

THE FIRST RAYS OF MORNING SPREAD YELLOW LIGHT through the room and across their faces, their bodies limp and entwined upon the warm and tousled blankets of the straw-mattressed bed. Wallace awoke with a start: sunlight!

He grabbed for his clothes, as she, too, awoke suddenly; she covered herself with the blanket and jumped out of bed, rushing to the window to look out, then drawing back quickly. "No one! Hurry!" she said.

He hurried to the window, leaned out, and saw a clear path down the wall to safety. He saw no guards along the base of the wall, no one between the castle foundation and the far rill where he had hidden his horse—and yet it was past dawn, already fully day!

In her arms he had lost all sense of danger, all sense of anything but her. And as much as he needed now to hurry, he stopped and turned to her and touched her face one last time.

He climbed out onto the ledge of the window. She touched his arm, and he lingered again. She had to ask him: "When we . . . did you think of her?"

He looked straight into her eyes and kissed her—her, not Murron—and climbed out.

She stood in the window and watched him all the way down the wall, across the heather, to the rill, until he was out of sight.

On his way back from the castle, William stopped at the secret grove where Murron lay. He remained there alone for many hours.

Night had fallen when he reached the cave and found Hamish and Stephen huddled by the fire, drinking whiskey. They watched as he tied his horse beside theirs and took his place at the fire. He said nothing.

"Scouting?" Hamish asked, though he knew where his friend had gone.

Still Wallace said nothing. Stephen offered him the jug, but Wallace shook his head and stared at the fire.

When the fire had burned to smoldering ash, and Hamish and Stephen lay asleep, Wallace still sat awake. Without sleep and without dreams.

When Hamish heard a rustling and opened his eyes to the chill gray light of dawn, he saw William saddling his horse. Hamish punched Stephen, who opened his bleary eyes and squinted painfully at the same sight. Instinctively both men lurched to their feet, staggering with their hangover.

"Too fookin' early!" Stephen groaned.

"Tell it ta God," Hamish mumbled.

"He ain't up yet," Stephen said.

Wallace mounted and rode off; Hamish and Stephen had to scramble to catch him.

61

THAT VERY AFTERNOON THEY ATTACKED AN ENGLISH TAXA-tion post, though it was broad daylight and the post was guarded by a dozen soldiers. Only a few stood to fight; the rest ran in all directions, recognizing the figure who charged them as the unkillable Scottish terror, William Wallace.

With the post still flaming behind them, Wallace led them on toward the garrison where the tax collectors were headquartered, reaching it before any of the escaped soldiers could and burning it to the ground as well. William, Hamish, and Stephen had more help than they needed; the villagers, when they saw Wallace riding past, his blond hair flying and his broadsword bright with blood, dropped what they were doing and ran to follow him.

They attacked for two days without sleep, zigzagging through the countryside, striking out at everything that represented Longshanks and his royal domination. On the second night Hamish and Stephen convinced William to steal a few hours sleep in the wool shed of a farmer they had known for many years, a clansman who had fought beside them at Stirling. But again William was up before the dawn, seeking more royal soldiers to attack and drive from his country.

They camped in the forest that night, bone weary, eating the few bits of bread and dried meat the farmer had been able to spare them. And once again, Wallace sat staring at the fire.

"Rest, William," Hamish pleaded.

"I rest," William said.

"Your rest is making me exhausted."

Stephen offered the jug; Wallace shook his head. "Come," Stephen urged, "it'll help you sleep."

"Aye. But it won't let me dream," William said.

He pulled a tattered tartan around himself and lay down.

62

THAT SAME NIGHT LONGSHANKS SAT BY A PALACE HEARTH, where a huge blaze burned. Still he was huddled beneath a blanket, and he coughed blood. But he ignored the ice in his lungs; his mind was plotting.

The princess walked her parapets alone, lost in her own thoughts.

Wallace lay in the forest, dreamless beneath the stars.

And Robert the Bruce climbed reluctantly to the uppermost room of his father's castle, summoned by a servant who said it was the old man's urgent request that he come. Robert reached the door, found it unlocked, and entered without waiting. Moving into the suffocating darkness, heavy with his reluctance to be there, Robert took his seat across from his father, already at the table. The single candle burned between them, and in its light young Bruce saw that his father was cloaked more heavily than before. "You wished to see me, Father?"

"Yes. We both did."

Robert heard a movement behind him and spun around to see Craig, leader of the Scottish council, standing against the wall behind Robert. Young Bruce was surprised to see that his father had revealed his disease to the old noble.

"Yes, I've shown him," the elder Bruce said. "I'm dying anyway, no use to hide. But Longshanks, too, is failing. We are becoming the past—as you become the future." The leper, feeling the weight of his infirmity —or was it the weight of something else?—sagged back and looked to Craig, who shifted forward, but only a half step; clearly he did not wish to be too close.

"Our nobles are frightened and confused," Craig said. "Wallace has the commoners stirred up again, from the Highland clans to the Lowland villages. In another six months Christ and the Apostles could not govern this country."

Robert glanced to his father; it was clear to the younger Bruce that his father had already been discussing something with Craig, and the two ancient noblemen, veterans of many decades of politics together, had agreed on something, something Craig was about to present.

But Craig was working up to it gradually. "Longshanks knows his son will scarcely be able to rule England, much less half of France. He needs Scotland settled, and he trusts you, after Falkirk. If you pay him homage, he will recognize you as king of Scotland. Our nobles have agreed to this as well."

From within his woolen wrap, he withdrew and extended a parchment bearing the noblest names in Scotland. Young Bruce barely glanced at it and said, "If I pay homage to another's throne, then how am I a king?"

"Homage is nothing!" Craig said impatiently. "It is the crown that matters!"

But young Bruce was intense with new clarity and the strength that came with it. "The crown is that of Scotland," he said. "And Scotland is William Wallace."

"Yes," Craig said, glancing at the elder Bruce, "that is another matter. For something else is required before all this can take place. You and William Wallace must meet. And make peace."

Robert was surprised. He looked to his father, who said, without lifting his cloudy eyes back at him, "Yes. At last I have seen that this is the way for both of you to have what you want."

63

In Lanark, where it all began, the villagers paused their baking and hammering and watched as three of Scotland's elder nobles, among them Craig, rode past their cottages. In the village square, on the very spot Murron was killed, the nobles stopped, and Craig announced, "We seek an audience with Wallace!"

The elders paused, staring around at the villagers, who had adopted fixed expressions that tried to say, "We have no idea who Wallace is or why you look for him among us."

Craig expected such a response. "We will wait beyond the village, at the edge of the loch!" Craig called out. "We will go to him however he wishes us to go!"

Craig and his comrades rode slowly past the silent villagers.

The half moon had risen into a clear, star-dazzled sky above the Scottish forest. In the hidden encampment where Wallace and a corps of his staunchest followers were planning the next raid, there was a commotion; the sentries had spotted the approach of a cluster of men and silently spread the alarm. Wallace and all the others were waiting with drawn swords as the nobles, their heads hooded, were led in on horseback by loyalists from the village. When Wallace stepped out from behind the trees, the nobles were stopped and their hoods pulled off. Nervously they glanced about them.

"Sir Craig. Out in the moonlight?" Wallace asked.

"Sir William. We come to seek a meeting," Craig said.

"You've all sworn to Longshanks."

"An oath to a liar is no oath at all. An oath to a patriot is a vow indeed. Every man of us is ready to swear loyalty to you," Craig declared.

"So let the council swear publicly then."

"We cannot," Craig said. "Some scarcely believe you are alive. Others think you'll pay them Mornay's wages. We bid you to Edinburgh. Meet us at the city gates two days from now at sunset. Pledge us your pardon and we will unite behind you. Scotland will be one."

Wallace glanced at Hamish and Stephen, who could barely hide their contempt. Wallace looked at the nobles. "One?" Wallace said. "You mean us and you?"

"I mean this," Craig said and reached to his pocket.

The surrounding Highlanders, any one of whom would felt honored to stab a dagger through a blueblood's heart, all lifted their blades. But what Craig withdrew was not a weapon; it was small, folded, limp. He extended it toward Wallace.

Then Wallace snatched it from Craig's grasp. It was the handkerchief, clean and bright, still bearing Murron's embroidered thistle, that Wallace lost at Falkirk in his encounter with the Bruce. Wallace stared at it, its soft folds bathed in the starlight, a relic he had thought gone forever, now returned to him from the unlikeliest source.

And he understood something else: the Bruce had found it, had saved it all this time. The significance of that, too, was not lost on Wallace.

When the Bruce had given Craig the handkerchief and told him to present it to Wallace as a sign of his sincerity, Craig had not understood what possible meaning such a simple object could have. But now he saw the effect on Wallace and said, "The Bruce will be there. He begs you to come and join him as a brother to unite Scotland as one family."

Wallace, Hamish, and Stephen retreated to the cave. Wallace had been silent since the nobles were rehooded and led away, and with every moment of Wallace's silence, Hamish's anger had grown. Finally, as Wallace stood at the mouth of the cave and stared up at the sky, Hamish could restrain himself no longer and blurted, "Why do you even pretend to wonder? You know it's a trap!"

"Maybe," Wallace said quietly. "Probably."

"Then . . . Then . . . ," Hamish could only sputter. He looked to Stephen for help, but the Irishman only shook his head.

"We can't win alone, Hamish," Wallace said. "We know that. Joining with the nobles is the only hope for our people."

"I don't want to be a martyr!" Hamish barked.

"Nor I! I want to live! I want a home and children and peace. I've asked God for those things. But He's brought me this sword. And if He wills that I must lay it down to have what He wants for my country, then I'll do that, too."

"That's just a dream, William!"

"We've lived a dream together. A dream of freedom!"

Hamish was shouting now. "Your dreams aren't about freedom! They're about Murron! You have to be a hero, because you think she sees you! Is that it?"

Wallace was quiet for a long moment. "My dreams

256

of Murron are gone. I killed them myself. If I knew I could live with her on the other side of death, I'd welcome it."

And that settled it. Hamish and Stephen saw that William was going to the meeting with the nobles, and nothing they could say or do could keep him from it.

64

WILLIAM, HAMISH, AND STEPHEN RODE TOWARD EDINburgh, talking little, not hurrying, knowing this could be their last ride. When they reached the top of the last hill, they stopped and looked down at the road leading into the city. Wallace handed his dagger to Stephen and unbuckled his broadsword and gave it to Hamish.

"No," Hamish said. "Keep these. We're going, too."

"No. One of us is enough," Wallace said.

"Nay. We decided it last night. We're comin' with you," Stephen said.

"I have to keep my courage. See, my hands already shake." Wallace held his hand out before them, and his friends could see the tremble, but it seemed to be from emotion, not fear. He said almost casually, "Whatever happens, if I know you're alive, I can bear it."

He leaned from his saddle and hugged them, Stephen first, then Hamish, whose great freckled cheeks bore twin rivulets of tears. But still Hamish seemed angry. "What will I do if I'm left alive and you're gone?" he demanded.

William looked at him for a long time. "Tell our story," he said. "Let our people dream."

With one last look at his friends, William Wallace rode away.

The house designated for the meeting was a two-story stone manor owned by Lord Monteith. The grounds around it were landscaped and manicured, but no servants were tending the gardens now; the house itself looked quiet as Wallace rode toward it.

Within the house, Robert the Bruce and Craig stood at the hearth of its central room, waiting. The Bruce had noticed that Craig had seemed particularly edgy since their arrival twenty minutes before, but then the Bruce was strained as well. He looked out the window; nothing yet.

"He won't come," Craig said.

"He will. I know he will," Robert said.

They heard the approach of a single horse. Robert looked out to see Wallace arriving.

"Here he is. And unarmed," the Bruce said. "My God, he has a brave heart."

They waited as Wallace reached the front door and dismounted, counting the moments as he tied his horse to the hitching post himself, since there was no groom waiting to do it for him. But before he could step to the doorway, two more riders appeared. "His friends," the Bruce said, looking out.

"No matter," Craig said. "They are welcome."

But outside, Wallace was not so welcoming; he glared at Hamish and Stephen, who shrugged off his disapproval of their presence. "We're here," Hamish said, dismounting. "That's all there is to it. So you may as well go right on, for we aren't leaving."

So it was three, not one, who entered the front door and then appeared at the broad opening into the house's main room. There Wallace stopped, facing the Bruce.

Wallace reached into his shirt and took out the handkerchief, a symbol now to both of them. They looked at each other, their eyes saying everything. Truce. Peace. A future for Scotland.

Wallace stepped forward to clasp the Bruce's hand.

And then the soldiers poured from every closet, every doorway, even leaping down from the balcony overhead.

Too late, Robert the Bruce understood. *"Nooo!!"* he screamed. But it did not matter. The soldiers— English professionals—were swarming Wallace and his friends. Wallace was stunned instantly by a man dropping onto him from above; Stephen was knocked senseless in the first rush; Hamish was smothered by three men—and sent them all flying like a dog shaking off water. One of the three bounced back from the wall, producing a dagger and plunging it high into Hamish's shoulder.

"No blades!" one of the soldiers was shouting. "All alive!" Wallace had already disappeared beneath a blanket of men; the others began clubbing at Hamish. Craig had darted back the moment the assault began, but the Bruce, at the edge of the melee, charged into it. Because of the truce, he had dressed without weapons, but he threw his fists into the faces of the soldiers. But they were ganging in from all sides; hiding such numbers within the house had been a marvel of cunning. They trussed Wallace like a netted lion, while their leader, with an expertly placed blow to the temple, dropped Bruce senseless.

The soldiers raised their clubs over the fallen Hamish and Stephen, ready to beat them to death. "Forget them!" shouted their leader, fearful that any moment more Scots would appear to fight for Wallace as they had in the past. "Go! Go!"

In a quick scramble, the soldiers hauled Wallace outside. A wagon with a team of horses was just then rattling up from its place of concealment within the manor's hedge maze. In seconds they had Wallace lashed down on the wagon's wood floor.

Stephen and Hamish, bloody and still stunned, staggered from the house in blind fury. Their horses were gone, and the wagon was already to the top of the hill.

Hamish ran after it.

Stephen knew it was hopeless. "You'll never catch them!" he shouted. "You'll never . . ." He watched Hamish running, ready to explode his heart in pursuit.

And Stephen ran, too.

65

DRIED BLOOD STILL MATTING HIS HAIR, ROBERT THE BRUCE surged up the stairs of his father's tower and tore open the door to the chamber. "You did this! You!" he screamed, grabbing at his father, too furious to flinch from the leprous flesh. "I hate you, you rotting bastard!"

His father was calm, no pain in his body, no pain anywhere. "Longshanks required Wallace," he said. "So did our nobles. That was the price of our peace. And your crown."

Robert shook him. "Die! I want you to die!"

"Soon enough, I'll be dead. And you'll be king."

"I want nothing of you! You're no man! And you are not my father!"

But the cold steel at the soul of the leper stiffened in him one more time. "You are my son. And you have always known my mind."

"No . . . no," young Robert said. "You deceived me."

"You let yourself be deceived. But in your heart, you always knew what had to happen. The only thing that could happen."

Robert's hands fell away from his father. He stepped backward; even his legs had lost their will. He staggered to the wall and groped at it for support. All he could think was that he no longer cared to live in this world. And suddenly it was his father who seemed to have all the strength.

"At last you know what it means to hate and how to deal with enemies," the elder Bruce said. "Now you are ready to be a king."

66

WILLIAM WALLACE WAS CONVEYED TO LONDON STRAPPED to the spine of an unsaddled horse, his head bare to the sun. A procession of heavily armed English soldiers paraded with him, as country people came out to jeer the Scotsman who had sent such terror through their bones.

"Don't look so fearsome, does he?!" some shouted, while others screamed, "Murderer!" and many more said nothing at all but threw rocks against his battered face and back or rotten fruit or worse.

While in the royal palace, Prince Edward inspected his father, who lay semiconscious in bed, his breath rattling ominously in his chest. The king knew of the successful capture of his hated enemy, at least he had been informed of it before he had another attack of coughing and smothering and his eyes began to roll separately from each other and he collapsed into the stupor in which he now lay. Longshanks was upon his deathbed, of that his son was certain.

Edward approved of this condition. He gave no instructions to the servants keeping vigil at the bedside.

As the prince left his father's apartments and stepped out into the corridor, the princess hurried up to her husband and followed him as he moved toward his own rooms. "Is it true?" she asked, barely able to keep her breath. "Wallace is captured?"

"Simply because he eluded your trap, do you think he is more than a man? My father is dying. Perhaps you should think of our coronation," Edward answered and continued his march down the hall.

"When will his trial be?" she persisted.

"Wallace's? For treason there is no trial. Tomorrow he will be charged, then executed." With a faint smile, he shut his bedroom door in her face.

67

WILLIAM WALLACE WAS TRIED IN WESTMINSTER HALL—IF what occurred can be called a trial. He was not allowed to speak during the proceedings meant to establish his guilt and his punishment, and neither he nor anyone who might have dared to step forward for him was permitted to offer any defense or arguments on his behalf. Wallace made no effort to object to these conditions and stood in silence, gazing up at the windows as six royal magistrates in scarlet robes decried against him, shouting accusations of an endless litany of atrocities.

The slaughter of his enemies, in battle or in ambush, Wallace would never deny. But one of the charges hurled against him that day bears witness to the posture of his judges. They repeated the claim—spread through all of Britain after the sacking of York—that Wallace had spared the nuns of that city in order to force them to dance naked before his troops. The lie in fact attested to a deeper truth, for the propaganda of the dancing nuns had been spread by Longshanks's advisors in an attempt to explain the fact, widely known, that Wallace had spared the lives of the nuns at York, whereas Longshanks, in sacking Scottish towns, had spared no one at all.

Finally the chief of the royal judges boomed out, "William Wallace! You stand in taint of high treason. You will be conducted to a place of execution, where you will be hanged, disemboweled, castrated, and beheaded! Have you anything to say?"

Wallace did not object to the punishment; it was the charge itself that he rejected. "Treason?" he asked. "Against whom?"

"Against thy king, thou vile fool!"

"Never, in my whole life, did I swear allegiance to your king—"

"It matters not, he is thy king!" the magistrate tried to shout over him.

"—while many who serve him have taken and broken his oath many times. I cannot commit treason if I have never been his subject!"

"Confess, and you may receive a quick death! Deny, and you must be purified by pain! Do you confess?" The magistrate's voice deepened with finality: *"Do you confess?!"*

"I do not confess," Wallace said.

"Then you shall receive thy purification," said the lord high magistrate who would oversee the execution. Then he added, "And in the end, I promise you will beg for the ax."

68

WITHIN THE TOWER OF LONDON, WILLIAM WALLACE WAS alone in his cell, still in the garish manacles of hand and foot he had worn for the last week. He could not stand to his full height; the chain connecting wrists to ankles had been shortened to force him into a slight stoop meant to represent a posture of submission. But that did not affect him now; he was on his knees. "I am so afraid," he whispered in his prayer. "Give me strength."

Outside the cell door, the jailers jumped to their feet as the princess, with not a single guard or attendant at her side, appeared at the base of the stone stairway and strode quickly up to them. "Your—Your Highness!" the jailor stammered.

"I will see the prisoner," she declared.

"We've orders from the king—"

"The king will be dead in a month! And his son is a weakling! Who do you think will rule this kingdom? Now *open this door!*"

The jailors obeyed.

The princess stepped into the reeking cell. She could barely contain her shock at the sight of Wallace. "On your feet, you filth!" the head jailer shouted as he and his partner snatched the prisoner upright.

"Stop! Leave me!" the princess demanded, but still they hesitated. "There is no way out of this hell! Leave me with him!"

Reluctantly the jailers shuffled out of the cell, but they could still see her back and hear her. She looked at Wallace's eyes and she couldn't quite hold back her tears—dangerous tears that threatened to say too much. "M'lady . . . what kindness of you to visit a stranger," Wallace said, trying to help her hide her grief.

"Sir, I . . . come to beg you to confess all and swear allegiance to the king that he might show you mercy," she said.

"Will he show mercy to my country? Will he take back his soldiers, and let us rule ourselves?" he asked her.

"Mercy . . . is to die quickly. Perhaps even live in the Tower!" Her eyes brimmed with tears and the illusion of hope. "In time, who knows what can happen if you can only live."

"If I swear to him, then everything I am is dead already," Wallace said.

She wanted to plead, she wanted to scream. She couldn't stop the tears. And the jailers were watching.

"Your people are lucky to have a princess so kind that she can grieve at the death of a stranger," he said.

She almost went too far, she pulled closer to him— but she didn't care. She whispered, pleaded, "You will die! It will be awful!"

"Every man dies. Not every man really lives."

Princess Isabella and William Wallace stared into each other's eyes. Neither knew or cared how long. Then she pulled out a hidden vial and whispered, "Drink this! It will dull your pain."

"It will numb my wits, and I must have them all. If I'm senseless or if I wail, then Longshanks will have broken me."

"I can't bear the thought of your torture! Take it!"

She pressed the vial to his mouth and poured in the drug. She heard the jailers shifting outside the cell door, trying to see what she was doing; she backed up, still looking at William, her eyes wide, full of love and good-bye. Then she turned, and keeping her face lowered, as if she could hide her tears, she was gone.

Wallace watched her go. When the door clanged shut, he spit the purple drug onto the stone floor of his cell.

69

LONGSHANKS LAY HELPLESS, HIS BODY RACKED WITH consumption. Edward sat against the wall, watching him die, glee in his stare. The princess entered. She paused at the door and watched the old king's chest

265

rising and falling; when she looked up at his waxlike face, she saw that he was looking at her. "I have come . . . ," she said, "to beg for the life of William Wallace."

"You fancy him," Edward said.

"I respect him. At worst he was a worthy enemy. Show mercy . . . oh thou great king . . . and win the respect of your own people."

Longshanks's body trembled; he was making a great effort—to speak? To lift his hand? His jaw worked and there was a gurgle from his throat, but no words came out. And then Isabella realized what the king intended: he was shaking his head.

"Even now, you are incapable of mercy?" she asked. But hatred still glowed in his eyes. The princess looked at her husband. "Nor you. To you that word is as unfamiliar as love."

Edward relished what he now had to tell her. "Before he lost his powers of speech, my lord king told me his one comfort was that he would live to know Wallace was dead."

Edward was smiling.

Isabella turned from him and moved to Longshanks's bedside. She leaned down and grabbed the dying king by the hair. The guards flanking the door started forward but the princess's eyes flared at them with more fire than even Longshanks once showed—and the guards backed off. She bent down and hissed to Longshanks, so softly that even Edward couldn't hear, "You see? Death comes to us all. And it comes to William Wallace. But before death comes to you, know this: your blood dies with you. A child who is not of your line grows in my belly. Your son will not sit long on the throne. I swear it."

She let go of the old king. He sagged like an empty sack back onto his satin pillows. Without even a look at her husband, she strode out of the room, with the rattling breath of the dying king rasping the air like a saw.

70

SMITHFIELD IS A SECTION OF LONDON LYING TWO MILES from Westminster Hall. In 1305 it was a place of butchery, where cattle were slaughtered and dismembered for the tables of the city dwellers. It was also the customary place of execution.

And so it was to Smithfield, on the twenty-third day of August of that year, that William Wallace was taken, strapped to a wooden litter and dragged by horses across the cobblestones. A crowd had filled the open, grassy square surrounded by the meat shops, and the people were in a festive mood. Hawkers sold roast chickens and beer from barrels, while street entertainers juggled and performed comic acrobatics in hopes of collecting halfpennies.

When the royal horsemen arrived dragging Wallace, the crowd fell silent. When they cut him loose and led him through the crowd, the people began to jeer and throw at him anything handy: chicken bones, rotten vegetables, rocks, empty tankards. Wallace did not react as the missles pelted off him. The bone rattling journey, bouncing across the cobblestones, may have stunned him already—or perhaps the pain of rocks thrown against his face seemed nothing to him compared to what he knew was to come.

Grim magistrates prodded Wallace, and he climbed the execution platform. On the platform were a noose, a dissection table with knives in plain view, and a chopping block with an enormous ax. Wallace did not look away from these implements of torture.

It was both to him and the crowd that the lord high magistrate announced, "We will use it all before this is over." Then his dark eyes fixed Wallace's. "Or fall to your knees now, declare yourself the king's loyal subject, and beg his mercy, and you shall have it."

He emphasized *mercy* by pointing to the ax.

Wallace was pale and trembled—but he shook his head.

The crowd grew noisier as they put the noose around Wallace's neck.

The princess heard the distant clamor from her room in the palace, and she lowered her head in helpless agony.

Helpless too were Hamish and Stephen, wearing the hooded smocks of English peasants, among the onlookers in Smithfield Square. They had come to this terrible place at this terrible moment because the only thing worse than being there was to not be there while this was happening, and they stood hoping to catch William's eye, as if in doing so they could somehow shoulder some of his pain.

Lying in his kingly bedchamber, Longshanks rattled and coughed blood, as Edward, the future king, waited for him to die.

Robert the Bruce paced along the walls of his castle in Scotland. His eyes were haunted; he looked south, toward London, and in his soul he heard the sounds of the horrible spectacle as clearly as if his own body had been pitched before the executioners.

All of them had become but observers of the event. All—the crowned heads, the nobles who contended for the thrones, the peasants, the priests, the acrobats, and the fools, even the lord high magistrate and his muscled assistants who were conducting the proceedings—were powerless and insignificant. And yet the man with his hands and feet manacled, his cheeks bloody, his heart pounding out the final rhythms of his life—he stood and faced his executioners as if the whole world turned on what he would—or would not—do now.

There on the platform, a trio of burly hooded executioners cinched a rope around Wallace's neck and hoisted him up a pole.

"That's it! Stretch him!" the crowd yelled.

The warrior who had fought alone and at the head of thousands, who had defeated great armies and sacked cities, who had struck terror in the world's mightiest nation, now dangled at the end of a rope, his face turning purple, his eyes bulging, the veins popping at his neck where the noose bit into his skin. The people cheered their approval. They knew this was not the end; much more was intended. But as the moments ticked on and on, the Scot at the end of the rope looked less to them like an enemy and more like simple flesh and blood. They grew silent, wondering at how much he could take, at how much his tormentors would extend his agony, before they lessened the torture—lessened it, that it could be extended.

The magistrate watched coldly. Even when the most experienced of the executioners gave him a look that said they were about to go too far, the magistrate prolonged the moment, then he nodded and the executioner cut the rope.

Wallace fell upon his face on the platform. The crowd cheered—not in support of him but in excitement. The sight was seductive, the lust for blood infectious. They hushed again as the magistrate leaned to Wallace and said, "Pleasant, yes? Rise to your knees, kiss the royal emblem on my cloak, and you will feel no more."

With great effort, Wallace rose to his knees.

The magistrate assumed a formal posture and offered the cloak.

Wallace struggled all the way to his feet.

"Very well then. Rack him."

The executioners slammed Wallace onto his back on the table, spread his arms and legs, and tied each to a crank. Goaded by the crowd, they pulled the ropes taut. The crowd grew quiet enough to hear the groaning of Wallace's limbs. Hamish and Stephen felt it in their own bodies.

Wallace wanted to scream, to try to blot out the agony that screamed through his body, but he would not let the sound go. The magistrate watched his struggle and smiled. "Wonderful, isn't it, that a man remains conscious through such pain. Enough?"

Wallace shook his head. The executioners drew hot irons from a fire box and pressed them to his bare body. The sound of sizzling cut through the air with the smell of the burning flesh. Some of those in the crowd groaned themselves and looked away. But still no cry escaped Wallace's lips.

Now the magistrate spoke only to him. "Do you really want this to go on? Are you sure?" And when the prisoner said nothing, the magistrate nodded to the executioners, who lifted the terrible instruments of dissection.

The disembowelment began. The magistrate leaned in beside Wallace's ear. "It can all end. Right now! Bliss. Peace. Just say it. Cry out. *Mercy!* Yes? . . . Yes?"

The crowd could not hear the magistrate, but they knew the procedure, and they, too, goaded Wallace, chanting, "Mer—cy! Mer—cy!"

Wallace's eyes rolled to the magistrate, who signaled for quiet and shouted, "The prisoner wishes to say a word!"

There was silence.

Hamish and Stephen were weeping as each in his own way prayed: "Mercy, William . . . Say 'mercy' . . ."

Wallace's eyes fluttered and cleared. He fought through the pain, struggled for one last deep breath, and screamed, *"FREEEEE—DOMMMMMM!"*

The shout rang through the town. Hamish, Stephen, everyone, on the square, heard it. The princess heard it at her open window. Longshanks and his son seemed to hear. The cry echoed as if the wind could carry it through the ends of Scotland; and Robert the Bruce, on the walls of his castle, looked up sharply as if he too had heard.

The crowd at Smithfield had never seen courage like this; even English strangers began to weep. The magistrate, angry and defeated, gave a signal.

The executioner lifted his huge ax—and Wallace looked toward the crowd.

He saw Hamish and Stephen, their eyes brimming and their faces glowing. He saw that he had won, and it was over.

The ax began to drop.

And in the last half moment of his life, when he had already stepped into the world beyond this one, he glimpsed someone standing at Hamish's shoulder. She was beautiful, smiling, serene.

She was Murron.

71

AFTER THE BEHEADING, WILLIAM WALLACE'S BODY WAS torn to pieces. His head was set on London Bridge, where passersby were invited to jeer at the man who had caused so much fear in England. His arms and legs were sent to the four corners of Britain as warning.

It did not have the effect that Longshanks planned. The story of William Wallace's torturous death and the courage with which he faced it kindled a fire in the bellies of the Scots, a blaze that could not be extinguished. They rallied behind the only man who seemed capable of leading them: Robert the Bruce.

Some Scots suspected him of involvement in Wallace's betrayal. Others found such suspicions unthinkable. All knew that Bruce was not Wallace, but he was the one, the only one, to whom they could look for leadership, for the other nobles, one by one, vacated their claims to the Scottish throne and announced their allegiance to the Bruce.

He accepted the remnants of the shattered Scottish army and declared that he would come to terms with England. And on a designated day, at the head of a ragtag army, he rode out to meet the English generals who had brought their army out onto the same field to witness and enforce the ceremony of submission from Scotland's new king.

Hamish, Stephen, and others who had fought alongside William Wallace were among those in Bruce's army that day. Also with the Bruce were the noblemen who had agreed to pay homage with him to Longshanks and to accept his endorsement of the Bruce's crown.

To the English generals, who sat upon their fine horses at the head of their polished army and looked across at the shattered remnants of William Wallace's forces, the ceremony hardly seemed worth the wait. The Scots looked ragged and defeated. Even the Bruce did, sitting slouched in his saddle. The English commander turned to the general beside him and said, "I should have washed my ass this morning. It's never been kissed by a king before."

Upon on the hill, Robert the Bruce looked down at the English generals, at their banners, their fine army.

He looked back at the ranks of his own. He saw Hamish. Stephen. Old MacClannough—though he did not know him. He looked at the faces there in the line.

Craig, among the other Scottish nobles mounted beside the Bruce, grew impatient. "Come," he said, "let's get it over with."

But the Bruce held something. Uncurling his fist, he looked at the thistle handkerchief that belonged to William Wallace.

The other nobles reined their horses and started

toward the English, but Robert looked up from the handkerchief to Hamish and Stephen, who had brought it to him, and were looking at him from the Scottish line even now, their eyes pleading for him to do what Wallace would have done.

"Stop," Robert said.

He tucked the handkerchief safely behind his breastplate and turned to the Highlanders who lined the hilltop with him. He took a long deep breath and shouted, "You have bled with Wallace!" He slid his broadsword from its scabbard. "Now bleed with me!"

A cry rose from the Highlanders as from a tomb: "Wal-lace! Wal-lace! Wal-lace!" Louder, louder ... *"Wal-lace! WAL-LACE!"*

The chant built to a frenzy; it shook the ground. The Scottish nobles could scarcely believe it; the English were shocked even more.

And Robert the Bruce, king of Scotland, spurred his horse into full gallop toward the English, and the Highlanders hurled their bodies down the hill, ready to run through hell itself ...

In the year of our Lord 1314, patriots of Scotland, starving and outnumbered, charged the fields of Bannockburn. They fought like warrior poets. They fought like Scotsmen. And won their freedom.

Epilogue

Edward the Longshanks died not long after the execution of William Wallace. He was buried as an exalted king within Westminster Abbey; he lies within a marble tomb behind iron gates to the left of the chancel.

Edward II had a brief and sad reign. He was blamed by noble and commoner alike for the loss of Scotland and for other reverses of the kingdom's fortunes. His wife opposed him in open rebellion; she escaped to France, recruited an army there in her homeland, and returned to England where she deposed her husband and had her son crowned in his stead. Edward II was privately executed by a method of torture that is unspeakable; his screams of agony, it is said, were heard for miles.

Isabella, queen of England, had a son. The boy, who became Edward III, was nothing at all like the man who is listed in the royal registry as his father.

And so we come to the end of my telling of the story of William Wallace. Whether I have told of him as he was or only as I wish him to have been, I cannot say.

But as I write these final lines, I think back to the last time I visited the place of his execution. The section of the Tower of London where he was imprisoned is known to this day as the Wallace Tower, and a visitor can stand in Westminster Hall and look up at the same windows he stared at when they condemned him, but it is at Smithfield, a place of slaughterhouses even now, where I have felt most reminded of how he lived and how he died; and it was the last time I was there when I felt it the most.

I had been there several times, always with others, but the last time, I went alone. I walked around the spot; a plaque hanging on an outer wall of Saint Bart's Hospital marks the area and commemorates Wallace's life as well as his death. There, too, is a small, ancient church, some of which was standing when William Wallace was put to death. On our first visit to Smithfield, my wife and I, thinking Wallace would likely have seen this church with his own eyes from the platform of his execution, entered the sanctuary; we found a beautiful, serene place, and there we stood in a majestic, beautiful, and tragic silence. On the day I last returned, I wanted to visit that sanctuary again to find a private place away from the crowded street, where people passed neither knowing or caring about the long-dead Scot remembered upon the plaque or the American who stopped before it, gazing up at it with tears in his eyes.

The church was closed that day. So I stood in the arched shelter of its entryway, beside its graveyard. I had meant to pray inside the church, but where I now found myself seemed no less fine a place for prayer. So I thanked God for my family and friends and for my calling as a storyteller. And I thanked God for William Wallace.

I wondered if William Wallace was just as grateful that I had come upon his story.

And then something strange happened. I can't say that I saw him; it may be an overstatement even to say that I felt his presence. But I felt . . . that I could talk to him there. And so I thanked him personally. I told him I had no idea if we were related by blood, but I had come to feel a kinship with him and felt that somehow I was meant to be there, seven hundred years after he was, to tell his story. I told him there were few promises that I could make him as to what would become of this telling of his tale, but I could make him the same one I had made to God and to myself: I would do my best to convey the truth as I saw it to those around me.

Maybe all that happened that day was that I talked to myself. Maybe the gift of any great person is the power to make us converse with our own hearts. And maybe as I stood there, I stood there all alone.

But when I walked away, I glanced one last time at the plaque. Someone had left flowers at its base. They were buttercups, and they were beautiful.